D1111938

After many years in public relations, advertising and marketing, **Blythe Gifford** started writing seriously after a corporate layoff. Ten years and one layoff later, she became an overnight success when she sold to the Harlequin Historical line. Her books, set in England and Scotland of the fourteenth to sixteenth centuries, usually incorporate real historical events and characters. The *Chicago Tribune* has called her work "the perfect balance between history and romance." Blythe lives and works along Chicago's lakefront and loves to have visitors at blythegifford.com and Facebook.com/blythegifford.

Jenni Fletcher was born in the north of Scotland and now lives in Yorkshire, UK, with her husband and two children. She wanted to be a writer as a child but became distracted by reading instead, finally getting past her first paragraph thirty years later. She's had more jobs than she can remember but has finally found one she loves. She can be contacted on Twitter, @jenniauthor, or via her Facebook author page.

Amanda McCabe wrote her first romance at sixteen—a vast historical epic starring all her friends as the characters, written secretly during algebra class! She's never since used algebra, but her books have been nominated for many awards, including the RITA® Award, Booksellers' Best Award, National Readers' Choice Award and the Holt Medallion. In her spare time she loves taking dance classes and collecting travel souvenirs. Amanda lives in New Mexico. Visit her at ammandamccabe.com.

TUDOR CHRISTMAS TIDINGS

———

**Blythe Gifford
Jenni Fletcher
Amanda McCabe**

HARLEQUIN
HISTORICAL

Recycling programs for this product may not exist in your area.

ISBN-13: 978-1-335-50575-0

Tudor Christmas Tidings

Copyright © 2020 by Harlequin Books S.A.

Christmas at Court © 2020 by Wendy Blythe Gifford

Secrets of the Queen's Lady © 2020 by Jenni Fletcher

His Mistletoe Lady © 2020 by Ammanda McCabe

This edition published by arrangement with Harlequin Books S.A.

For questions and comments about the quality of this book, please contact us at CustomerService@Harlequin.com.

Harlequin Enterprises ULC
22 Adelaide St. West, 40th Floor
Toronto, Ontario M5H 4E3, Canada
www.Harlequin.com

Printed in U.S.A.

CONTENTS

CHRISTMAS AT COURT

Blythe Gifford

To Holly and Amy with much love.

Dear Reader,

Christmas! There is magic in the very word, even for us today.

To get myself in the right historical mindset, I always assemble a musical playlist, as accurate as I can make it. When I did that for this book, a surprising number of the songs were familiar. I was comforted and amazed to realize my characters would have known "Coventry Carol," "There Is No Rose of Such Virtue" and "God Rest You Merry, Gentlemen," although sung in different versions during Tudor times.

Long ago, the celebration continued, literally, for the Twelve Days of Christmas. I love that idea, that those days are set apart as a respite from ordinary life. Even today, there is some sense during the season that time stands still.

But for my characters, "Christmas at Court" does not turn out to be the seasonal reprieve they hoped for...

Blythe

Chapter One

The first Christmas
Christmas Eve 1483—Westminster Palace

The messenger entered the chamber and, with the smallest of nods to her, began to speak. 'I have a message for Lady Alice. From Dame Elizabeth.'

It took Alice a moment to recognise the name. Until a few months ago, 'Dame Elizabeth' had been Queen of England. The one who had been Queen when Alice was born.

'I am Lady Alice. Give me the message.'

The messenger, taller and older than most who did such duties, looked around. 'The message is only for your ears.'

She motioned her attendants to leave, then clasped her fingers so he would not see them tremble. Her father had warned her that Christmas at court would be treacherous.

Until this year, she had known only one king: Edward, fourth of that name, who had been sure and steady and warm as the sun. A man full of life and a happy family, overflowing with children. Her parents had been often at court. And while she had heard there had been fighting over the throne, that had been no more than a distant memory with a happy ending.

But, suddenly, this year, King Edward had died. And nothing was as it had been. Or should be.

She studied the messenger, who stood, eyes downcast, waiting.

'Now,' she said, uneasy, 'what have you to say?'

'Dame Elizabeth summons Lady Alice to a meeting concerning a matter of great personal importance for your future.'

'You will need to be brave,' her father had said, before she left. *'You will hear from our former friends. Honour them.'*

Was this what he meant?

Alice frowned, looking out of the window towards Westminster Abbey, looming black against the winter-grey sky. The former Queen had fled to the Abbey six months ago, after Richard had killed her brother and seized her two sons along with the throne.

No one had seen the boys since.

To protect her daughters from a similar fate, the former Queen had claimed sanctuary at the Abbey's Abbot House. Would a visit to her there raise the very suspicions her family was trying to avoid?

But Alice could not ignore the message, nor would she want to. She and the oldest royal daughter, also Elizabeth, had played together in the nursery. Ali and Bessy, they had called each other.

Still, such a visit could be dangerous.

She studied the messenger, wondering how the former Queen knew him well enough to send him with this summons. His face was all bones and angles, cheeks, brow, chin. His expression was hardened, even suspicious.

Well, this was not the time to be too trusting.

'Is it allowed? For me to visit?' Sanctuary, they called it, but the former Queen's situation had more in common with prison. Monks guarded the door. Priests and doctors could visit, but few others were permitted.

He nodded. 'Come alone. You are expected before vespers.'

A little time, then. She glanced down at her dress. Not the one she would choose for a meeting with royalty, current or former.

She looked back at the man. His piercing eyes were not

helping her concentration. She straightened her shoulders and met his gaze. 'Tell Her Grace… I mean, Dame Elizabeth…that I will be there.'

A pause. He waved a hand above his head. 'Without the…'

She raised a hand to her headdress. Tall, horned, distinctive. The height of fashion. It would draw unwanted attention.

So her visit might be allowed, but must not be noticed.

She nodded. 'I understand.'

Did he smile as he bowed and left? And could his information be trusted?

Her parents had trusted her to come to court alone. Now she must justify their trust.

A few hours later, garbed in a gown of green velvet, Alice was admitted to the Abbot's House tucked close to Westminster Abbey. The black-robed monk at the door waved her in. A woman visiting a woman…well, he saw no great threat there.

Though only a few steps from Westminster Palace, the Abbot's House was far from the comforts of the court. The large hall was full of mismatched chairs, tables and trunks, taken hastily when the Queen fled, now piled as if in a storeroom.

And at the end of the room, Elizabeth, the former Queen, sat on a simple stool.

Alice dipped a knee, even though she was the length of the hall away. The Queen, for so Alice still thought of her, motioned her ahead.

Alice glanced around as she walked the length of the hall, hoping to see Bessy, but there was no one else, not a single attendant, in the room. So, it seemed, the visit, as well as the message, was for her ears only.

Stopping, at last, before the woman who had summoned her, Alice made her inclination. The Dowager Queen was as fair and lovely as Alice remembered, still with royal bearing and composure, though her family had been of humbler stock.

The silence stretched, but it was not for Alice to speak first.

'The Earl and the Countess of Oakshire—they are well?' The woman's face softened with the question. Alice's parents had been respectful of this Queen when many had not. She had been a Lancastrian knight's widow and her father was of the gentry, so many of the nobility resented her family's rise to royalty.

Sometimes, Alice thought her parents' fondness for the King and Queen stemmed from the fact that they, too, had married for love, as her parents had.

'My mother is ill and my father chose to stay with her, so they sent me to represent the family. But they said if I saw you...' she looked around, again satisfied they were alone '...to give you their greetings. And to say they are sorrowful about...'

She could not say the words *about the Princes*. After the King died, his brother Richard had become Protector, ruling on behalf of his young nephew. But within months, the young King and his brother had been taken to the Tower of London.

Then, they seemed to disappear. Her father, like most men, assumed they were dead.

A queen, but first a mother, the woman closed her eyes and gave a small nod of thanks. The rest must be unspoken.

She opened her eyes, a queen again. 'We haven't much time. I have called you here to give you good news. You are to be betrothed on Christmas Day.'

Christmas Day. Tomorrow.

The world stilled. 'What?' Not the answer she should give, but she was too startled for subtle words.

'You are to be betrothed,' said again, slowly. 'On Christmas Day.'

So soon? Shouldn't such news come from her own father and mother? 'My parents said nothing of this.' Of course, at seventeen, she was of an age to wed, but in a year that had seen three kings, her marriage had been of little consideration.

A wave of the hand. 'It is agreed. They wanted me to tell you.'

Alice paused, struggling to understand. Her parents had told her this season at court would be important for her future. That was the reason they had allowed her to come alone.

'If the Queen summons you...'

They must have known. But why the secrecy?

'It will be a treacherous time at court. We trust you to navigate difficult waters...'

Yet they had given her no compass.

She lifted her chin. 'To whom?'

'To John Talbot, son and heir of the Earl of Stanson.'

She recognised the name. From the north of England, where the current King had much support, far from her family and their sympathies. Had she seen him at court in the past? It did not matter. It was not her place to object. The affection her parents had shared was a luxury few could afford, especially in these uncertain times. A marriage was an alliance, a matter of life and death, not trifling emotion.

And yet, the questions tumbled through her mind. Why this man? Why now? When would they actually be married? Why was the Queen the one to tell her?

But among them all, she asked only one. 'When do I meet him?' She had never expected to have a say in choosing her husband, but she had hoped to at least see him before they were wed.

The Queen raised her eyes and looked behind Alice. 'Now.'

She turned.

There, at the door, wearing the fur-lined cape and cap of

a physician, stood the man she had taken for a messenger only a few hours ago.

He looked not at all pleased.

Sir John stepped into room, jaw clenched so no words would escape. Lady Alice stared at him, wide-eyed, and his impression remained the same as when he had seen her earlier.

Young. Naive. Pretty. Tawny hair. Gentle, innocent blue eyes…

But as he watched, her expression shifted. Not angry. Not yet. But bewildered, as if she was watching the sun rise in the west.

He could tell the moment she recognised him and realised what he had done. As she did, her gaze sharpened, narrowed, and he knew she would never be so naive again.

Better that way. These were dangerous times.

He stepped forward and bowed, a gracious gesture, he hoped.

She glanced at the former Queen, then back at him. 'So it seems you are neither the messenger nor the physician you pretend to be.'

He forced a smooth reply. 'I am a knight, son and heir of the Earl of Stanson.'

She inclined her head not an inch more than necessary. 'May our union honour both our families.'

Words by rote. As was his answer. 'We shall do everything we can to make it so.'

Silence. Awkward. Though he could see countless questions in her eyes.

She glanced back at Dame Elizabeth. 'Is this to be announced to the court, then?'

He met the glance of the former Queen and left her to speak.

'The betrothal ceremony will be a private affair, though

word will become known, of course. However, my involvement must remain secret.'

The puzzled furrow between Alice's brows deepened. 'And the King's approval?' she asked.

'Has been obtained.'

She did not look as if she believed that, he thought. Not a dull-witted woman, then. So it was as well she did not know the priest who would preside was a secret ally of Henry Tudor, who was gathering an army in exile to take England's throne.

He watched as she forced herself into composure. 'Christmas is tomorrow. Certainly the ceremony can wait until my parents can be present.' Her voice held the lilt of a demand.

Dame Elizabeth waved her hand, as if she still reigned and the audience was over. 'No. It cannot. Sir John, please see that Lady Alice returns safely to the palace.'

One final bow and they left the hall, side by side.

Winter darkness had fallen. The court would soon gather for the Advent meal, breaking the fast of the day. If they were careful, they could return unobserved.

The wind from the river whipped around the Palace, blowing skirts and scarves awry. Beside him, she shivered. He reached out his arm, sheltering her with his fur-lined cloak, pulling her close.

With her body next to his, he thought of her, suddenly, not as a pawn in this game, but as his *wife*. Married, he would be free to explore the soft warmth of her, to press against her, to touch her hair and her breasts and...

If. When. Maybe. So many unlikely things must happen first.

She pulled away. The cold wind whipped the strands of her hair away from her scarf and across her face. 'You deceived me. Why?' Asking as if she deserved an answer.

Guilt prickled his spine. He was deceiving her still. 'I am a warrior. I like to assess the field before battle.'

Wide-eyed again. Lips parted. 'You see this marriage as a war?'

What was he to say? The country was at war with itself, even if no swords were drawn today. 'I just wanted to…see you before you…knew.'

A smile, finally. Unexpected. 'You mean, before I donned a disguise?'

He raised his brows, startled. 'Disguise?' It had not occurred to him that she, too, might…dissemble. It should have. Men sat puffed up on the throne, but women, in the shadows, made their own plans. About this marriage. And more. 'I hope you will not find that necessary.'

She shrugged.

And for once, he regretted her silence.

They entered the Palace, suddenly engulfed by the smell of fish and the scent of Yule greenery, and she stepped beyond his reach. 'We are not yet betrothed. Leave me to enjoy the last night of Advent.'

She turned away, leaving him alone.

He let her go, wishing her a night of peace. There was still much she was not to know.

Not yet, at least.

Chapter Two

In her chamber, Alice studied herself in the mirror, then smoothed her eyebrows and dabbed her lips with beeswax, wanting to look her best this night.

Her last as an unwed woman.

Christmas would be very different for a betrothed woman than for one unmarried.

What foolish hopes she once had for this season. Her parents had warned of treachery, but after this long and terrible year, she had thought only to smile and dance and laugh with one young man, then another, to release all the cares and worries.

The twelve days she had anticipated had shrunk to twelve hours. And as it was the Vigil of Christmas, there would be no dancing tonight. Only more fish and endless prayer.

Her attendant helped her with the steeple headdress, which wobbled uncertainly until properly centred and attached. It forced her to move deliberately and slowly, keeping her head steady. Good practice to fight the uncertainty about her betrothal on the morrow.

A betrothal was not a wedding, but it was so binding that it would prohibit marriage to anyone else, even if those betrothed did not marry each other.

That was the argument King Richard had used to declare his brother's children illegitimate and Queen Elizabeth a concubine and not a wife—all based on a prior betrothal of King Edward that had conveniently come to light just in time for Richard to seize the throne.

So, once betrothed, Lady Alice would be married to Sir John, or not at all.

She descended the stairs, slowly, balancing her head-wear. She had wanted to enjoy the festivities, but instead, she would disguise her disappointment with a smile and the lift of her head.

'We know you will do the right thing.'

What else had her parents known? And *was* this betrothal the right thing?

As she entered the hall, uncertain laughter, out of harmony, clashed with the music. No one knew what to expect from this celebration, the new King's first Christmas.

Last year the former King, joyous, generous and draped in a robe trimmed with sable, had fed two thousand people at Christmas. Surrounded by his wife and children, he had kept the season with perhaps more celebration than religion, but to little complaint.

The new King could not afford such generosity. As they gathered at the table to break Advent fast, conversation was hushed. Lute and harp and recorder played softly, and if some silver and plate items were missing, sold to raise ready money to pay for the celebrations, well, it would not be wise to mention it.

Even though he had been crowned five months before, King Richard still looked uncomfortable on his perch at the high table. With reason. Only a few months ago, his most trusted supporter had turned against him, fighting to remove Richard and put Henry Tudor on the throne.

Why? Had the man's conscience finally caught up with him or was he just angry that he had not been more fully rewarded? No one was sure, not even her father, who knew more than he said. But when Richard defeated and beheaded his former friend, many who had joined the rebellion fled across the channel to rally around Henry Tudor, living in exile in Brittany.

Many around her family's Oakshire lands in south-east

England had taken up arms. Her father, thankfully, had not, so was spared punishment and exile, but the King still had his suspicions about the Earl's loyalties.

With more reason than she wanted Richard to know.

So when the King summoned her to him after the meal, she took a breath and kept her smile steady.

'Your father is not here, Lady Alice.' A frown showed his displeasure.

You are our only child. You must represent us.

She hid her shaking fingers in the folds of her skirt and bent her knee before the King.

'To his sorrow and regret, Your Grace. My mother fell ill and my father stayed to tend her. They sent me to pay our homage.' She held her breath. Had she spoken aright? It must be clear that their absence meant no disloyalty, though even loyalty was no protection from this King.

Richard's Queen reached to touch Alice's hand. 'I hope it is not serious. I had to leave my son…he is ill…'

Alice murmured something comforting. The couple had only one son.

Only one heir to the throne.

'I understand,' the King said, interrupting, 'that your family wishes you to join with the Earl of Stanson's son.'

She swallowed and nodded, trying to gather her wits. So the King did know. Had she alone been ignorant?

My involvement must remain secret.

She must measure each word. 'It is time for me to wed, Your Grace.' A statement of fact. Only the disruption of the year had kept her from being promised earlier. 'With the permission of Your Grace, of course.'

And if it did not come…?

A frown. 'Stanson has been unfailingly loyal. I hope your family will be the same.'

'Do not let there be a question of that, Your Grace.' Certainly she must do nothing to raise one. Her father had found little to admire in King Richard, but he had, for the most part, held his tongue.

Dangerous to do otherwise.

'Ah!' The King looked up, distracted. 'There's Sir John. It is time to hang the holly and ivy. You will want to help him.'

She wanted no such thing, but she forced a smile and turned to greet him, only to see the man dressed in new garb. Neither doctor nor squire nor even knight—this time, he wore a rich blue brocade doublet and woollen hose.

Was this really the man any more than the squire or the physician she had seen before?

But the King was not finished. 'After the greenery is hung, it will be time for prayer. None of the licentiousness we have seen in Christmas past. See to it, Sir John.'

Having handed her to an 'unfailingly loyal' man, Richard moved off, leaving them alone.

John took her hand, his grip strong and sure as if he already possessed her.

'He knows,' she whispered. 'Of our betrothal.'

'You mentioned it?' As if she should not have.

'No, he did, but he approves,' she added, 'as you said.'

Unfailingly loyal. Did the King suspect her family was not? Was this man, loyal to the King, sent to spy on them?

He smiled. 'Cause for celebration, then. Yet you look ill at ease, Lady Alice.'

Trying to read her thoughts. Succeeding.

Well, if they were to be married, he would have to learn to hear her speak freely.

'I had hoped,' she murmured, softly, so she would not be overheard, 'for a season of joy and dancing and merriness before I became a wife. Instead, I have only tonight and that is to be filled with vigil, fasting and masses. After that, we shall be betrothed and I will be ever bound by whatever your desires might be.'

The word *desires* echoed between them.

She bit her tongue.

His hand was warm on hers, but his hard, sharp gaze assessed her as if she were an enemy. 'We do not always get what we desire. Come. A basket of holly awaits. There are a few ways we can spend the coming hours pleasantly.'

She shivered. This man, this John who would be her husband—was he as ruthless as the King? Who could be trusted now? Her parents? The former Queen? The current King?

Or this silent man who continued to slip into disguises?

Amid the laughter around them, John studied Alice as she carefully picked up each piece of holly, placed it one way, then another, as if there were some perfect angle where it must rest.

She kept her attention on the greenery, not on him.

Her family had told her nothing, apparently. Did they not think her wise enough to know? Were they trying to spare her? Perhaps they were just cautious in the same way his father was. The Earl did not always reveal every plan to his son. The less he knew, the more guiltless he could appear.

He had thought her naive. Perhaps she had just been protected.

John was the Earl's heir. He had not had the same luxury.

He had seen men shift sides as swiftly as a spinning weathercock. York. Lancaster. They were only names. Badges one could don or take off. Fealty seemed no longer sacred. For when a man wanted power and someone stood in the way… Well, he might switch the badge of a white rose for one with a white boar as casually as reaching for a new cup of wine.

This King had certainly done that. Calling himself a York, then usurping the throne from the rightful York ruler, his own young nephew. He had been named Protector of the boy by his brother, but the only thing he had protected was his own power.

He was a man who demanded loyalty and gave none. Hence, in John's opinion, he deserved none.

So, when the rebels rose up a few months ago, John was ready to ride with them. Only luck and his father's stern hand had saved him or he, too, would have been executed or exiled instead of lifting a cup of wassail at the Christmas court.

Our time will come. Wait.

By next Christmas, he hoped to toast Henry Tudor as King.

But Richard knew, and must know, only of their family's past, unshakeable allegiance. He must not discover the secret promises made to the former Queen and her allies.

John looked back at Lady Alice, trying to assess her without being distracted by her full lips and the swell of her bosom. Her parents had trusted her to come alone. That must mean something.

Would she be a help and support to him? Or a danger? Was she a simple fool or as wise and devious as the former Queen and the mother of Henry Tudor?

And which would be better? If she were a fool, he could simply leave her to tend to domestic matters. But if she were shrewd? Well, the former Queen and Henry Tudor's mother had taught him not to underestimate what a woman could accomplish behind the scenes. But he must be certain that her family's interests and his would align.

And consider what to do if they did not.

For this marriage was about more than him and her. More, even, than Stanson and Oakshire. Nothing must put that at risk.

'Ouch.' A small cry and she popped her finger in her mouth.

He reached for his handkerchief. 'Let me see.'

'The holly… I was careless.'

He took her hand. The cut was no bigger than one a pin might make. A wound no warrior would notice. The bleeding barely spotted the cloth before it stopped.

But he did not release her hand. Close now, he inhaled

the scent of her, some mix of flowers and spices. It scrambled his thoughts. As soon as tomorrow he might kiss her. Why not tonight? Why not now? He bent closer, let his lips hover…

She pulled away and he let go a breath, grateful for her strength. He was the naive one if he allowed lust to rule when the throne was at stake. Edward had done that and too many noblemen had never forgiven him for taking a common woman as Queen and favouring her family over those of noble birth. That simmering resentment had helped Richard rise.

A safe distance away from Lady Alice, he could speak again. 'Is that better?'

She nodded. 'It will not prevent my hands pressing together in prayer as the King demanded.' This was said without a smile. 'I shall withdraw to begin.'

'Wait.'

She raised her brows.

He did not want her out of his sight. Nothing must go wrong before tomorrow when they were pledged.

'The King may prefer prayer, but there are other ways to spend the final hours before midnight mass. Perhaps, a game of cards?'

'On Christmas Eve?' Her voice, shocked. But the edge of a smile teased her lips. 'Cards are not allowed until tomorrow.'

She could be tempted, then. Good. This way, he could watch her, without raising her suspicions. 'We but hasten the celebration by a few hours.'

'And your parents? Will they not have plans?'

They were at court, but with their own responsibilities. Lady Alice was his. 'They will expect me to keep you company, since yours are not.'

A hesitation. And then she nodded.

With heads bowed to hide their smiles, they left the hall and found a small room with a fire that could be rekindled. When he pulled out his cards, he was gratified to see her eyes widen. He was proud of them. Paper layered for stiffness and strength. Hand-painted with coloured ink and touches of silver and gold. Each a work of art.

She touched one, gently. 'Who is your card maker?'

Ah, a woman familiar with cards. So he must confess. 'They come from Burgundy.'

'You defy the law?'

Importing cards was prohibited, the better to protect card makers in London. 'They were a gift and I could not refuse.' He played with them casually, as if they were of no consequence. 'You will not order me seized for having them, I hope.'

Her laugh, deeper and richer than he had expected, was a comfort. 'I will not. But now I understand why their import is forbidden. The Worshipful Company of Playing Card Makers can produce nothing so beautiful.'

Fortunate that she had not asked how he had got the cards. Even prohibited luxuries could be obtained for a price, if you knew men who were slipping secretly back and forth across the narrow sea. 'We are lucky the priests are no longer burning cards as evil.' Words spoken lightly as he shuffled.

Playing at cards was the least dangerous thing they were doing.

'High card wins?' he asked casually.

She nodded. 'Three count.'

More experienced than he had thought. 'What stakes? A kiss?'

She studied him for a moment, looking neither shocked nor insulted, but… 'Let us wager something more valuable.'

Now he was the one startled. 'Do you not value your virtue?'

'Why wager something that you will be able to take freely tomorrow? I would prefer something else. Truth.'

He held back a shiver. No. Not naive at all. 'Truth?'

A firm nod. 'If we are to be betrothed, I should like to know more of you than your name.'

'All right.' Cautious. Maybe she was only curious to know how he liked his meat prepared.

She reached for her cards and pulled them to her. 'Begin.'

One. Two. Counted out face down. The third, face up.

His was a two. Hers a three.

'So,' he said, with unease he had not expected, 'what would you like to know?'

Chapter Three

Alice smiled at his question. What would she like to know? Everything. But she must start carefully, lest he become wary. 'Tell me of your home.'

Ah, she had surprised him. A feeling of satisfaction, as if she, too, might know a bit about assessing the field. Assuredly, he had expected a more difficult question.

'The castle guards a river crossing and is well fortified, with sturdy walls and many towers so no force can come upon us unawares.'

She sighed. Asked of home, he described a fortress. 'I do not want to know its strength, but how it is situated. If I am to live there, a place I have never seen, I want to know what I will see day after day. Is the river large and placid or full of racing rapids? Can you watch the sun rise? Or set? Does it streak the sky with angry red and gold or gentle pink and yellow?'

At her words, his gaze softened, as if he saw his land with a lover's eye. Ah, so beneath all the hard edges, he cared for something. If she ever saw such love in his eyes when they looked at her, she would know herself blessed.

'It is high on a hill, commanding a river full of the fattest fish in England, surrounded by green, lush forests full of deer. The breeze comes from the south-west and it is the fairest land in Christendom.'

Now, she was the one surprised. More than a warrior. A poet, it seemed. Loyal to his land, as much as to his King. 'It sounds beautiful.'

He blinked as if waking, a bit of red touching his cheek. 'Aye.'

'And you love it very much,' she said.

'Doesn't every man do anything he must to protect his home?' His voice held the trace of a burr she had not noticed before.

A reminder of how far from home she would be once they wed. Her father had been loyal to the York family, though sceptical of King Richard. In the north, they had been loyal to Richard himself, even when he was the Duke of Gloucester.

The stern man with the sharp gaze had returned and he picked up the cards. 'Now, I have answered. We play again.'

Silent, he rearranged the cards, dealt one, two, three to each of them. She held her breath as they each showed their cards. Hers a queen. But this time, he showed a king.

Of course, she must lose at least a few rounds. Yet now, she held her breath. What would he want to know?

'Are you a woman who can keep a good home?'

Release of breath. Relief and disappointment. So, spared questions she had feared—about her family and their loyalties. But about herself? All he wanted was a helpmeet, a handmaiden to be at the service of his beautiful castle.

And so, she replied, 'Yes.'

Foolish man. He had asked a question that could be answered yes or no. She would give him no more. Certainly she could boast of supervising the staff of kitchen and cupboard, garden and pantry. She could organise the household for travel and for the welcoming of guests. All this was what he had the right to expect from her.

But did he not care that she could recite the opening lines of *The Canterbury Tales*? Or that she had learned to pick a melody on the lute?

Ah, well. She, not he, was the foolish one, to expect more than safety and protection from a husband.

'Yes?' he said. 'Is that all?'

'You asked. I answered. Let us go again.' This time, she took the cards, thinking that, if she shuffled them, they might be kinder to her.

One. Two. And…she lost again.

'What would you know?' With a sigh.

For a moment, he looked puzzled, as if he could think of nothing else to ask of her. Then, something shifted behind his eyes, a realisation of what he truly wanted to know…

'A kiss.'

The words were growled. From deep in his throat.

Startled, she searched his eyes. Did he simply want to stop her from talking? Was this the obligatory nod to the Yuletide mistletoe? No. Something deeper stirred him. As if what he wanted was not the obligatory kiss a wife would owe, but something beyond that. Something that kindled desire she had never felt before.

He moved closer. She leaned to meet him. Heat, his chest, ready to press against hers, his arms locking her close, where she would not be able to move…

'A kiss,' she said, 'is not a question.' Her words were ragged.

He stopped.

For a moment, his eyes cleared. But he did not release her. Her breasts pressed against his, as they might some day in the marriage bed.

'Would. You. Kiss. Me?' His words rougher than hers.

But he had asked. And she wanted, she so wanted…

'Yes.'

Why had she thought a yes-or-no question was so foolish? For the answer was not a single word, but the heat of his breath on her cheek, her lips pressed to his, and her body, too, as if the kiss extended the length of her, as if the kiss alone joined them, more tightly than a betrothal would.

John was the one who broke away, breathing heavily as he might in battle. What had he been thinking? He hadn't.

But the kiss was what he had wanted since he first saw her, watched the shape of her body, all the time trying to hide his gaze, fearing she would see the hunger in it.

And yet she had not. She had seen no more than a messenger, someone she did not even recognise at first when she saw him again. But the curve of her waist, the tilt of her head, had immediately seared his brain. And when he had held his cloak around her, felt her heat near his heart, he knew that this would be no simple marriage.

Nothing like the formal union he had wanted.

This betrothal was only one move in a large, uncertain game of chess, a promise made by others for reasons that had nothing to do with him or her, but only to bind two families to promises they hoped would change the future of the country.

Nothing personal in it at all.

At least, there hadn't been.

Now, it was something he wanted, passionately, enough that he had allowed it to cloud his judgement, rouse his passions and expose her to his desires. Desires which might never be satisfied until they *were* joined…

She moved in his arms and he let her go quickly.

'I think,' she said in a voice more calm than he could muster, 'that I must win the next round.'

Her pointed headdress was askew. He reached to right it, instead knocking it further awry. She laughed and reached to catch it, her fingers grazing his hands instead.

He pulled them away and forced a smile he did not feel.

She lifted off the headdress and put it aside, without looking at him, then turned back to the table and laid out the cards again, silent.

He could not tell whose fingers shook more.

One. Two. Three. And she did win this time.

Uneasy, he watched her assess him. What was she going to ask?

'Have you been with a woman?'

He had feared many things she might have asked. He had not thought of this one. Awkward. How was he to answer? He opened his mouth…

'I mean—' as if she had just caught herself '—tell me about the women you have been with.'

He laughed, relieved, remembering the mistake he had made. 'You cannot change your question now.' Only one word to answer. That made it simple. What man had not been with a woman? Or two. Or more. 'Yes.'

The bell started pealing, summoning all to midnight mass. She swept up his cards, shaped them into a neat pile, pushed them towards him and stood.

'Then pray for forgiveness tonight.'

Alice had slept little between the midnight and morning masses. She told herself it was because she was to be betrothed on Christmas, but that was only partially true.

Each time she closed her eyes, she felt his kiss again, not just on her lips, but on her skin, in her blood. Even—dared she think it?—in her soul. Everything had changed and suddenly she was jealous of those other women, the ones he had been with before she even knew him.

She tried to think, instead, of the betrothal and what she had been told to do. They both were to linger after the morning mass, then move to a small chapel at the side of the church, where they would plight their troth.

She made her way to the Abbey as light touched the dark sky, a reminder that Christmas brought the birth of Jesus, the light of the world. A dark world now, that needed light more than ever.

She listened to the familiar Latin, thinking of the former Queen and her daughters, on the other side of Westminster's wall. She understood that a visiting priest had been allowed to give them Christmas communion—the same priest who would soon stand before the altar to join her with John.

Was the priest somehow connected to the secret involvement of the former Queen?

Mass over, she stayed on her knees, silent. No one would question why she lingered in prayer. Finally, she felt the stillness of an empty church and opened her eyes. On the other side of the aisle, John rose.

When he left the sanctuary, she, too, stood and made her way to the small chapel of St Erasmus, where John waited for her before the altar. The priest was there, too, frowning, no doubt cross to be kept from breaking his fast.

Her own stomach growled and she put a hand on it, as if to quiet the noise.

Betrothals were to be witnessed, but the witnesses who stepped forward were John's parents, keeping the circle of knowledge small. A ceremony not secret, but discreet, for reasons she still did not understand.

That, she realised, belatedly, was the kind of question she should have asked John when she had the chance, not some silliness about other women.

She studied his parents. Like his son, John's father, the Earl of Stanson, was a man hard and lean, but with a face that had known more years of war and betrayal. His wife moved to Alice's side and patted her back as if she were a child.

What kind of marriage did these two have? What would John expect marriage to be?

Suddenly, she felt John take her hand. Comforting. Strong. She looked up to meet his eyes. A bit gentler this morning. A bit sleepy. Some day, she would wake beside him in bed. They might kiss again…

The priest began, speaking hurriedly. Promises made before God. Not to be broken. They spoke the words, with no more emotion than if they were answering the Latin mass. John's father, brow knitted, overlooked the procedures, frowning, as if he were uncertain of the rightness of it.

And her absent parents? What if she had been wrong? What if they did not approve…?

And just like that, it was over.

'When,' Alice said, 'are we to be wed?'

Awkward silences. Glances exchanged.

John was the one who answered. 'That has not been decided.'

His parents put on practised smiles as they left the chapel and murmured meaningless congratulations.

She asked no more questions.

John assessed the room as they entered the feast hall unnoticed. While Richard and his Queen sat quiet and apart, his parents, along with the rest of the court, apparently had decided that, having survived the year with their heads, it was time to celebrate.

He could not.

This betrothal was a gamble, a high-stakes risk. His family had, literally, bet their lives on it.

But to stand silent would draw attention he did not want, so he took two cups of ale, handed the second to Alice and lifted his to her.

She raised her eyebrows. 'To what do we drink, my lord?'

'To long life.' He touched his tankard to hers. 'Together.' Just a bit late. He would be lucky to survive the coming year.

Her expression, too, was sombre, but she lifted her cup and met his.

He put on a practised smile. She matched it. 'Are we to remain…together through the day, then?'

He shrugged. 'That isn't necessary.' The need to watch her was lessened, now that they had completed the ties, and he might better be separated from temptation, for as important as the betrothal had been, it must not become a consummated marriage. Not yet.

So they parted, each circling the Hall separately, though neither, it seemed, spent much time with any other person.

See. Be seen, but not remarked on. Enough music and good cheer that conversation beyond a happy expression was not necessary.

When they met again, however, and stood silently looking out over the crowd, he felt strangely at home with her. Even the shared awkwardness was comforting.

It took his mind off kissing her.

Poor Scogin, the jester who had served the last King, was desperately trying to make the current one laugh, as if his life depended on that laughter. And though he had known Richard for years, he seemed to have no more certainty than the rest of the court what the King might do.

John had seen the King's gaze follow him around the room, seeming to relax only when he rejoined Alice. Well played, then. Joining a family loyal to the former Queen to a family loyal to Richard seemed to reassure him. Just as it was meant to.

It should have done just the opposite.

Alice turned to look at him, not boldly, but with a new... assessment.

'We are now betrothed.' Her voice pitched low, the meaning of her words for his ears only.

John nodded. He had learned that she said little without some purpose.

'And this betrothal goes beyond the uniting of our families.'

Definitely not so naive, then. More worldly-wise than he had expected. He looked away. Could he trust her with the truth?

When he met her gaze again, he lost his thought as he looked in her blue eyes, wishing this betrothal was free of conditions and uncertainties. Wishing he were not so alone...

Another sip of his beer, a look over his shoulder and he motioned her into the corridor, away from the hall, but with a clear view, so he could see anyone approaching.

Then he leaned in, his lips tantalisingly close to her ear. Anyone watching would see only a smiling couple, a seasonal dalliance.

'Yes,' he whispered. 'It does.'

Chapter Four

'*Yes. It does.*'

Alice had known even before he said it. Otherwise the former Queen would not have been involved. There would have been no need for dancing on the edge of secrecy. All these had been clear markers.

'*We trust you,*' her family had told her. '*Be brave.*' But they had not told her what the danger was. Now, she must be brave enough to face it.

She met John's gaze. Her husband, but with motives as disguised as he had been when first she saw him. Why? 'We are betrothed. My fate is bound with yours into eternity. Tell me.'

He studied her face and she tried to read his in return. Their union was a lie and it had not even begun. Could there be any trust between them?

He whispered, urgent, 'Today, Henry Tudor will stand before his supporters across the Channel and vow before God that when he takes the English throne, he will marry Elizabeth of York.'

She struggled with his words, which seemed unrelated to her question. Henry Tudor, ostensibly a claimant to Richard's throne, had not even set foot in England for years. The rebellion that might have removed Richard from the throne had been crushed, its leaders were dead or exiled. Her childhood friend Bessy, the one he vowed to marry, was isolated in sanctuary, unable to leave. She would be allowed to marry no one unless King Richard approved.

What could such a declaration mean? Nothing.

'But Henry Tudor is in France,' she said, not adding that his claim to the throne was superficial at best. 'He has no power. No army. His forces were defeated. What does it matter if he promises to marry a York he has never even met...?'

A York.

Henry had descended from the Lancaster line.

Her breath stopped. Lancaster and York.

Suddenly the fanciful story made sense. Such a marriage would truly unite the families that had warred against one another for decades. If a Lancaster and a York married and took the throne together, there could be no question of their children's right to rule. The endless to and fro of war might finally be over.

The understanding must have shown on her face, for he nodded.

But there remained a mystery. 'What does that have to do with you and me?'

John's smile carried a hint of conspiracy, though his words were banal. 'Both our families want to see a York on the throne.'

A York. But not *this* York. Not Richard. The throne should have gone to Edward's children, not Edward's brother. So if by supporting Henry, they could be sure that Edward's daughter Bessy would sit on the throne, well, that would be worth...everything.

That would be reason enough for the former Queen to support their union.

She dared not even speak such a thing. And he had not said it. Yet, she knew. 'A pledge. Our betrothal is a pledge of your family's support and mine...'

Support for Henry Tudor to invade and seize the throne.

He nodded. 'We marry only when, if...'

'If...' Now she understood. They would marry only if Henry became King *and* married Elizabeth of York.

To her surprise, her first reaction was not relief, but dis-appointment. This betrothal she had been so hesitant to make, that she had assumed had closed the door to the rest of her life, was no certainty at all. It was contingent on events far beyond their control.

The list was dizzying. First, Henry would have to invade England with enough men to challenge the King. Then, his forces would have to fight Richard. They would need to at-tract additional support from men still in England, ostensi-bly loyal to Richard. After all that, they would have to win.

And they would have to do all this having failed to do it once already. Who would rush to a cause already lost? Who would stand up to the forces of a king who had already crushed a rebellion and beheaded its leaders?

Even if all that happened and Richard was dethroned, the new King Henry would have to fulfil his promise to marry Elizabeth, so Elizabeth must remain unwed for as long as it took for all this to come about.

A list so nearly impossible, it was absurd.

And so she laughed. Laughed as if they had not just discussed the overthrow of the government, betrayal and treason. Laughed and reached to touch the hand of her be-trothed, a hand that might never really be hers. 'Then we need not worry about how we shall live together, shall we? That will come no time soon, if at all.'

John stepped back and pulled his hand away. How could she laugh about the fate of the nation?

How could she laugh when he had just admitted to being a traitor? That's what both their families were. Or would be.

He could not speak the word. Could barely form it in his mind, but there it was. He would be false to the King who should hold his fealty.

And for what? Was she right? Was this all impossible? Her laughter, her smiles, were they because she was certain Henry would never hold the throne and so she would be, ultimately, free?

But he knew things she did not. Things he did not yet trust her enough to share.

Already, Henry had gathered many of Richard's former supporters to his side in Brittany. This pledge was made to them. And to the ones still in England who would be tempted to rise up. His family. Hers.

Those who had gathered around Henry in France included some of the most revered lords of the south, former neighbours of her family. Richard had already seized their lands so they had now pledged their sacred honour to Henry Tudor. And when they returned to England, armed, as they would, his family, and others the King counted on, would support them.

But the surprise of her laughter unleashed his harboured resentment of the entire effort. He had been forced to marry a woman and ally with her family in order to support a king who did not yet exist. He was risking everything, even his life, and she was laughing to think it all might fail.

At his stern silence, her laughter faded. 'You look sombre.'

He frowned. Was he now to be studied by this woman every minute? But he would give her no reassuring smile. Instead, he shrugged. 'I am by nature a serious man.'

That only made her look at him more deeply. 'All the more reason to seek joy when you can. What brings you joy?'

And the vision that came to him was of her. As his wife. In his bed, open to his kisses. And more—

Dangerous to think of that now. He could touch her, of course. Stand close to her. Even whisper in her ear. In fact, many betrothed couples went further. Much further. Betrothal was as binding as marriage.

Almost.

But he knew, and, now, she did, too, that their pledge

was only as good as Henry's. Their marriage depended on him. So they must not wander too far into temptation, or they would risk the fate of the kingdom.

A consummated betrothal *was* a marriage. It would no longer be a pledge that bound their families. Or Henry.

'Joy is not something a man should seek,' he said.

'Is it not? Did God put us on earth to be miserable? Then why do we celebrate Christmas with joy?'

A foolish woman, to prattle of joy when she had never faced death in battle. 'Being alive is gift enough.'

'If so, then we ought to rejoice in each breath.'

And her lips parted, taking that breath. They were sweet and round and welcoming and made him forget the argument he had planned to make.

He steadied himself. She was ignorant of all they faced.

'When the season is over,' he said, 'I will return to Northumberland and you to Kent. I do not know when next we will meet.'

'All the more reason to enjoy the days we have.'

Enjoy. Not a word he much used. Yet life, death, war, the fate of the nation—they controlled none of that right now. They had only each other. And their shared secret.

He must take his mind off her temptation, the fate of nations, all of it. He must think of something mundane and meaningless that would allow him to smile through the Christmas feast. 'What is your favourite dish?'

Brief, wide-eyed surprise. 'I am particularly fond of peacock.'

Now he was the one to laugh, stretching muscles unaccustomed to use. 'Peacock?' One of those dishes designed for the eyes, not the tongue. 'My lady, you may eat my share of peacock if I can enjoy your helping of roast boar.'

He held out his hand.

'I see,' she said, putting hers on top of his, 'that we shall get on very well together this Christmas.'

And, perhaps, if God blessed them, long after.

The twelfth day of Christmas, Epiphany

It seemed to Alice as if she had no more than blinked and the last day of Christmas arrived. A more pious celebration than usual, but still, the season of joy she had longed for had come to her, not as a single woman, but as the betrothed of a man she had never seen until two weeks ago.

She had thought she must pretend joy. Instead, the joy she pretended had become real, but remained her secret. Twelve days was too short a time to fall in love, surely.

Could she trust her feelings?

And did John feel the same? She did not know and dared not ask.

He had not kissed her again. That, she understood, would take them too close to temptation. But there had been moments when they stood, side by side, her breath echoing his, and then their eyes would meet...

Now, the end was here, and she sat with him at the banquet, holding tight to each moment.

King Richard, in an expansive mood, had put on a final feast, more celebratory than all that had come before. The Great Hall was filled not just with members of the court, but with the guild leaders of London who had been helpful to the King.

Sometimes, more so than those of his own class.

The King sat high at his table, touching his crown occasionally, as if to make certain it was still in place. He had presented London's mayor and the aldermen with an extravagant gold cup and cover, encrusted with pearls. It was no doubt paid for with money they had lent him, but he gave a pretty speech about keeping it in the Guildhall in commemoration of the friendship between himself and the people of London.

Promises scattered like autumn leaves.

Amid the noise and laughter, Alice and John sat side by side, silent.

'I leave in the morning,' she said, finally.

He nodded. 'He has called a Parliament to meet next week.'

And so, the shelter of the season would be gone. Her father would be forced to come to London and play his part in the government. 'What will happen?'

He shrugged. 'Rumours only. But Parliaments are about money, always.'

And this King needed money.

'So your father,' he said, 'and mine will sit among the lords, forced to vote aye to whatever he asks.' Sad wisdom gained beside the joy. Both must keep Richard's confidence, and their heads, until Henry gathered men and ships.

But today, in this great hall, with a vigorous man in the prime of life wearing the crown, Richard III's grip on the throne seemed unassailable.

She turned to John. 'We shall not see each other again until…'

There was no answer, she knew. No guarantee that they would ever see each other again. Or, if they did, whether it would be to marry or to mourn.

He shook his head, while beneath the table he covered her hand with his. How quickly they had paired. How strange it seemed that she was forced to leave him.

'What shall I tell my parents?' she said.

'Tell them you did your duty and we are prepared for whatever happens.'

But she was not prepared. Not at all. She wanted to howl and scream and march up to the Bishop and demand they be joined now. Only a matter of days ago, she had, in child-ish innocence, thought the world was as it must be and her life would flow ahead.

Now, she could see that nothing was certain. In fact, John seemed the most certain thing in her life.

She was staring at him and he at her. Too long. No words. Yet…

He squeezed her hand. 'Meet me.' He motioned his head. They had a favourite alcove in the corridor, where it was possible to whisper unseen. 'I'll go first.'

He slipped away. At a discreet distance, she followed. A guard stood at the entrance to the hall, but the corridor was empty.

John held her hands in his, lifted them to his lips and kissed them. His face blurred through her tears.

'You must not cry.'

She gave a rueful smile. 'First you do not like my laughter. Now, you object to tears. Of all the things I must or must not do, I think I am entitled to cry. Can we not, perhaps, see each other? Some time—'

He shook his head, not letting her finish. 'You. Me. The fate of the kingdom is more important. This is our part to play. No matter how uncertain the outcome.'

'But if we were together...'

He put a finger to her lips. 'You know what must happen for us to be together. And if it does not go well, it must be on my head. Only mine.'

She shook her head. Now he was being naive, for if the plan was discovered, her family, his and she, too, would pay the price.

A draught. Cold air. The doors to the palace opened and a travel-weary man entered, escorted by two guards. One stayed with him. The other hurried towards the hall.

Suddenly, John was at attention.

'What is it?' Alice whispered.

He waved for silence. No one arrived on Epiphany without good reason.

They stood motionless in the shadow of the alcove, barely breathing.

One of the King's most trusted men came from the hall to question the new arrival. 'What news?'

'Henry Tudor gains strength. More followers have pledged to him.' The messenger reeled off the names of the lords in exile, some of the most senior houses of England who had been banished or fled across the Channel when the rebellion failed. She recognised the names of former neighbours. 'They call him King. And he promises them he will marry the young Princess of York when he is.'

She held her breath against a surge of joy. Henry still in exile, pledged to Elizabeth. The first step taken, as promised.

Her moment of joy was cut short by the next words from the King's man.

'We'll put an end to that when Parliament meets. He and all his supporters will be condemned—stripped of their lands and titles. The former King's marriage will be declared void, his children labelled bastards, including the young Elizabeth. There will be no path to the throne for any of them.' He clasped the man on the shoulder. 'Now come. Feast. And speak to no one of this.'

The words echoed behind them as the men entered the hall.

Alice looked at her betrothed. 'What if...?' If Henry did not come or could not marry...

John kissed her question away, his lips hot and hungry, holding her close and hard, so she could feel his heart beating, quickly, in time with hers. Saying with his body all they must not speak.

And when he let her go, only a few words. 'I *will* see you again.'

But he did not say when.

Chapter Five

John was late to court. Travel had been wretched. He would have apologies to make.

A year had gone by and much had changed, but the most important thing had not. Richard III still wore the crown.

As John entered the Palace, he did not know what to expect. He had heard things. Fact? Rumour? Hard to know. The Dowager Queen had left sanctuary in the spring even after Parliament had formally declared her marriage illegitimate, her children bastards and Richard and *his* descendants, not Edward's, as the rightful Kings.

Just as John had overheard last year.

Yet all those manoeuvrings had been no defence against fate. Now, Richard *had* no descendants. His son had died in the spring, his wife was weak and the succession was again in doubt.

There were rumours that the King was now smiling at the nieces he had labelled bastards. He had promised them protection. Even invited Elizabeth of York, the woman Henry had promised to marry, to join him at court, though John was certain her mother would never allow that. After her brothers had been put in Richard's care, they had disappeared.

And Henry Tudor? Henry was still across the Channel.

John looked around the Great Hall, searching for Alice. He had not seen her since last year except in memories and dreams more frequent than he had expected. Until his eyes found her, he had not realised how much he feared she would not be here.

She looked up, as if he had touched her with his gaze, and moved towards him.

'You are here,' she whispered, when she was close enough. Words near breathless. 'When Christmas came and you were not here, I feared you would not come.' She glanced over her shoulder and her voice lowered again. 'I heard nothing from you all year. I did not know...'

He could not speak for a moment, taking her in. She had grown a bit taller, a bit rounder in the last year. And the eyes that had seemed so innocent were shadowed with new sorrows.

'The journey was long. The ground was near frozen from Northumberland to London,' he said. Some said God would send brimstone to destroy the world, but this year, it felt as if He had decided to freeze the earth instead. 'Hay for the horses was near impossible to find. Or afford.'

He was babbling of nothing. As if she cared for the feeding of his horses. Looking down, he realised he had taken her hands in his and pulled them to his heart. He dropped them and stepped back. He was a warrior. He knew better than to rush to the field without assessing the risks.

And the risks this year were many.

She pressed her hand on his arm and whispered, 'I have not spoken to Bessy.'

Bessy. Elizabeth of York.

He looked back at her, sharply. He had discounted the rumours. Perhaps he had erred. 'She is here?'

Wide eyes. A look of surprise. 'She sits at the royal table. Beside the Queen.'

He raised his eyes to the royal table, shocked at what he saw. Elizabeth of York, the woman Henry Tudor had vowed to marry, was sitting at Richard's table next to Richard's wife—a seat of honour only a member of the royal family should hold.

At the sight, John felt as if he had stepped on to a battlefield crowded with knights wearing neither livery nor badges, unable to distinguish friend from foe.

Did this mean the Dowager Queen had switched allegiance from Henry's cause to Richard's? If so, then Alice's family had surely done the same. And if that were true, they might already have betrayed his family for plotting to replace King Richard.

And he might be escorted to the Tower at any minute.

Last year, he had misjudged Alice as naive and let his passion cloud his judgement. He could afford no such mistake now. He must learn the way of things while keeping his head attached, all the while assuming anything he said to her might reach the King's ear.

Stifling his emotion, he reined in his words. 'But I must first wish you a gracious Yuletide.' Words for a stranger, not for his betrothed, but in truth, they were strangers again.

Were they enemies, as well?

She matched his shift, stepping away and shielding her expression. 'And to you,' she answered, words as meaningless as his. Her expression, too, was guarded, as if all the promises they had made, the trust they had built, had disappeared across the months.

For good reason. No one could be trusted now. Even—especially—his betrothed, despite the temptation of his unruly body.

'I heard of your grief,' he said. Her mother, who had been ill the year before, had died in the spring.

Alice blinked, tears threatening. 'We mourn her still. My father remains at home. It is hard to see all this…' She waved her hand.

He looked around, absorbing for the first time the extent of the celebrations. Last year, Richard had gazed around the hall with pious frowns, condemning the lively Christmas court kept by the former King.

This year, the Feast of St John the Evangelist was being celebrated with all the wine the occasion demanded. Saint John had survived after drinking poisoned wine, so his feast day provided an excuse for high and low to lift a cup of wine, or two, or three, to his memory. And so they were.

All this despite the fact that Richard and his Queen had lost their only child—the heir to the throne—earlier in the year. Yet except for Alice's sorrow, there seemed to be little mourning in this court.

'Is your family with you?' Alice asked.

He tensed, wondering whether there was more in her question than courtesy. 'The extended cold has created… problems. My father was needed at home.'

He and his father had battled over who should come and what should be said, but in the end, that was the story they had agreed to tell. In truth, John had come alone so that both of them would not be in Richard's grasp at the same time. And it seemed the decision had been a wise one.

Alice was looking at him, silent, as if trying to see what he had not said.

That he could not allow.

Fighting temptation, he pulled his gaze from her face and looked up at the royal dais. 'I must present myself,' he said.

Step by step, he approached the royal table. Draped with three layers of cloth, it was dressed as sumptuously as those who dined there. The King and Queen sat on chairs under a canopy, but Elizabeth, next to the Queen, had also been honoured with a high-backed chair instead of a stool.

Sitting at the royal table. Treated like royalty.

Gold and silver cups and basins crowded the table and the King's fingers caressed the most absurd salt cellar, sitting at his right. Gold, in the shape of an elephant carrying a castle and two damsels, the salt-cover handle was a diamond-set white rose. Two women and the York white rose. Did it carry meaning?

'Your Grace,' John said to the King, with a deep bow.

'You're late. Where's your father? I expected you both to be here.' Suspicious. Did he suspect, or worse, know something?

John recited his apology. The weather. Hard journey. The need to take care of things in the north.

The King waved him away. So, he was not to be clapped in the Tower of London. At least, not now.

Jaw clenched, John turned to greet the Queen, sitting beside Elizabeth. Seeing them together was startling. Not only did they share fair hair and light blue eyes, but, in violation of sumptuary laws, Elizabeth was dressed in a gown identical to the Queen's. One which only royalty should have been allowed. Certainly not one permitted to a woman Richard had labelled the bastard daughter of an illegitimate king.

Richard's wife was older, true, but they looked as if they were sisters instead of sharing common great-grandparents. They resembled two matched chess queens, looking as if one could be exchanged for the other.

The thought chilled him. Was that Richard's plan?

But as he faced the Queen, bowing, he realised he had been wrong about one thing. She did not share the merriment of the rest of the court. Instead, she smiled but weakly, her face full of weary grief, the death of her son weighing like a lingering illness.

The face of Elizabeth of York, in contrast, was radiant, as fair and comely as her mother's. And today, back at the royal table, she indeed looked like a queen.

Was she anything more than a pawn?

He had not met the woman before and, as he presented himself, he wondered whether she would even know who he was. But her eyes widened in recognition. 'A pleasure, my lord.'

Then she *did* know him. Was that a good sign, or a dangerous one?

'I have not spoken to Bessy.'

What promises had persuaded the Dowager Queen to leave sanctuary and let her daughter join the court of the man who had murdered her sons, stripped her of her title and income, and declared her an adulteress and her children bastards?

And what secrets had been revealed as a result?

Richard reached across his wife to touch Elizabeth's arm and point to the new jester across the hall. She laughed, then tried to encourage the Queen to look and smile.

John backed away, unnoticed.

Richard held a firm grip on the throne. Elizabeth, the woman who was to validate Henry's claim, was laughing with her uncle, dressed as if she were a queen.

Clearly Henry's plan was in jeopardy.

Alice watched John approach the royal table, struggling to make sense of it all. In that first, unguarded moment, he had seemed glad to see her. Then his face became again unreadable, devoid of emotion.

How foolish, truly, she had been last year. Playing at cards with him, thinking only of whether or not he might 'love' her, when she should have been worrying about her family's fate.

Just a few days ago, in Westminster Abbey for Christmas Mass, she had looked longingly at the chapel where they had taken vows last year. They had parted with trust and longing, expecting Henry Tudor to land soon and sweep the old regime away. The world had been full of hushed plans, secret expectations and imminent change.

But Henry had not come.

And the former Queen, who had said last year that Alice's betrothal to John was of critical importance to the future of throne, country, and family, had seemingly changed sides and sent her daughter to celebrate Christmas at Richard's court.

Alice had trusted last year that her family wanted her to enter into the secret pact that the betrothal implied. Her father had confirmed this when she returned home. Outwardly, joining with a family known for loyalty to Richard would protect her family, disguising their secret support for Henry Tudor.

Now, she feared even her father had been deceived. Perhaps the real plan had been for John to expose her family's part in the plot and send them all to the gallows.

Alice's father, mazed by grief after his wife's death, had retreated from the world for most of the year. It was hard to know if the plan was still alive. He had said only that he had received a message: *Be patient.*

He did not say from whom.

And he did not say how long patience must last.

So, for months, she had waited with no other word about her fate, that of Henry Tudor, or the throne.

Did John know more than she?

'My lady.' As if conjured, he appeared beside her, stern-faced as a stranger. And yet she could not help but smile.

He did not return it.

Her smile faded. 'Sir.' A greeting as formal as if they were linked only by their joint attendance at court. Perhaps that was now the truth. Perhaps all the plans had crumbled, leaving their betrothal as just another piece of chaff, discarded on a pile of shifting loyalties. 'It is good that you arrived safely, despite the difficulties of travel.'

His expression darkened. 'I am here at my King's command,' he said.

Which king?

She bit her tongue against the question. Dangerous, to refer so frankly to the conspiracies of last year when she knew not where his loyalties might lie today. But she must learn what she could in order to protect her family.

And even with all the danger, just to stand beside him made her heart beat faster. She felt again the warmth of his nearness, remembered their kisses, wanted to move closer...

She looked away, out at the glittering spectacle of the Great Hall, and tried to speak as if commenting on nothing more grave than the recipe of the sauce on the pudding cake.

'Elizabeth of York remains unwed,' she said. A statement of fact only.

He did not answer immediately, but she felt him turn to study her.

'She does,' he said, finally.

Not a word more.

'As do her sisters.' The former King and Queen had a bevy of daughters, some barely out of the nursery, though that would not prevent marriage agreements being made.

'The King, no doubt, has plans for them.' Smooth, safe words.

But any plan of Richard's would not involve Henry Tudor.

She wanted to grab his arm, shake him and ask what he knew, but even if he had not switched sides, the King had ears everywhere. She must choose safe words. Words that would not betray them.

'No doubt he does,' she said. 'Marriages can serve a useful purpose.'

He turned to look at her and, this time, she met his eyes. Did she imagine a hint of longing hidden there?

'Sometimes.'

They were breathing in the same cadence and, for a moment, she lost her thought, remembering...

Then she clenched her fist, digging her nails into her palm. She must keep her wits or she might lose her head. 'And when I spoke to Queen Anne, she mentioned I was unwed.' The mention had seemed innocent at the time.

His startled face reassured her. 'Did she say more?'

Alice shook her head. 'My father has been…silent on my future.' Not the complete story, but all she would risk sharing. In fact, she knew little more.

Be patient.

She was not, by nature, a patient woman.

So when John did not answer her, she had to press. 'And yours?'

'My what?'

Impossible man. 'Your father. Has he spoken of your future?'

Not a question she should be asking. And yet…

'His attention has been on other things,' he answered. 'The new Council of the north, the truce with Scotland, the visit of the King…'

All important, but none relevant to what she had asked.

'So,' she said, softly, slowly, aware she should be saying nothing at all, 'perhaps plans have not changed since last year…'

She dared to look at him, only to see his eyes seeking hers. There was a flash of desire in his, as fierce as that she felt.

'In my experience,' he said, 'most plans require change.' But still he did not look away. He did not break the bond of hope that held them.

Did the words mean something? 'Change, but how much…?' She searched his eyes, as if they held truth his tongue did not. Could it be true? Could they still…?

But the invisible visor came down, his eyes no longer burned with truth and all that remained were words, floating on air. 'And sometimes, plans must be abandoned altogether.'

Abandoned? Did he mean Henry Tudor had abandoned his plan or was it only the Earl of Stanson? The King had visited Stanson earlier this year. Something could have happened when they met. Perhaps the earl had changed his mind and revealed her father's support of Henry Tudor. If that had happened, she and her father were both in danger.

She looked away. 'Sometimes, it is hard to know which path is right.' Too painful to hope when she did not know whether the biggest danger was to long for this man or to reject him.

So they stood together, silent, and she understood, truly for the first time, the limbo on the edge of Hell, reserved for those born before the coming of the Christ and for un-baptised infants. She felt like one of those innocents: saved from the worst of Hell, but barred from Heaven, too.

Still, she forced a smile. 'Life is full of uncertainty, so we must make merry at Christmas, while we can.' Foolish words. She had never seen John 'merry' and he did not look so now.

'As if tomorrow does not matter?' His face broke into a surprising smile, as if he, too, were pretending all was well. Pretending they could spend these days together, happily, even if plans had changed. Or been abandoned.

She wanted that. Fiercely. The King, this cruel usurper on the throne, was feeling expansive and mirthful. Riotous almost. Who would notice a kiss in a dark corner, or not be willing to overlook it if they did? All part of the celebration of the season, nothing more. Something, perhaps the only thing, she might have to remember later.

And if that meant she could keep him close and spy on him in an attempt to protect her family? Well, she would tell herself that, too.

Just as she told herself she would resist the temptation of his nearness, of his kisses...

'Verily!' she said. 'Let us enjoy and celebrate this Christmas as if it might be the last.' A statement too forward for a woman. She did not care.

'As if...our last,' he echoed.

And she did not know whether the rush of her blood was of anticipation or dread.

* * *

John steeled himself against temptation. Christmas merriment. Dance. Drink. All dangerous.

And so, it seemed, was his betrothed.

John stood beside her, tense, trying to decipher her intent. Was she no more than a giddy woman, thinking of dancing and kisses? So she had said last year, as well.

He near laughed at his own foolishness. He had underestimated her last year. Had he learned nothing?

But last year, they had, ultimately, been on the same side. Pledged, in secret, to support a plan to overthrow the King that now seemed less and less likely to happen, or to succeed if it did.

One word to the King about his family's promise and he, and his father, would be parted from their heads. Had her family ever been in earnest? Or had they been part of a scheme to destroy his?

He had trusted her, finally, last year, because he had let his body rule his brain. He should not make the same mistake again. Foolish emotion had no place when life and death were at stake.

'Tomorrow there is a disguising,' Alice said. 'We may be asked to play some part.'

He shook his head. Every day this season would be a disguising, but he did not know who played what part.

'Attend! Attend all!' The Lord of Misrule stomped his staff on the floor. 'It's time for a game of Hoodman's Blind.' He pranced towards John, then grabbed his arm. 'And this man will be it!'

Chapter Six

Suddenly, John was pulled into the crowd, a hood thrust over his head and he was spun around until he was dizzy.

When the man let go, John staggered, fighting panic. Dark beneath the hood. Impossible to see. Hard to breathe. Spun around until he did not know one direction from the next. Even to stand was uncertain. One unsteady step and he would fall.

He held out his arms like a blind man, reaching for something to hold on to.

Something hit him from behind. He stumbled. It was a cruel game, the players all invested in bringing him to his knees, while his job was to catch someone and identify who it was.

Cruel, deliberately, to put the hood on a man who had arrived in court less than an hour before. How was he to know anyone?

Now, people crowded close, but when he tried to grab someone, they all scuttled out of reach.

'No running out of the hall or up the stairs,' the Lord of Misrule called, his words muffled by the hood on John's head. 'Give the man a fighting chance.'

This time, instead of rushing him all at once, one person, then another, came close, laughed and ran away. Tantalising.

He grabbed an arm. A man, he was sure, and strong enough to pull himself away. Next, a woman. She could not escape.

He pulled her closer. Not Alice. He knew instantly. How? Her height? Her scent? But he knew it was not.

Closer, the woman did not resist. He put his hands on her face, felt her breath on his fingers, but did not know her.

What a fool they had made of him.

He pulled her closer. Did she lift her face, as if to be kissed? Cheek close to his. Lips near his ear. The hood, safely separating them.

Then, a whisper. 'Beware.'

And she slipped out of his reach.

Who? What?

He raised his hands, ready to tear off the hood. Behind him, two hands clasped the edges of the hood, holding it close to his shoulder.

'No cheating,' the Lord of Misrule said. 'Only if you guess right can you remove the hood.'

He must not guess at all. Someone had tried to warn him. Anyone he named, right or wrong, might put them both at risk.

Lies. Intrigue. All hidden so that a man did not know friend from foe. He longed for an open field of battle, with the enemy in clear view.

'You are all long at court,' he said, words muffled through the hood. 'And I have not had time to put my hands on many women here.'

As he intended, the remark sparked laughter, loud and appreciative.

'Well, then we should give you the chance,' said Misrule, behind him. 'Ladies, come within reach! Let's see which one he can identify by touch!'

Now, the laughing increased, breathlessly dancing close and away. He had learned to hold his head up and cast his eyes down to the floor, trying to glimpse the edge of a gown, struggling to remember who was wearing what.

What colour had Alice donned this evening?

But he did not need that clue when he caught her. Knew

her the minute his hands were on her waist. She let him pull her close. Though she leaned away from the waist up, below, she was tight against him. And his body did not care that they were in the midst of the entire court…

Hoots from the crowd.

'Lady Alice!' he called, glad to have it over.

Applause, but some rude remarks about how he knew her. 'My betrothed,' he called, hood off, frowning. As far as anyone knew, that was still true. 'What other woman should I know?'

'Then she is the next to be blindfolded. But this time, you are not to be among the men she tries to catch.'

He felt his stomach turn and tried to protest. But it was Christmas and the Lord of Misrule was master of all and even the King was cheering.

Alice glanced at him, frightened, as the hood went over her head.

Twirled around and pushed as he had been, she teetered, waving her arms, struggling for balance. Now the crowd around her hit her with rolled-up fabric. She staggered. He lunged, wanting to stop them, to stop this.

Two men held his arms, preventing him from moving.

'Beware.'

Who had said that? And what did it mean?

'Be brave,' her father had said, though she did not think he had expected this.

It was a game. Nothing more. But unable to see, knowing John was prevented from rescuing her, as she had him, she did not feel brave at all.

Her breath quickened, stealing her calm. Someone pushed her. She almost fell.

No. Shoulders straight. Breath steady. She would best them all.

She reached for something. A man's hand. He pulled it

away. The edge of a full tunic. That, too, snatched out of reach.

Laughter from the Lord of Misrule. 'Now, men, you must not try too hard to get away or we will be here until it is time to break fast.'

So instead, all laughing, they surrounded her. To make it easier, they claimed. But all of them, taller, stronger, closing in, too close…

And then, the space around her cleared, as if they all had moved away.

She reached, grabbed. An arm. Fur at the end of a velvet sleeve. Fur allowed to only one man.

She sank into an obeisance. 'Your Grace.'

Her hood was removed so she could see the King's smiling face coming close, closer, and then he kissed her lips.

Laughter all around her. She dare not move until the King did. Then, he, too, laughed, enjoying the jest played at her cost. So she must smile, hide her embarrassment. And her disgust.

The attention of the court shifted and she breathed again, then fled the Hall, unable to face John. What would he think of such a display? Would he think she was now allied with King Richard?

Was he?

'I trust you,' her father had said. The burden felt heavier, even more fraught with danger than last year. Bessy had not spoken to her, but she had whispered something to John during the game. Did they plan a secret meeting? Was his family now allied with the former King's family to carry out some new plan?

Alice was still perplexed the following morning as she joined the other lords and ladies of the court in preparations for the disguising. Perhaps Bessy had been fully drawn into this wanton court. Certainly, she, the King and the Queen were the intended audience for the disguising, so Alice was protected, for the moment, from facing Bessy.

And she could be sure, for the moment, that John was not plotting with Bessy, for he, too, had been forced to participate in the entertainment. She thought him a man accustomed to disguises, but he looked distinctly uncomfortable as they made him stand still while the servants searched for his costume.

There was no chance to speak to him and she was grateful for that. She needed to subdue her emotions first.

She had not fully admitted, until forced to confront her own future, that she had wanted a marriage like that of her parents, as full of love as of duty. No woman, or man, could expect that. And if you were lucky enough to find love, it would only bring you grief in the end. Her father's pain at her mother's loss would never end.

No. Better to make a marriage like a move on a chess board, with an eye on the overall game, not for the personal feelings of the pawn.

A chess piece had no feelings. Or did not admit them.

But Alice did. And feelings were dangerous, as well as painful.

She had been wary of John last year, but in the end, she had let down her guard. She must not make that mistake this year.

Final whispers of preparation. A disguising was something like a painting brought to life. Nothing to do but stand as instructed. So she had paid little notice to what was being presented. Then, someone thrust something into her hand, closed her fingers around it and turned away.

Brought back from her thoughts, she looked down. A white rose. She was wearing a white gown and carrying a white rose.

Pushed from behind, she walked into the hall and saw John entering from the other side, robed in purple, with a crown on his head.

Dressed as if he were the King.

Her breath stopped. Had her fears been realised? Would the King rise and denounce them as traitors to be taken to the Tower?

She glanced at King Richard, fearing a frown, but he was smiling and nodding at the master of entertainment.

'Go. You must walk,' the play master hissed. 'Join your hand to his.'

She took a step. John's robe of purple and the crown. That could only mean one thing. He was supposed to be King.

King Richard.

She looked down at her dress. White. Just as the Queen and Elizabeth had worn last night.

Surely Alice was to represent Richard's Queen, a touching tribute.

But John's face…she had never seen it so hard, so angry. And the flower in her hand? It was a white rose.

Elizabeth. She was supposed to be Elizabeth.

Appalled, she looked at the Queen, sitting beside her smiling husband as if she had been propped up in the chair. Her gaze was weak, vacant. Beside her, Elizabeth shone even more brightly—beautiful, young and vibrant. Was her stiff smile, too, a disguise? Surely she could see what this was meant to be.

A picture of a marriage of Richard and his niece Elizabeth. One that would violate the laws of God and man.

But the herald, behind them, finally spoke, explaining the scene was the union of Richard and the House of York to the throne of England, now and for ever.

The King laughed and clapped and cheered. Anne and Elizabeth clapped without strength. Richard's personal priest sat to the side, frowning and mute.

John gripped her hand, as if signalling her to hold steady. She looked up. Despite his clenched jaw and the stern anger on his face, his eyes touched her gently. And for that moment, the illusion of marrying a man she loved shimmered before her again. If this were a real marriage, their marriage—

Then, before her eyes, the anger returned to his face. Had the gentleness been a disguise?

At the high table, the King reached over to Elizabeth, as if to encourage her appreciation. She smiled and nodded, clapping harder than before, laughing now, as he seemed to demand.

Alice frowned. Had Bessy been threatened? Was she smiling at Richard under duress? Or had she truly changed her allegiance?

There was only one way to know. She must talk to Bessy, alone, and trust her to tell the truth for the sake of their friendship.

She hoped she would not regret it.

On the fifth day of Christmas John had to get away from the palace.

King Richard's evil infused Westminster's very air, poisoning it just like the wine that Saint John drank. The mysterious warning to beware, the unnatural marriage portrayal, the uncertainty about Alice… He needed clear air.

And a clear head.

The anger that had surged through his blood when the King kissed Alice was jealousy, yes, but more. Disgust. Hatred. A tinge of fear? A justification for all his suspicions. And yet, he was certain she had not invited, nor wanted, the kiss. But then, the next day, the mock marriage and its calumnious implications…

Even then, when he looked at Alice, it seemed as if their marriage could be real, that she would be his and, for a moment, he thought of nothing but her—

A man could go mad from it all.

So he crept out of the palace to stretch his legs on the streets of London, glad of the cold wind. He would have preferred a hunt—hours on horseback, matching wits against his prey. The simple world of life, death and truth. Not the brainsick, distorted intrigues of Richard's court.

It filled him with fury: the deceptions, the machinations, the plots, the waiting. He was ready for battle. If only he knew on which side…

And which side Alice was on.

'I have not spoken to Bessy.'

Was that even true? Elizabeth was Alice's childhood friend. If she had now thrown her lot in with Richard, surely Alice would have done the same.

'Beware.'

Of Alice?

Leaving, even for a few hours, was a risk, for he did not know what she might do when he was not watching her. He headed north along the river, surprised to see so many people on the streets. Already he longed for the hills of home, realising for the first time how often during the last year he had pictured showing them to her.

At last, tired and cold, he ducked into a tavern. He had come out wearing no livery, nor any evidence of rank, so he did not attract questions. The owner, unable to afford to close for the season or greedy to earn some extra coin, poured him a cup of ale and he took a sip. Harsher than the brew served at court.

Around him, the customers were merry. Drinking, singing. Some on their way to Canterbury in honour of the martyr Thomas Beckett. From what he could overhear, these were palmers, paid by others to take the trip on behalf of their souls, so travelling for coin, not holiness.

'Let's drink to King Richard!' said one. 'And the end of the beneficences!'

He stilled to listen. So did several others. The beneficences, a nice word for taxes, that the previous King had imposed had not endeared him to the lesser classes. Richard was wise to lift them.

A mug was raised. A few more. Slowly, as if reluctantly. Cheers were few. And muted.

'Despite that,' someone muttered, 'he's an unnatural man.' Shaking his head. Others joined.

'Rumours,' scoffed the first.

'Not a rumour that he's been courting his niece in front of his ailing wife. My cousin works in the kitchen. He's seen it. And worse.' He leaned forward and whispered.

John leaned back, casually, trying to hear.

Poison.

They thought the King was poisoning his wife.

Even he had not thought to accuse Richard of such evil. True, the Queen seemed more frail by the day. And the attention Richard had lavished on Elizabeth, the implications of yesterday's mock wedding, were…unnatural. But did he truly intend…?

The job of a king was to protect his people from enemies on earth and in Heaven. No man, certainly no king, had a spotless soul. But a man who would kill his nephews, poison his wife, marry his niece… Such a man would be abandoned by God.

What havoc, then, might befall his country?

If Richard's people already thought him so vile, perhaps they would, indeed, welcome Henry Tudor as King.

A reminder of the real mark. Marriage to Alice was unimportant except that it would help Henry Tudor take the throne. If, to ensure that end, John had to spy on Alice, even to remove her as an obstacle, he would.

Chapter Seven

So, once again, John was forced into subterfuge, keeping Alice close as he tried to determine whether she was now friend or foe.

Once again, he must struggle not to enjoy it so much.

Standing at the edge of the Hall that night, he thought her unusually quiet. Yet he, too, remained mute, unable to think of anything to say except those things he must not speak.

Have you turned to Richard's side? Do you now plot against me?

There seemed to be fewer in attendance than last year. Perhaps other men had made excuses, as his father had. A year and a half into his reign, Richard had made it clear that he rewarded loyalty. Yet the rewards he gave were land and money seized from some of his once-loyal supporters—men he had killed when they turned against him.

Not a policy designed to foster steadfast support. Surely the men who got the spoils must wonder when their 'loyalty' might also be rewarded by death.

The extensive Stanson holdings would be tempting indeed to use as a reward for another man's loyalty.

He would raise the issue aslant, to see what she might say. 'King Richard seems to be celebrating mightily this season,' he said. His words sounded flat, even to his own ears. 'He seems comfortable on the throne.'

Not afraid that Henry Tudor would replace him, certainly.

She glanced at him, sharply. 'You have been away,' she

replied, 'so you may not know that Henry Tudor has left Brittany and now resides in the court of the French King.'

He had said nothing about Henry. She must have mentioned it to see whether she could discover what he knew about Henry Tudor's plans. 'So I heard.'

He knew much he would not say. Henry had, indeed, left Brittany, just ahead of a troop of men King Richard had sent to capture him. The network of spies working on Henry's behalf had been just moments quicker than Richard's men.

But Alice had more to say. 'This new alliance with the French King angered King Richard so deeply that he issued a proclamation against all the exiled lords in France supporting Henry. He has called them murderers, adulterers and traitors.'

'Oh?' He sounded surprised. 'When was this?'

'Just a few weeks ago.'

'Word had not reached us in the north.' North, the home of Richard's strongest support. If Richard branded the exiled lords as traitors, he would not hesitate to do the same to those still on English soil. His father was supposed to be Richard's right arm, but this step had been taken deliberately without his consultation.

Was she trying to warn him of danger?

She continued, in a voice too deliberately careless to be believed. 'Richard accuses Henry of promising to relinquish England's right to the French throne in exchange for the French King's support. He claims,' she said, 'that if Henry invades, it will be as if France is rekindling the war. And winning.'

He tried not to snort. France? It was Englishmen who were supporting Henry's plans. The French King was a corbie messenger, late to come with his support. But though the war between England and France, which had dragged on for more than a hundred years, was officially over, the hostility remained. Richard was wily to take advantage of that. The support of the French King was not going to endear Henry to many in England, even to those who thought Richard a child murderer.

'Interesting speculation,' he said, in a tone he hoped did not betray his anger at the suggestion. 'But we seem a long way from either of these things.'

Longer than he would have liked.

She met his eyes now, somehow insistent. 'But Henry has written letters to those in England,' she said, 'asking for support of his "just quarrel". And he has signed them *Henricus, Rex*.'

Henry, King.

No past ruler had called himself King before he defeated the current occupant of the throne. Was it hubris or confidence? Perhaps the fact that the French King had recognised Henry as the rightful King of England had emboldened him.

'We did hear,' he spoke cautiously, 'that de Vere has joined Henry.'

She shrugged, giving him no indication of how the King viewed this development.

Perhaps she did not realise the importance of it. De Vere, key leader of the Lancaster military forces during the earlier wars, had been in prison for ten years in Calais. He was a seasoned, respected commander. At the head of Henry's troops, he would be a threat.

Had John's father helped his release by providing money to bribe a guard? Best not to ask. What he did not know, he could not reveal.

Were Alice's revelations a sign of trust or a trap? He let the carol music fill the lull as the dancers filled the hall. Imprisoned by forced silence, he shrugged frustration from his tight shoulders.

'Another card game, perhaps?'

Her question startled him into laughter. 'And let you fool me again?'

Did her cheeks burn or did he imagine it?

But she met his eyes, not retreating. 'It is only…if we are

wed, we will have many hours together. We should learn how we might fill them.'

Hard, hungry thoughts tore through him of how he would like to fill those hours. And her. 'If?' Did the word carry significance?

'No date has been set for...anything.'

Was she speaking of their marriage? Or of Henry Tudor's plans? 'You think I know something,' he said, tired of being circumspect.

'Do you not?' she asked.

He didn't. But he should not have spoken so bluntly. 'I know that neither of us knows much of the other,' he said, with a smile that belied harsh words, 'And we stand across from each other on a battlefield.'

'Or a dance floor,' she said, with a smile of her own and a nod towards the floor. 'Which is much more pleasant.'

'Then shall we join the carol ring?' A chance to move, at least, instead of trying to joust at conversation.

Her eyes widened in surprise. 'You dance?'

Of all the things they had shared last year, never a dance.

'Do you think me a Scot barbarian?' Defensive words. He might not have a courtier's graces, but he had been trained as befitted his station.

Her eyes lowered, a semi-apology.

He took Alice's hand, fighting the rush of heat raised by her touch, and led her into the gay celebration.

And then, shocked, he saw the King lead Elizabeth of York to the floor, leaving his wife behind without a glance. *Poison.* Exchange one woman for the other. It now seemed that he should fully consider that possibility.

Beneath his hand, he felt Alice's curl into a fist. He turned to look. She wore a calm smile, again, disguising the tight pressure of her lips as she watched the King with Elizabeth.

Surely Alice disapproved. She could not possibly be part of such a plot.

Or was that just what his unruly body wanted to be true? He must keep the danger in mind, instead of craving a kiss...

The dance began with them hand in hand, following the line of dancers, with the King and Elizabeth in the lead. Then, the King turned to the left, Elizabeth to the right, each followed by the men or women behind them, forming separate circles, which then mixed and mingled in patterns that had been ingrained in him for years.

But that meant each person was, even briefly, close to countless others. Did Alice whisper something to that man? Did that one pass a message to her? Would someone come to stab him in his sleep that night?

But as he watched her, he realised she was not speaking to those she passed in the dance, but following him with her eyes as closely as he was watching her.

Spying as he was?

Her nearness, tempting, always lulled him into trust. He needed to keep a close watch on her, yes, but he needed time apart. Time to put his mind again in charge of his body.

And his heart.

Or he might lose his life.

Instead of watching her steps or her passing partners, Alice found her eyes following John, trying to read his intention. He had left the palace today, she had learned, yet said nothing of it to her. He must be hiding something. Conspiring with people he did not want her, want anyone, to see.

She had been foolish to speak to him of Henry Tudor's plans, perhaps, though she had said nothing that was not public knowledge. Yet she'd been surprised at what he did not seem to know.

Finding his eyes, in turn, on her, she saw little of longing there. Instead, he watched her with suspicion that matched hers.

Now, their betrothal floated uncertainly on dangerous

waters. Still a fact, but one that garnered neither attention nor action. No time, now, for fantasies of marrying for love. Foolish to think of the kisses they had shared, memories that still warmed her dreams.

This night, as King Richard danced with Elizabeth, a marriage between Bessy and the upstart Tudor seemed impossible. And so did theirs. She would be lucky if no more than the betrothal was lost.

Be brave. Better that she beware.

The dance ended and they were handed a cup of warm, sweet hippocras wine. She sipped, revelling in the smell of cinnamon and ginger as the King signalled the end of the evening.

John, with only the briefest of bows, left the hall without a word to her. A relief, but more proof, if she needed it, that he had secrets to keep.

'Ali?' Bessy's voice.

Suddenly, her friend was walking beside her, as if by chance. A smile, as of old. Bessy reached to squeeze her hand, quickly, then let it go. 'Are you having a happy Christmas, Ali?'

Alice looked at Elizabeth, uncertain how to answer. The laughing, careless friendship of childhood seemed beyond reach. And yet… 'I miss my mother, of course,' she said. 'And you? You must enjoy being out in the world again.'

Sanctuary, they called it. It must have been more like prison, since no one could come or go without the King's knowledge. And consent.

Bessy averted her eyes. 'Yes. Yes, it is.' Was there a hint of desperation in her voice. Or was it guilt?

'And your mother? She is not here?' Could her absence be a sign that she and her daughter now had different plans for the future?

Now, a sharp look. 'Do not judge what you do not know.'

Alice knew nothing. That was exactly the problem. None of this made sense. Unless it was as she had feared: Richard had killed Bessy's brothers. He must have threatened her. And her mother.

And perhaps even his Queen's ill health might not be sent of God...

Alice looked to the floor to hide her fear. This betrothal that had seemed so far-fetched last Christmas suddenly seemed as dangerous as battle. 'For the friendship you bore me...please...'

A sharp whisper. 'Shhh.' Then, head bowed. 'Tomorrow. After supper.'

'Tomorrow. After supper.'

Alice went through the sixth day of Christmas as though she were holding her breath. John was avoiding her and she was glad, since she did not have to think about what to say, or not say, to him. She found if difficult enough to concentrate on playing her own role at court.

Made even more difficult because the Lord of Misrule, given sway over the court, was turning the world upside down, trying to force unbridled cheer on the festivities. But at the high table, Richard, who had laughed at everything the day before, sat glumly, without a smile.

He had been said to change moods at the drift of a shadow. She could see that today.

The Queen was absent from court. Whispers of her ill health were growing louder. The physicians, it was said, had told the King he could no longer share her bed. Was the man mourning her? Or thinking of a new wife?

Richard had gone to great lengths to be sure Parliament named his own children successors to the throne. Now, with no heir and a sickly wife, who would reign after him?

Henry Tudor?

The new jester, tasked with raising everyone's spirits, had a hard time of it. Even when he tried to toot a carol tune with farts and the assembled laughed, the King, always a jester's main audience, did not.

Desperate, foolish, the man made some comment about an archer who shoots arrows which never find their mark and so bear no fruit. Under normal circumstances, such a remark, too close to home as a suggestion of the lack of manhood of a childless man, would be greeted with laughter, perhaps a little too loud to mask the disease of the insult.

Not today.

But, unwisely, the jester, gambolling about the Hall, made an even more pointed joke.

'Who sits in a high chair? A judge or a murderer or a king?'

There were titters, the room not certain whether they should laugh or not.

Alice looked at Richard's face. There was no laughter there. The man was pale with fury, sweating as if anger seeped through his skin.

The jester, ever vigilant, switched his tune. 'A king, of course!' A few backward flips. Applause.

Alice did not watch. She kept her eyes on the King.

Richard motioned his head. The Lord of Misrule came to his side. A few whispered words. Then Lord of Misrule disappeared.

Within a few minutes, so did the jester.

The pipers began to play, a little too loudly. The King nodded his head in time. Everyone let go a breath and took a stiff gulp of wine. The murmur of conversation began again, but no one dared ask aloud what had become of the jester.

No, there was no question that Richard remained uneasy about his grip on the throne. Anyone he suspected was a threat would be in danger.

Across the hall, Bessy met her eyes and gave a quick nod. *Tonight.*

Chapter Eight

Late. Dark. At the Abbey, Matins prayers were over and the monks had gone to rest. In the Palace, knights, pages and squires slept in clumps around a dying fire in the Great Hall. Even the servants had gone to grab a few precious moments of rest. All was quiet and Alice could move unseen.

She knew where Bessy would be—in the same room, overlooking the river, where they had played and prayed together as children. Alice needed no candle to find her way there.

Dangerous to be about, but more dangerous, she feared, to remain ignorant.

She took a deep breath and scratched at the door. 'Bessy?' No one else would use that name.

The rustle of fabric. The door opened and she was pulled inside, quickly. The room so dark, she could barely be sure who was there.

'Shhh.' Bessy's voice. 'I told the maid I wanted to be alone tonight, but she may return. I think she gives reports to him…'

Him. No need to say more.

'Tell me true, Bessy. Is King Richard your choice?' For King? For husband? Was there a difference now?

She thought she saw a shake of the head 'no'. 'You don't know what it has been like. He killed my uncles, my brothers. He made me a bastard by law…' The words trailed off.

Alice reached out, enveloping her in a hug, heedless of the years and changes in rank that had passed. The cruelties Richard had inflicted, hard to comprehend. The woman was the daughter of a king and queen, yet he had created a wild lie and persuaded Parliament to accept it, for no other reason than his own lust for power.

Elizabeth pulled away, steadying herself. 'Mother did not know how long it would be before he became impatient and would no longer honour sanctuary. We would not be safe...'

'But he vowed to protect your family.' A public pronouncement, loudly, before they left for the sanctuary.

A bitter laugh. 'And you believe him?'

'But you seem to be...' what was the word? '...happy.'

'If I have fooled you, I hope I have fooled him, as well. I have tried to grasp some moments... Is it wrong to want some joy in life?'

How could it be? She had wanted only that herself, last year, when Elizabeth was still imprisoned next door. When Alice should have been thinking of bringing food to her friend instead of whether she would be allowed to dance. 'But the disguising, the implication that you, the King, that you might...'

'Marry?' The word curdled. 'Surely the Pope would not give dispensation for a man to marry his niece. Besides...' another mirthless laugh '...he has trapped himself. He knows I am a legitimate royal heir. My husband would have a path to the throne. That is why he created legal lies to "prove" we were illegitimate. Now, he cannot marry me and keep the fiction.'

No great plan. Nothing for the good of the nation. Just reactions, schemes, lies, one after another, meant to elevate himself, no matter what the cost.

'So you still plan to marry Henry?'

A stifled laugh. 'None of this is in my hands. My mother and the mother of Henry Tudor...these women make the plans. Until the Tudor man triumphs, I must stay alive. Today, that means smiling at a murderer so he will not murder me.'

As she feared, Bessy had been threatened. 'But there is still a plan?' Was the question a prayer? 'For you to marry Henry and me to marry…' *John*. His name would burn her mouth if she spoke it.

'Someone, I'm sure, still plans that. I only hope I am still alive and unwed when, if, Henry triumphs.'

'And what should I do?' Alice asked, like one witless, desperate for answers that did not exist.

Bessy hugged her. 'Oh, my dear Ali. Do what you must to stay alive.'

A chill reminder. No one was safe.

But was all the danger from the King? 'Do you know… has the Earl of Stanson changed his loyalties back to Richard?'

She asked about the Earl, but Alice really wanted to know about his son.

'Richard still thinks him loyal. Is he?' Bessy shrugged. 'He is a man, like Richard, who shifts to stay alive. But then,' she said, sadly, 'so must I.'

All Alice had feared, real.

Staying alive must be her concern, not some foolish dream of love. She must make certain that she and her family would live long enough to see her married. To anyone.

John roamed Westminster's dark halls, unable even to pretend to sleep. Questions roiled in his brain. He wanted to believe he could trust Alice and that she was still to be his, but the plan's success depended on secrets being kept on all sides. Tonight, the real intentions, of the former Queen and of Alice's family, were as hard to see as the corridor before him, lit only faintly by the moon.

Suddenly, a shadow. One he knew was Alice. Far from being safely abed, she, too, was creeping through the palace.

Near the room of Elizabeth of York.

All he had feared, happening. A conspiracy to foil the Tudor plan, his family betrayed—

He stepped to block her and she gasped.

Unable to see her clearly, he had to speak. 'What are you doing?' If she answered, would she say the truth?

He could hear her breath, steadier than he expected. Silence gathered. Long enough to make him uneasy.

'Why,' she said, finally, 'should I trust you enough to tell you?'

Her words an echo of all he had just wondered. She, too, might believe his family had betrayed the cause. And if each was suspicious, who would trust first?

'Because,' he replied, 'we are bound together for life before God?'

She laughed. Not the joyful sound of last year, but a short, sharp signal that she had lost all faith. 'So are we to be the sole members of court who keep our vows?'

Certainly the King had not.

He wanted, craved, to believe her. He wanted to believe in something. He was tired of carrying the distrust like an extra suit of armour, weighing heavier with every step. He wanted to believe that if he just held her in his arms, just kissed her, he would know the truth...

He reached for her and she held out her arm, keeping him at a distance.

'Tell me—' he said.

'Who goes there?' An unfamiliar voice. A shaft of candlelight. A guard? The King so paranoid that he had armed men roaming the halls, thinking someone would kill him in his sleep.

Alice stiffened at the sound.

He stepped closer, wrapped her in his arms so she could not move, and whispered urgently before he took her lips, 'Please.'

Then he kissed her. Long. Hard. The kiss he had wanted for days. The kiss that was its own truth, that made him dizzy enough to forget the guard, the fear of betrayal, forget everything but that this woman, despite everything, belonged to him.

Over his shoulder there came a chuckle and the sound of the guard sheathing his knife while lifting his candle. 'A little Yuletide cheer, eh?'

John held her head to his chest, hiding her face, and turned to scowl. 'Can a man not kiss a woman in peace?' His voice rough, ragged with desire unfeigned. 'Without interruption?'

'As long as the woman is not mine,' the man said, laughing. But he did not leave.

John arched a brow. 'Without an audience.' There was a deliberate touch of humour in his voice. One man to another.

The laughter he had hoped for came. 'Enjoy! I'll stay blind.' Footsteps faded with the laughter.

Both of them breathed and melted against each other. She, at least, was shaking.

'He did not see you,' he whispered.

She nodded, without raising her head.

'It's all right now.'

Wordless, she lifted her arms around his neck and pulled him into another kiss...

Not for show. Not this time.

Thanks? Relief? Desire? But now he could not stop his hands, running down her back, pulling her hips closer, as if they might truly be alone in their own bed.

And at this moment, that was all he wanted. Her. Him. A bed, a life, that was theirs. No logic to the thought. No fighting the urge. Other women? Yes, as he had told her. But nothing felt this way.

He told himself to resist. But thoughts, logic all dissolved in hot blood and pounding hearts. His head was scrambled by lust, but this might be the only moment they would ever have. And, he had to trust someone...

Finally, he relaxed his hold, let their lips part and she rested in his arms, his heart, hers, beating as one. Peaceful.

With her in his arms, a new emotion flowed through him. A fierce desire to protect her. Something wholly apart from the alliances and plans that had brought them to this point. But he could not unless he knew...

So he, too, must be brave in a way no battle had ever demanded.

'The fact that you and I now fear each other says much about this King,' he said, 'and how he chooses to rule. I do not think things between us have changed as much as either of us fear, but I cannot help you unless we both take a chance.'

Was he putting himself—worse, his family—in harm's way? He wished he could see her eyes. He wished courtiers wore badges that reflected their true allegiance. He wished...

'Trust me,' he said. 'I will not hurt you. Or your family.'

She released a breath and stepped back, then looked up, as if trying to read his expression in the dark.

'I spoke to Bessy. She is, I think, still my friend,' she said. 'And she is afraid.'

Alice held her breath. She had said little that a rational man could not guess. But in front of the court, Bessy had looked full of gaiety. To suggest otherwise...

Had she said too much? Had she imperilled Bessy, her family and the entire Tudor effort?

The minutes in John's arms had felt endless. No thought, just feeling. A kiss, but just beyond it, so much more. And she wanted that. Wanted it all.

When, finally, he relaxed his hold and let their lips part, she had rested in his arms, hearing his heartbeat, and felt... at home. She had wanted to marry for love. But now, love had meddled with duty and she wondered whether she knew who to trust.

Who to love.

But her father had sent her to court alone. Twice. Trusting her to navigate its perilous currents as if she were an emissary, sent to a foreign land.

Now she must trust herself.

And John.

He did not push her. He did not look anxious or angry, but simply glad to be next to her.

But he said nothing.

'I did as you asked,' she said, the words unsteady. 'Do you trust me enough to do the same?'

Did he? What would he say?

He did not speak right away and when he did, she did not understand.

'The Bishop of Ely has gone to Rome.'

Were the words in cipher? 'What does that mean?'

'He goes to prepare the way. Henry and Elizabeth still need dispensation.'

Suddenly, she *did* understand. Her gaze had been so fixed on the relationship between Richard and Elizabeth, she had forgotten that Henry and Elizabeth, too, shared an ancestor, four or five generations and more than one hundred years past. Their marriage, too, would need dispensation.

That meant the wedding, the invasion, all of it was still planned. And Elizabeth, or her family, were still committed to Henry Tudor.

So hers and John's? That, too, would still be expected, however unlikely.

Yes, last year, she had nearly laughed at the idea that so many impossible things must happen. Now? Now, she had fixed all her hopes on those very things. To hear that the plan had not been abandoned…no gift could have brought her greater joy.

'Then,' she said, 'we have hope.'

He kissed her forehead, somehow as much a vow as when he met her lips. 'Yes. Hope.'

The twelfth day of Christmas, Epiphany

The news from France came on the Twelfth Day of Christmas. Impossible to keep secret, though Richard tried, at first.

Finally. Henry planned to invade.

The news sent John's blood coursing through his veins and for a moment, it was not clear which caused the greater thrill—that he might succeed in restoring the proper King to the throne, or that he might finally marry Alice.

He was on his way to find her when the page gave him a summons to the King's chambers. He made his way there with a sense of dread. Had he been wrong to trust Alice?

Little ceremony today. The King was pacing.

'My spies say he will invade, but they don't know where. Kent? Wales? I am coming north. We must plan. Tell your father to be ready. We will need to raise an army. And money.'

No hint of anything but belief that the Earl of Stanson was Richard's most loyal supporter. John breathed again. 'I will tell him,' he said. He did not say he would stand by the King.

Would he? For all his doubts about Alice, he knew his father was a shrewd man, unlikely to openly declare allegiance too soon. For if Richard ultimately retained the throne, the Earl would be free to abandon the young upstart.

For John, it was easier to fool the King when he was unsure of his own father's intentions, but harder to suppress his own hopes.

For a better king.

For his promised bride.

But when he found Alice, ready to tell her of the coming invasion, she looked pale and shaken.

'There is news,' he said. 'Henry is coming.'

Grabbing his arm, she leaned close, whispering as if he had said nothing of importance. 'I have talked to Bessy.

Richard speaks of marrying her to the Portuguese Prince. She begs you to tell your father. If that happens…'

Move. Countermove. Richard already planning to block Henry's path to the throne with more than swords.

'Your father must send a message to Henry,' she continued, urgently, 'to let him know Richard's plan. Henry must not misunderstand her intentions, but he must hurry…'

Chapter Nine

The third Christmas
December 23, 1485—Westminster Palace

A new Christmas, a new king. Surely a miracle, that all of the impossible things that had to happen before he and Alice could marry had come to pass.

Almost all of them.

Henry had defeated Richard on the battlefield in August. John's family, and Alice's, had played their promised parts. Parliament had recognised the new King, he had celebrated a proper coronation and, now, Henry Tudor sat on the throne.

No, John reminded himself, as he entered the gates of the Palace. Henry the Seventh, not Henry Tudor, was now King.

Yes, almost everything had come to pass except one thing: Henry and Elizabeth had not wed.

Yet.

But as John handed the reins of the horse to the page, even Westminster Palace seemed new, full of clean air and fresh possibilities.

The guest list this year was smaller and more select. Henry, from the beginning, had recognised and rewarded those who had risked all to support him, but he allowed only a select few into his inner circle.

John was not yet one of them.

When he entered the palace, the first thing he heard

was his father's voice. 'Son!' The word echoed along the stone walls.

They embraced, awkwardly and spoke of John's journey, as they walked to the room the Earl had taken.

They had seen little of each other since the battle at Bosworth Field in August. There, the Earl of Stanson had done as agreed and kept his troops apart. Denying Richard their support no doubt helped make Henry the victor that day.

But despite all pressure and warning from his father, John could not refrain from battle. He broke away, leading his own small group of men into the melee to join Henry for the final assault. A decision irrevocable, in direct defiance of his father's order, but he was weary of the cautious games his father played.

And in the end, his father could not protest, for John had picked the winning side. Now, just one thing remained.

John held his tongue until they were alone, behind closed doors. 'When will the King marry Elizabeth?'

A shrug. 'I helped persuade Parliament to officially endorse the match. He only awaits the dispensation to arrive.'

'It's been a year,' John muttered, remembering when he had told Alice the Bishop had left for Rome. 'Did the Pope object?' Of all the obstacles, he had worried more about war than God.

His father shrugged. 'The hierarchy of the church is more complicated than that of the law. And had I not seen Henry in battle, I would have guessed him a lawyer. He has insisted that every legal obstacle be addressed and solved. We had to reverse the Act of Parliament that made her illegitimate, without saying she had been declared illegitimate, then we had to—'

'I don't need to hear each step,' John said, impatient. 'What remains to be done?'

His father sighed. 'Tedious business, yes. But a request has now been sent to the Papal Legate who is in Edinburgh. I hope he will act quickly. And once the wedding is set, we will have completed our part in putting Henry on the throne. There will be no need for you to marry the Oakshire woman. I see a different alliance to be much more advantageous.'

A different alliance? He must have misunderstood. 'What do you mean?'

'Our neighbour has a daughter ready to be pledged.'

'I am already pledged.'

'Yes, and that arrangement accomplished its purpose. But their land abuts ours upstream. It is pasture we need to feed the sheep…'

His father continued to talk. John stopped listening. All the machinations, the plotting, the moving of people as if they could be controlled like chess pieces, and, in the end, to break his word? He was done with it.

'No.'

'What?'

'No.' All his life he'd trusted his father's wisdom while ignoring his own. And now, on the battlefield and the field of the heart, he was defying the man. 'I am betrothed. That is an unbreakable contract.'

His father chuckled. 'No contract is unbreakable.'

'Does Henry feel that way?' Had the King's marriage been delayed because he had changed his mind?

'His agreement to marry Elizabeth is more like a treaty. We can find a reason to walk away from a simple betrothal. Maybe she has decided to enter a nunnery.'

'Alice does not want to enter a nunnery.' Of that, he was certain.

'She doesn't have to stay. Just retreat for a while. After a year or two, she can come out and marry whom her father pleases.'

John's anger flamed. The thought of Alice being forced, even temporarily, to be exiled to a convent… And for what? For his family's convenience.

For his family's power.

'We won't say anything until after Henry and Elizabeth

wed, of course,' his father said. 'But once they have, we will have fulfilled our parts. Henry is on the throne and will be married to Elizabeth. Our promise made that possible. That was enough.'

The promise was enough. Words were enough. Well, there had been deeds, too, but a promise not kept *was* only words.

And what man could trust himself if he did not keep his word?

This was everything he had railed against. But this was not just any man. It was his father, clearly more interested in power than honour. How had he not seen that before?

Because he had seen only the venality of the man on the throne.

'I will not break the betrothal.'

His father raised his eyebrows, but kept his temper. 'Don't be so quick to decide. I have not spoken to Oakshire yet, but I wouldn't be surprised if he would be open to a different alliance for his daughter, now that we have our preferred King on the throne.'

Something in the tone of his words... Was it Alice who wanted a different alliance? Perhaps he had misread her. Perhaps, she, too, was ready to abandon their vows. Perhaps he had been the fool to trust all along.

He stopped his thoughts. If he was to defy his father, he must know her mind.

As eager as Alice was to see John, she was far more nervous than she had ever been in the Christmases past. This year, what had been no more than promises and speculation was to become real.

She had passed John's father in the hallway. His greeting had seemed cursory, but he had more important things to do than exchange words with her. The Earl of Stanson had been busy with his duties in the House of Lords. No doubt he had meetings with the King.

King Henry.

Still difficult to realise…

She had seen too little of the man to judge him truly, though even an imperfect man was to be preferred over the monster Richard had been. But allowedly, her thoughts were first of Bessy, not the country. Would Henry be a good husband?

Both John and the King were expected at Westminster soon, so, late in the afternoon, Alice and Bessy gathered in Bessy's rooms to wait.

Bessy looked ready to be happy.

'You like him,' Alice asked, 'don't you?' A silly question. What difference did that make to her duty? And yet, it did.

Bessy's answer was given shyly. 'I do. And I *think* he likes me.' She sighed, with the hint of a pout. 'But even after an Act of Parliament we remain unwed. And he had his coronation without me!'

Alice hugged her. 'He must have good reason,' she said, with a confidence she did not feel. 'Look at the wonderful clothes he has ordered for you.'

'And for himself and his entire household!' Bessy's tone was short.

While Alice was wearing her familiar green velvet gown, new clothes for the King and his family were part of the season's expectations. Still, every single piece seemed newly stitched. Was he an extravagant man who would waste money on finery?

Then Bessy shook her head. 'Forgive me. He needed each piece. He had no more than what he was wearing when he arrived.'

A reminder of the miracle that had made him King. An exile, a man who had nothing, embarked on a quest worthy of Arthur and gained it all. 'But you have spent time with him now. Is he…? Do you…?'

'Do I love him?'

Alice blushed. Not a question she should ask a queen.

Yet Bessy's answer was kind. 'How often is that possible for a king and queen? And even when it comes it can be…'

She did not finish the thought. Bessy's parents had loved each other. Once.

She let the words fade and faced Alice. 'You love John, don't you?'

Alice's first thought was *yes*. Her first impulse was to deny it. So she fell back on a simple statement. 'I have only seen him twice for a short time over the last two years. Here, at court, amid the seasonal madness. How can I know whether we will suit?'

'And I have just met Henry this year. Yet I may learn to love my duty.'

Her duty to marry. As Alice's was. She had always thought she wanted love. Had she forced that feeling with John? After all, she had seen him for less than three weeks in two years. Perhaps it would be better, easier, not to love him, but only to do her duty. After all, her father still mourned the loss of her mother. Did their years of joy out-weigh his pain at her loss?

'Lady Elizabeth.' A page, out of breath. 'The King…he asks for you.'

And suddenly, Elizabeth of York looked more nervous than royal. She stood, smoothing her hair.

'And Sir John is looking for the Lady Alice to meet him in his privy rooms,' he continued.

Now she, too, rose, bumping into Bessy as they both reached for the mirror.

Then she laughed. 'You look beautiful,' Alice assured her.

'As do you,' Bessy answered. 'And I think you do know that you and John will suit.'

Their laughter mingled as they left the room.

Finally, John saw at his door, the one thing he most wanted to see: Alice. He knew her shape, recognised the silly steepled headdress pointing aslant and when he saw her face it was as if he had come home.

Did she run? Did he? They moved into each other's arms and did not let go.

Then, a mutual sigh.

'You are safe? Unharmed?' Not willing to take his presence as proof, she touched his head, his arm, looking for wounds. 'I heard you fought for him. I was afraid. So many died…'

He nodded. 'Both our families did their part.'

Alice's father, as promised, had prevented the King's supporters in the south-east from joining his march to the final battle while sending some of his own men across the country to join Henry.

She gripped John's hands. 'And now Parliament has blessed, even begged, for this match. The Lords stood, bowed their heads and beseeched him to honour his promise! Why have they not wed?'

The impatience in her voice matched his own. 'And yet,' he said, barely able to think as he looked at her, 'they are as married as we are. It takes only one thing…'

A king and queen must have a public wedding. Other couples could consummate the marriage without any ceremony beyond the privacy of the bed…

She blushed. 'Then we could not be put asunder.'

The vision that had teased and tormented him for a year was now too close. If only they…

He straightened his arms to hold her a safe distance away. 'Alice, do you *want* to marry me?'

Alice blinked at his question. Struck dumb for a moment. 'How can I answer? We have not been given a choice. Like Henry and Elizabeth, we do what we must. For the greater good.'

'What if you were given a choice? What would you choose?'

The world slowed down. Her heart beat faster and seemed to move up to her throat. All this time, the irrevocable promise had been a wall, a fence, a barrier unmovable, trapping them together, no matter what they might want.

Had he changed his mind? She had thought it had become more than a duty for him. Had she been wrong? All this time, she had wanted love so badly she had been sure he had wanted the same. They had shared kisses at Christmastime, yes. What man would resist a kiss? But she had thought there was more. And now…

But he had asked what *she* wanted. As if that mattered. As if he cared what her choice would be.

She took a deep breath, searching his face. Something had changed, but she did not know what. 'Why do you want to know?'

'Because I want to know the truth.'

And if she told it? If she told him she loved him and discovered he did not love her in turn? What then? But if she did not try, she did not deserve the love she wanted.

And suddenly, it no longer mattered. For if she had learned anything over these past two Christmases, she had learned to trust herself. More than family, country or even God.

'Yes. Yes, John Talbot of Stanson, I *do* want to marry you.'

'Even if we no longer are forced to?'

Laughter now. There was nothing to lose but him and she had already won, or lost, that. 'Especially if we are no longer forced to!' So close. They could make it real. 'It only takes one thing,' she whispered. No longer ashamed to want it.

Now he was the one who blushed. 'Are you willing?'

'Yes!'

He picked her up and swung her around. 'Then, my lady, let us wed and let no one put us asunder.'

And when he put her down, he barred the door and came

back to kiss her again and neither one noticed when her headdress was knocked to the floor, nor cared where it landed.

As John led her through the palace well after dark, they heard, from behind the King's door, murmured, happy voices, including one Alice recognised...

She smiled. 'I guess we are not the only ones ready to consummate a marriage.'

He burst into inappropriate laughter and the voices beyond the door stilled.

Chapter Ten

The next day the King sent for John to come to his privy chambers. The twelve days of Christmas would begin tomorrow, but the business of the kingdom would not wait, it seemed.

In the aftermath of lovemaking, John felt woolly headed, certain the evidence of his night with Alice must be plain as if displayed on his shield.

He struggled to stifle his smile as the yeoman before the door checked to be sure he had been invited.

Personal protectors for this King, it seemed. Not for Henry the expansive openness of Edward, who had been known to invite commoners in. This King would have layers of people and ceremony. That might serve his reign well.

But what would it mean for John?

His father was right about one thing. For a man who had seized the crown, literally, on the field of battle, he was going to great lengths to be sure the business of the realm was conducted by law and not by force.

John could only hope that this unknown Tudor, this man who carried Arthur's banner of the red dragon, would be in truth an improvement over the murderous tyrant before him.

'Your Grace.' A bow. A deep one. He wanted no question as to his loyalty.

The King looked at him, assessing. 'You are to marry Alice of Oakshire when I marry Elizabeth.'

'Yes.' Relieved to hear that the King, at least, had no doubts.

'Her family fought for me.'

'Indeed.'

'Your father did not.'

So he had relaxed too quickly. 'My father did as he said he would and withheld his troops, denying Richard the support he had expected.' No need to add that his father, as a result, would have won no matter who triumphed on the field. 'He did not fight for Richard as had been expected. That allowed you to win.'

The King frowned. Impolitic to imply his father was solely responsible, but why was he asking John about his father's actions? 'I, Your Grace, did bring my men to ride beside you.'

'You think I have called you here to give you your reward.'

A blunt statement. But right now, the only reward he wanted was Alice. His father, of course, had quite a different perspective.

'You are the King. You may call me before you for any reason you like.'

Eyebrows raised. 'You are not a man discreet with words.'

'I am a soldier, Your Grace, not a courtier. I say what I mean.'

When I can.

'Unlike your father.'

'Now you are the one not discreet.' And that made John ill at ease.

'The privilege of a king. So… What reward do *you* want?'

'Your Grace?'

'You. Not your father.'

What did he want? 'Marry Elizabeth, as you have promised, and allow me to wed Alice and you will have my undying devotion.' With the King's official approval, his father would not be able to abandon his promise.

He only prayed the King would not say no to a marriage already consummated.

The simple request seemed to startle the King. 'Is that all?'

'All?' John had to smile. 'No, Your Grace. I would like a long life, peaceful days of hunting in my own woods, nights with my wife and children, even with grandchildren at my feet.' And he wanted these things far from the centres of power, on his own piece of ground. 'But that is all you have the power to give. The rest is up to God.'

The King smiled. 'Well, I do have a few other things in my power.' He studied John, silent, for a moment. 'What if I were also to give you responsibility for keeping the peace in your corner of the Scottish Borders?'

John was shocked by the surge of desire he felt. 'I would consider it an honour. And do my best to fulfil your trust. But my father...'

'Unlike you, your father is a courtier. He is a man I would like to keep close. Here. At court.'

Where the King could keep an eye on him, no doubt.

'So, Sir John, Elizabeth and I will be wed in January and you will have what you desire: your castle, your lands and your bride.'

John bowed, deeply, in gratitude, discreet enough to refrain from mentioning that he and Alice had already wed.

January 18, 1486

And so, two days after the Papal Legate's dispensation arrived, John and Alice watched as Henry and Elizabeth took their vows, sharing similar smiles.

Henry was a careful and thorough man, but even so, he married without waiting for the final word from Rome. John had a feeling the King's impatience had matched his own.

As they left the church, the King and Queen paused to greet John and Alice. 'You are to be wed today as well?'

'Yes, Your Grace,' John answered. 'May the Lord shine his mercy on both our unions.'

'And on our country.' The King smiled at his new wife, then turned back to John and held out a small piece of cloth. 'A token of our admiration for your support.'

It was a badge, worn to show loyalty, but the symbol on it was a new one. Not a white boar, like Richard's, or even a red dragon, such as Henry had carried into battle. Instead, it was a flower, similar to the Yorkist white rose. But this flower also had red petals.

He looked at the King, puzzled.

'The pattern is new,' Alice said.

The King nodded. 'No longer Lancaster and York.' He hugged his wife's arm closer. 'It is a Tudor rose, now.'

A Tudor rose. John smiled. 'Long may the name rule.'

* * * * *

Author Note

As is often the case with history, the strangest stories are the true ones. Though John and Alice are my creation, much of what surrounds them is true.

Certainly there has been much debate about the character of Richard III. I have chosen the interpretation of his actions that I believe and that fits the events of my story. To my mind, many subsequent events do not make sense unless the two Princes, Edward IV's male heirs, are acknowledged as being dead by late 1483.

Henry Tudor, in Brittany, did promise on Christmas Day 1483 to marry Elizabeth of York. And Richard got the news on the twelfth day of Christmas. The next year Richard III was suspected by some of plotting to poison his wife and marry his niece, and the celebrations at court, with all three of them there, were considered scandalous in some contemporaneous reports. Henry's miraculous escape from Brittany just ahead of Richard's men is also true.

The entire plan for the two to marry and take the throne was reputedly orchestrated from behind the scenes by Elizabeth, Edward's Queen, whom we meet in Chapter One, and Margaret Beaufort, Henry's mother. Though I did not put Margaret Beaufort on the pages of this story, those who have read my books will understand my pleasure at the fact that Margaret, a fascinating woman in her own right, is the great-granddaughter of Katherine Swynford and John of Gaunt, who appear in *Rumours at Court*.

A major ally of Richard's held back his troops at Bosworth—a key factor in the Tudor victory. Even stranger, this lord's wife was Margaret Beaufort. I could not attempt to cover that level of complexity in a novella!

Alas, however, the Tudor rose is partly legend. Henry, attuned to the importance of symbols, did indeed invent and promote it. But, while the white rose of York was well known, the red rose of Lancaster was largely invented by Henry as part of the story of the Tudor rose.

More than one hundred years after my story, writing in the reign of Henry's granddaughter, Queen Elizabeth, William Shakespeare created a scene in the play *Henry VI, Part 1* that seared the idea of the War of the Roses, the red and the white, into cultural memory. And at the end of the play *Richard III*, Henry Tudor, triumphant at Bosworth Field, promises to 'unite the white rose and the red' and asks Heaven to smile on 'this fair conjunction'.

The story of the dispensations to marry that Henry and Elizabeth received is more complex than I have told, or than most readers would find interesting. In fact, Henry Tudor and Elizabeth got some four dispensations, from two different popes, each emphasising a slightly different aspect of the union. But they did marry two days after the Papal Legate brought one in January and before the final one arrived from Rome in March.

Elizabeth bore their first child eight months after the wedding. Whether the royal couple started early, as I suggest, or the baby was born early history will never know, but I enjoy my own speculation. The marriage was said to be a happy one. Elizabeth died from complications of childbirth and Henry, according to biographer Thomas Penn, was 'shattered' and 'would never be the same again'.

They had seven children—some sources say eight—including the next King of England: Henry VIII.

SECRETS OF THE
QUEEN'S LADY

Jenni Fletcher

Dear Reader,

It's obviously a huge understatement to say that society has changed in the five hundred years since the reign of Henry VIII, and yet many of the elements of a Tudor Christmas are familiar. It was the biggest festival in Tudor times, with celebrations beginning on the day itself and continuing for twelve days with a holiday period of plays, feasting, wassailing, carol singing, gift giving and even mince pies. Christmas trees were a Germanic rather than English tradition, but since my story is set mostly in the household of Anne of Cleves, I've sneakily managed to include one.

I really enjoyed my research for this story, but I honestly think that as you get older, celebrating the festive season becomes less about gifts and more about traditions and hope for the future. Because of that, I wanted to write a heartwarming story about second chances, reconciliation and love overcoming obstacles. I hope you enjoy it and have a very happy Christmas.

Jenni

Chapter One

London—December 1540

'Welcome to Richmond Palace, Sir Christopher.'

The words were preceded by the shadowy outline of a woman as she emerged from behind a wooden screen at the far end of the hall. Silhouetted as she was, with only the light from a few beeswax candles and the amber glow of the fireplace to illuminate the scene, Kit recognised her voice at once. The low timbre of it made his heart leap unexpectedly.

'Lady Philippa?'

He was vaguely aware of his jaw dropping open. He'd heard that she'd become a member of Lady Anne of Cleves's household, staying behind in Richmond even after most of the other English gentlewomen had left, but he'd never imagined that she'd be the one sent to greet him. After yet another confrontation with his brother that morning, the sight of her was like a breath of fresh air, lifting his mood and giving him the fanciful notion that he'd just found the answer to a question he'd been turning over in his mind for days, months even. As she moved closer, her still-slender figure seeming to glide rather than walk towards him, he could see that her distinctive heart-shaped face was just as beautiful as he remembered, framed by glossy, chestnut-coloured hair that hung loose beneath her hood. For a few seconds he felt utterly knocked off balance, too surprised to do anything but gape, only belatedly remembering to remove his hat and bow.

'My lady.' He hoped that she hadn't noticed his momentary lapse in manners. 'You haven't changed at all.'

'In ten years? You flatter me, sir.' Sparkling green eyes danced with amusement. 'For which I will be eternally grateful. It makes me doubly happy to see you again, although I confess I might not have recognised you without being informed of your identity. Whatever happened to young Kit Lowell?'

'He grew up, although he's still known as Kit to his friends.' He made another small bow, taken aback by just *how* pleased he was to see her again. 'I still consider you one of those. You were one of my very first friends at court, as I recall.'

'Was I?'

She smiled and he bent over her hand, pressing his lips to the back of her knuckles for a few moments longer than was necessary, acutely aware of how mud-stained and windblown he must look after his ride. 'Yes, I remember the day we met quite clearly. I was seventeen years old and lost in Whitehall Palace when you rescued me. You took my arm and led me to the King's privy chambers, all the while pretending it was because you felt faint. Then you made a remarkable recovery in the doorway.'

'I remember!' Her face lit up with a look of delight, one that seemed to warm his insides. 'And all these years I thought I was such a good actress!'

'You were very kind. It meant a great deal to me.' He cleared his throat, afraid that he'd just revealed too much, but she waved a hand dismissively.

'Whitehall is such a maze it took me weeks to find my own way around, but you've done well for yourself since then. You've travelled most of Europe on the King's business, I understand?'

'Yes, my sense of direction has improved immeasurably.

I lose my way only every other day now.' He grinned. 'As it happens, I've just returned from a tour of the German duchies, Cleves among them.'

'I'm sure that my lady will be glad to hear the details. I know that she misses her homeland.' Lady Philippa shook her head, her gaze wandering over his face with an expression of wonderment. 'You look so different. The same, but different.' She laughed, her cheeks flushing slightly. 'Forgive me, I'm not expressing myself very well. I mean that you look very handsome. And there, now that I've repaid your compliment, to what do we owe the pleasure of your visit?'

'I've come with an invitation from the King. He and the Queen would like Lady Anne to visit them at Hampton Court in the new year.' He quirked an eyebrow at her suddenly frozen expression. 'Is something the matter? Do you think she will not wish to attend?'

'No,' she answered too hastily. 'It's a great honour and I'm sure that my lady will be most pleased to accept. Only...' Her brows knitted with a look of concern. 'Would you permit me to ask a question? As old friends?'

'Ask anything you wish.'

'Thank you.' She threw a swift glance over her shoulder before lowering her voice. 'Is everything quite well at court? We heard that the King is happy with Queen Katherine, but has he found some fault with my lady?'

'None that I know of. He only wishes for his royal sister to visit him at Hampton Court.'

'His sister.' A look of relief passed over her face. 'He still regards her as such, then?'

'Yes, my lady, as the terms of the marriage annulment state.'

He grimaced, wishing he could retract the words the moment they were out of his mouth. They sounded too severe, as if he were admonishing her for the query, but defending the King's behaviour had become second nature in his career as a diplomat. It would have been treason to do otherwise. Not many men would refer to a discarded wife as a *'most beloved sister'*, but the King had long ago made his own rules when it came to women.

'Of course.' Lady Philippa bent her head in acknowledgement. 'Thank you, Sir Christopher.'

'Kit, remember?'

'Kit.' Her gaze warmed again. 'Then you must call me Pippa, as *my* friends do. Come, let me take you to Lady Anne.'

He followed behind, admiring the gentle sway of her hips as she led the way back towards the screen and then up a winding staircase, its walls hung with ornate tapestries of fantastical unicorns and griffins while the plastered ceiling above was painted in dazzling shades of red and silver. He had a feeling that he would have recognised her by her walk even if he hadn't been able to see her face. The graceful way that she moved was one of the things he'd remembered most about her—and he'd remembered more than he'd realised. They'd spoken on only a few brief occasions before he'd left for the Netherlands, but she'd always struck him as the very epitome of a perfect court lady, exuding an aspect of calmness, elegance and dignity. She still did. He'd never been quite sure of her age, but at a guess she was probably no more than seven or eight years his senior, halfway between thirty and forty perhaps, but aside from a few faint lines across her brow, she looked just as lovely as she had on that first day. Lovelier even.

The fact struck him as particularly strange considering how *much* had happened in the time between. Ten years before, the King had still been married to his first wife, Catherine of Aragon, and the country had been tied to Rome. Kit's own father had still been alive, keeping an increasingly precarious rein on the political ambitions of his eldest son, George, while allowing *Kit* to lead the life of travel and adventure he'd always craved. Lady Philippa, meanwhile, had been married to Sir Nicholas Bray, one of the King's favoured companions and a victim of the ague that had swept through London the previous year. Kit thought that his loss must have come as a terrible blow to her. From what he remembered, they hadn't had any children, but they'd always seemed a devoted couple.

'So tell me, what was your favourite place on your travels?' Lady Philippa asked, pausing to walk beside him as they entered a long gallery lined with oak panelling on one side and an impressive array of glass windows on the other.

'The Italian states,' he answered at once. 'I visited many of the great cities. Venice is like something out of a dream.'

'The city on the water,' she murmured wistfully, the evening light streaming in through the windows bathing her face in a wash of gold. 'I've seen paintings, but I'd love to see the reality myself some day. I doubt that such a journey will ever be possible, but it sounds magnificent. Milan, too. They say...' She gave him a sidelong look and stopped walking abruptly. 'Kit? Is something the matter?'

'Forgive me.' He gave a jolt, realising that he was frowning. 'I'm afraid that Milan has bad memories for me. It was there I received word of my father's death.'

'Ah, I'm sorry.' Her expression softened. 'I know that he's greatly missed at court. He was a good man.'

'He was. England isn't the same for me now.'

'But your mother and the rest of your family are all in good health, I hope?'

'My mother has gone to stay with my sister Judith's family in Cambridge for a few weeks and my brothers...they're both in good health, yes.' He paused tactfully. 'I was grieved to hear about your husband, too. He was another good man.'

'Yes.' A shutter seemed to descend over her face, the light behind her eyes disappearing like candles being extinguished, though not before he saw the flicker of pain inside them. 'Thank you.'

She moved on quickly before he could say anything else,

leaving him to regret his words for the second time that evening. He could hardly *not* have said them, but they seemed to have cast an immediate gloom over their reunion. After just over a year of widowhood, she was obviously still grieving and, after ten years of growing up, he was still just an awkward and lost boy around her.

'Come.' She glanced back over her shoulder at him, her smile somewhat strained now. 'My lady is waiting.'

Pippa hastened her steps along the gallery, her hands folded across her stomach, taking deep breaths to try to restore her inner sense of calm. The slightest mention of her husband always depressed her spirits, but being offered sympathy made the feeling even worse. She ought to have expected and braced herself for the words—everyone had thought Nicholas such a fine man, *such* a gallant knight errant—but they'd still caught her off guard, stirring the dark well in her soul until the memories threatened to swell up and overwhelm her. She'd hoped that, over time, it would have become easier to control her emotions, but today it seemed harder than ever.

Perhaps it was because she'd been enjoying herself in Sir Christopher's—*Kit's*—company. She'd been genuinely pleased to see him again, remembering the day that he'd mentioned—the day they'd first met—as clearly as if it were only a few short weeks and not years ago. She'd come across him looking lost in a corridor and stopped to show him the way to the King's chambers, though she'd tried to soften the blow to his youthful pride by feigning dizziness. She recalled his good-natured smile and his gratitude for her help, his obvious intelligence as they'd discussed the newest poetry by John Skelton, as well as his enthusiasm for the idea of travelling abroad. They'd spoken only briefly afterwards—she'd always been too aware of Nicholas watching to offer much more than a greeting—and then he'd left a few weeks later to join the English ambassador's household in Amsterdam. But their meeting was a rare, bright and surprisingly vivid memory from an unhappy time—a time when the stark truth of her marriage was becoming more and more evident.

He still *seemed* good-natured—she could feel his concerned gaze on the nape of her neck as she hurried ahead—though it was almost impossible to believe he was the same gauche youth she'd met so many years before. The boy she remembered had grown into a man and an extremely attractive, virile-looking one, too. When he'd smiled at her, she'd felt her heart stutter in a way that she'd almost forgotten was possible. He'd been handsome enough at seventeen, but now he was mesmerising, like a young lion, with a slim, athletic physique, hair the colour of a sun-gilded wheat field and eyes of shimmering grey, as if there were smoke swirling inside them. He'd acquired an air of confidence, too, a new kind of stature, as befitted a man who spent his time travelling around Europe's great cities. The contrast made her feel old and suddenly weary.

Overall, it was a relief when they finally reached Lady Anne's withdrawing chamber and she was able to announce him, then step aside, half-concealing herself behind two other attendants.

'Lady Anne.' A lock of golden hair fell across Kit's forehead as he bowed and repeated the King's invitation. It made him look almost boyish again and, incredibly, even more handsome. There had been an audible murmur of appreciation from the gathered ladies when he'd entered, as well as a few discreet nudges, ones that were echoed and repeated again now. Pippa could hardly blame them. It was difficult *not* to admire the way his breeches fitted so closely to his thighs and his shoulders filled his doublet to sleek perfection.

Quickly, she diverted her attention to her mistress, wondering how she felt about the King's unexpected invitation. Lady Anne's expression was everything that it ought to be, everything that a courtier who reported to the King might expect to see, but then her ability to control her features so consummately was one of the qualities Pippa admired most about her. Even when those features themselves had been criticised so cruelly and publicly, Anne had maintained a calm and dignified demeanour. It was doubtful that she could feel any real enthusiasm for returning to court, despite her graciously worded acceptance. It had been only a year since she herself had arrived in England to marry the King and yet now she was being asked to visit her *successor*, a girl of not yet twenty who'd once served as her own lady-in-waiting. No woman in the world could feel pleased at such a prospect, but there was no way to refuse the invitation either. Which meant a return to court for all of them, the very idea of which made Pippa shudder.

Unfortunately, at the very moment her shoulders heaved, Kit turned his head, his piercing grey gaze finding its way past the other attendants and straight into her own, his quizzical expression seeming to catch light and smoulder suddenly. It was only the briefest of moments, surely no more than a second or two, but she caught her breath as the rest of the room seemed to dim and fall silent. It was as though they were completely alone again, standing facing each other as they had in the hall, only this time with a new sense of intimacy and awareness between them.

Then Lady Anne reclaimed his attention, the light and noise returned, and she was left to wonder what had just happened.

Chapter Two

The gardens were Pippa's favourite place at Richmond. There was a deer park surrounding the palace, too, but the enclosed terraces, with their marble statues and fountains, neatly trimmed hedges and topiary sculptures lent a reassuring sense of shelter and security. In the distance, the sky over London was streaked with ribbons of pink, threatening rain or worse to come, but at this early hour of the morning, the frosty air felt bracing and salubrious, clearing her head and restoring her inner sense of calm.

She'd had a disturbed night, dreaming of a pair of slate-coloured eyes in a strong-jawed face, framed by sharply arched brows and a mane of golden hair. She'd pulled back her bed curtains and come outside even earlier than usual, exasperated and shocked by the wanton nature of her own imagination. It was mortifying to have been so affected by a moment that she'd surely imagined! Not to mention by a man so many years her junior! She hadn't thought about any man in that way since…well, not since the earliest days of her marriage almost twenty years ago.

At thirty-five, she was among the oldest of Lady Anne's ladies, ten years older than Anne herself, and even if she *had* been reasonably attractive once, she was now long past her prime. Kit might have said that he was pleased to see her again, but only as what he'd called her, an old friend, which meant that whatever intensity she'd *thought* she'd seen in his eyes the previous evening had simply been concern, that was all. It was ridiculous—shameful!—to imagine it might have meant anything more. She only hoped that he hadn't noticed anything too revealing about *her* expression.

She turned into a narrow avenue bordered on both sides by towering walls of yew hedge. The path between was an apt metaphor for her life now, she thought ruefully, mercifully calmer and more predictable than it had been and yet confined and occasionally lonely, too—a path she was destined to walk mostly alone. Which was just as it should be, she reminded herself, skimming her glove across the prickly surface of the thicket, just as she'd promised herself it would...

A twig snapped and she looked up, her heart slamming to a halt as she saw Kit striding from the opposite direction towards her. She stopped, half in surprise, half in embarrassment, the merest sight of him undoing all of her carefully restored calmness and turning her mind into a riot of conflicting emotions. He hadn't yet seen her, walking along with his eyes fixed on the ground as if he were deep in thought, so that for a moment she was tempted to turn around and flee, but such behaviour would only confirm her foolishness. What would she say if he caught her? She had no quarrel with him, after all, and it was ridiculous to be so aware of him as a man. No, the best thing she could do was to stand her ground and act normally. He would either laugh or make a hasty retreat back to London if he guessed even half of what she was thinking!

'Good morning.' She dipped into what she hoped was a suitably modest curtsy, relieved by how steady her voice sounded.

'Pippa?' His steps faltered as he lifted his head, looking equally surprised to see her. 'You're outside early.'

'Yes.' She stiffened, the sound of her name on his lips sending a shiver of awareness rippling down her spine. It seemed too intimate somehow, even though she'd told him to call her by it. Of course that had been yesterday, *before* the moment in Lady Anne's presence chamber...the moment she'd surely imagined… 'I like to enjoy the peace of the gardens before everyone else is awake.'

'As do I.' He held on to her gaze for a few seconds, his own searching. In contrast to his friendly behaviour yesterday, his attitude now seemed faintly guarded. 'Perhaps we might walk together for a while?'

Pippa twisted her head in the direction of the palace. Only the high, four-storey turrets and elaborate crenellations were visible above the top of the hedge, meaning that in their current position they were effectively hidden from view, but a walk out in the open was more likely to be noticed and at this time of the morning it could easily be mistaken for an assignation, no matter how ridiculous the idea sounded. Lady Anne had strict rules for behaviour. Even after the annulment of her marriage, it was imperative that she and her household remain untouched by scandal. The King's favour was a precarious thing.

'I'm afraid that a walk might not be appropriate…' If she wasn't mistaken, she saw a flash of disappointment in his eyes. 'But there's a small pavilion close by. Perhaps we might sit there for a while? It's not too cold, I think.'

'That would be pleasant.' He inclined his head, clasping his hands behind his back as he fell into step alongside her.

'You're outside early, too,' she commented after a few moments, relieved that he hadn't offered her his arm.

'Yes. It's my first visit to Richmond and I wanted to look around. It's a beautiful palace.'

'It is. Peaceful, too.'

'Indeed.' There was a frown in his voice, as if he were preoccupied with something. 'Speaking of peaceful…you were very quiet at supper yesterday.'

'Was I?' She blinked in surprise. As a guest, he'd been seated beside Lady Anne at the high table and had seemed very attentive. Every time she'd looked across he'd been either talking or smiling. She certainly hadn't thought that he'd been paying any attention to *her*. 'I was tired.'

'Is that why you chose not to play cards afterwards?' He glanced sideways to look at her. 'It wasn't because I upset you? Because I thought perhaps—'

'But how could you have?' she interrupted, twisting her fingers into the folds of her cloak and willing him not to mention her husband again. 'I told you, it's good to see you again.'

'Ah… That's a relief.' He sounded unconvinced, though thankfully he didn't pursue the subject.

'Here we are.' She darted through a gap in the hedge, then up three steps into a stone pavilion completely hidden from view of the house. A domed roof was supported by four external pillars and one in the centre, the base of which was carved into a circular bench. Pippa sat down, arranging her cloak and skirts with undue care in an attempt to distract herself from Kit's proximity. Several lurid episodes from her dreams were already replaying themselves in her mind and there was a strange constricting sensation in her chest that was making it something of a challenge to breathe normally.

'Will you be returning to court this morning?' She smiled politely.

'Shortly, yes, but I'll be returning soon for your Christmas celebrations. Lady Anne invited me last night and I accepted.'

'You did?' Her steady voice seemed to have turned into something higher-pitched and panicked-sounding all of a sudden. 'But what about the festivities at court? They'll be much grander than anything we can offer here.'

'Grander doesn't necessarily mean better and I've been promised authentic German gingerbread. That makes it hard to refuse.' His smile faded as his gaze honed in on hers. 'Unless the idea of my returning displeases you?'

'Of course not.' She shook her head quickly. 'I just thought that your family might miss you.'

'Only my eldest brother is at court at the moment. He can represent the family. It's what he does best.'

'Ye-es…' She didn't argue with that, though she was taken aback by the sudden sharp edge to his voice. George Lowell's advancement at court had been swift and some said ruthless. By the sound of it, his younger brother had his own opinions about that.

'Then you have no objection to my returning?' A muscle clenched in his jaw.

'It doesn't matter what I think.'

'None the less, I wouldn't want to displease you.'

'You would not. I'd be delighted to see you again,' she answered truthfully, since it *was* the truth, even if it ought not to be. It would be far better for her peace of mind if he stayed away completely, but she could hardly say—or explain—*that*. 'Lady Anne's gingerbread is delicious. She makes it herself, as well as spiced biscuits.'

'Even better.' He smiled again, his tone mellowing. 'Tell me, does Lady Anne like her new home?'

'She does now.'

'Only now? You mean that she did not at first?'

'Oh…' She bit her tongue at her own indiscretion. 'No, it wasn't that she didn't like it, just that things were difficult to begin with. The King sent her here to protect her from the ague, but…it wasn't what she expected.'

'Meaning that she assumed he would follow her?' He lifted an eyebrow, his gaze knowing, and she nodded.

'Yes.'

'And he never came?'

'He had good reasons, of course, and she's happy here now. And I believe that she intends to make a progress to some of her other homes in the spring, too. The King was most generous with the properties he gave her.'

'Indeed.' His eyebrow was still raised. 'I understand that Hever Castle is among them?'

'It is.' She averted her gaze, swallowing a sharp comment. Hever had been the childhood home of Anne Boleyn. It seemed a somewhat tactless and inappropriate gift for another discarded queen, although no more tactless and inappropriate perhaps than the properties previously owned by Thomas Cromwell, the man who'd brokered Anne's alliance to Henry in the first place. Pippa sometimes wondered if the King had included them in the settlement as a kind of veiled threat, intended to warn Anne what would happen if she refused his terms or earned his displeasure afterwards. Both Anne Boleyn and Cromwell had met their ends at the hands of an executioner.

'I was in Cleves when her brother, Duke Wilhelm, received news of the King's intention to seek an annulment,' Kit said suddenly.

'You were?' She jerked her head back towards him in surprise. 'That cannot have been easy.'

'It was one of the more challenging diplomatic situations in which I've found myself, I admit, and I could hardly understand it any more than they could. The ministers there believed that Lady Anne's pre-contract with the son of the Duke of Lorraine had been satisfactorily dissolved years before and I'd heard good reports of the lady.'

'Yes.' Pippa hesitated over her next choice of words. To doubt the King's reason for annulling the marriage was close to treason, although it would obviously have made far more sense for him to raise doubts over the legalities of their union *before* the wedding. 'But the King said that he couldn't accept her as his wife in his heart when he believed she already belonged to another.'

'So I gather.' Kit gave her a look that suggested he understood perfectly the words she wasn't saying. 'However, I'm glad to find that she's happy now.' He dropped his voice to an undertone. 'Some might say more so than she would have been otherwise.'

'Yes.' Pippa spoke in a matching murmur. 'Some might say so.'

They were silent together for a few moments, equally complicit in their condemnation of the King before Kit moved suddenly, placing one booted foot on the bench beside her and leaning across it.

'What about you? Are *you* happy in her service?'

'Me?' The question caught her off guard. She couldn't remember the last time anyone had asked if she were happy. She had a sudden fleeting image of her childhood nurse, though surely it hadn't been *that* long? 'I am content.'

'Is that the same thing?'

'It's enough.'

'Then what made you stay in Lady Anne's household? I heard that most of her English ladies left to join the new Queen's.'

Pippa pursed her lips before she could stop herself. It was hard not to see Katherine Howard as the real reason behind the King's desire for an annulment, especially since he'd married her only a month afterwards. 'I confess that I'm not a great lover of court. It holds too many memories for me—besides, I like Lady Anne. She's a kind mistress and I feel better suited to her service.'

'I believe you are, too.' His voice softened in a way that raised goose pimples on her skin. 'You know, I've thought about you over the years.'

'Oh.' Her mouth seemed to turn dry, rendering speech impossible, although she had no idea what to say either. Since she'd been married, he ought not to have thought about her at all, though surely he didn't mean the words in *that* way. Still, she couldn't help but feel a warm glow in her chest all the same.

'I was always grateful for the kindness you showed me.'

Ah. The glow faded. *Grateful*, as he would have been to a friend... She touched her tongue to her lips, trying to moisten them. 'I only showed you the way to the King's chambers.'

'It was more than that. I remember feeling utterly miserable that day. I'd come to court for adventure, but there were so many rules to learn, so much politicking and back-stabbing and standing around. It wasn't what I'd hoped for my life. I was feeling lost and disillusioned and you rescued me. You smiled and made me feel as if things would get better—which they did. I believe that I've seen you as the perfect woman ever since.'

'A long way from perfect.' She shook her head self-consciously, trying to laugh the compliment away. 'And isn't that honour supposed to go to a boy's mother?'

'You obviously haven't met my mother.'

She had to stifle a smile. In fact, she'd met Lady Low-ell on several occasions, remembering her as a hard-faced woman with a rigid spine and even more rigid opinions. It seemed incongruous somehow that this earnest, good-natured man could be so closely related to such a woman, but then his father had always been kind-hearted. Theirs had been a curious marriage, as she recalled, as well as an obviously unhappy one. She knew all the signs of those.

'Well, I'm glad that things have improved for you.' She steered the conversation back on to safer territory. 'You seem to be quite the courtier now.'

'Only on the outside, I assure you. I'm still not comfort-able at court, but I've grown better at hiding the fact. I enjoy a life of travel much more. In truth, I'm little more than an envoy, but it suits me.'

'And how do European courts compare to ours?'

'I'm afraid that backstabbing seems universal.'

'So what brought you back to England?'

'Ah, that was my brother's doing. He and my mother have a marriage in mind. They're determined to make a glittering match for me.'

'I see.' She feigned a smile, aware of a definite sinking feeling, one that she had absolutely no right to feel. 'But that's good news, surely? A wedding is always a joyful occasion.'

'For others maybe. Personally, I'm reluctant to have my bride chosen for me.'

She dug her teeth into her bottom lip, unable to argue with that sentiment. Nicholas had been chosen for her when she was still in the cradle. She'd never been offered a choice about their union, although if she had…no, she couldn't pretend that she would have acted differently even then. She'd been so young and he'd seemed so dashing and honourable. Everyone had called her fortunate and she'd agreed—for the first few years anyway. She hadn't learned the truth about his true nature until afterwards.

'It's the way things are done.' She sat up straighter, folding her hands in her lap before her thoughts could stray too far down that path.

'The wrong way.'

She hesitated for a moment before agreeing. 'Yes.'

'Forgive me, perhaps I should not speak so candidly.' He dropped his foot off the bench and sat down beside her, close enough that she could feel the heat of his body through his doublet and cape. If she tipped her head, she could rest it on his shoulder, she thought distractedly, could just close her eyes and rest it there. It was the least of what she'd imagined in her dreams and it would be so easy. The whole side of her body felt as though it were tingling, her stomach clenching and unclenching as if there were an invisible string tugging her towards him, drawing her closer…

'There's nothing to forgive.' She had to concentrate on keeping her spine ramrod straight. 'I understand what it's like to have your life arranged for you. Perhaps things would be better if we were all so candid.'

'Exactly.' He gave her a sidelong look. 'It's strange how easily I can talk to you, Pippa. I remember thinking the same thing ten years ago. I enjoyed our conversation that first day. I always wanted to talk to you more.'

'I enjoyed talking to you, too.' She met his gaze and

quickly turned her face away, staring fixedly at one of the pillars. 'As a friend, of course.'

He didn't answer and she cringed inwardly, instantly regretting the clarification. As if he would have thought otherwise!

'So you've come home to marry.' She struggled to pull her scattered thoughts back together. 'Who is your bride?'

She thought she heard a soft sigh before he answered. 'Lady Cecily Acton.'

'Lady Cecily?' She feigned yet another smile. 'Oh, but she is a pleasant girl. Extremely pretty, too, and from a good family. It sounds like a very eligible match.'

'So my brother tells me. The eldest daughter of an earl is a great match for a second son, more than I could have expected, or something to that effect.'

'He's right.'

He made a scornful sound. 'From what I understand, the earl has some financial difficulties that my brother has promised to alleviate.'

'Have you told your brother how you feel?'

'I've told him that I like my life as it is now, but he just fixes me with a stare and then carries on scheming as if I haven't said a word. He says I need to do my duty to the family.' He laid his forearms over his knees and shook his head with a brief look of frustration. 'The worst part is that he's right. So I can either carry on with a career that I love and let down my family or do my duty to them and marry a woman I don't love. It's hard to decide which is the lesser of two evils. Is it wrong to do violence against your own brother, do you think?'

'I think it depends on the brother. I admit I've occasionally felt the same impulse towards my own.'

'Really?' He looked interested. 'Why?'

She hesitated for a moment before answering, but he was right, it was *so* easy to talk to him… 'After I was widowed, my brother and his wife made it clear that I wasn't welcome back in my family home. That's how I came to join Lady Anne's household in the first place.'

'And they say we have a duty to family.'

'Yes, we do! That was why I...' She stopped mid-sentence, the words *why I married Nicholas* frozen on her lips. Given the circumstances, it wasn't a very persuasive argument.

'But we have a duty to ourselves, too, do we not?' His voice seemed to contain a new sense of urgency. 'People tell you that love grows over time, but what if it doesn't? My parents' marriage wasn't a love match. They had nothing in common and in the end they led separate lives. I've never been close to my mother, but my father was the best man I've ever known. One of the unhappiest, too, and all because he married out of a sense of duty to his family.'

'You think he was wrong to do so?'

He drew a deep breath and then blew it out again between his teeth. 'I don't know. I believe he had deep regrets, but he loved his children and he did his best to make us happy instead. He was the one who arranged for me to join the King's ambassador in the Netherlands when I begged him to let me travel. I think—I believe—that he would have wanted me to marry for love, too, only I never asked him. Now I wish that I had. Why *shouldn't* the rest of us follow our hearts when the King does it often enough?'

'Kit!' She gave a startled gasp. 'We cannot compare ourselves with the King.'

'No, I suppose not...'

He was looking at her strangely, she noticed, a second before she noticed the position of her hand on his bicep. She must have put it there instinctively to quiet him, but now she was very aware of the stiffening of the muscles beneath her fingertips. His eyes looked very dark all of a sudden, too, as if they were black instead of grey, locked on to hers with the same intensity she'd seen—*thought* she'd seen—

the previous evening… Heat flooded her veins, making her skin feel scorching hot beneath her woollen cloak and gown.

'Have you spent much time with Lady Cecily?' she blurted out, quickly removing her hand and curling it around the edge of the bench.

'No.' He cleared his throat, his voice noticeably huskier-sounding than before. 'We've spoken twice and we talked about the weather on both occasions. I'm afraid that the rest of my life will be spent discussing the possibility of rain.'

'She's probably nervous.' Pippa felt compelled to defend the other woman, if only to pretend that the last thirty seconds hadn't happened. 'Courtship is more difficult for women. Men are encouraged to go out and gain experience of the world. Women are kept locked away from it. We sew and read and talk, but we're not allowed to actually *live*. Maybe Cecily didn't know what to talk to you about. Given time, I'm sure you'll find things in common.'

'Maybe. She seems pleasant enough, only so young.'

'A lot of men would see that as a virtue.'

'Maybe a lot of men only want to be obeyed.'

She tensed at the words, knowing the truth of them all too well. 'At least as a husband, you'll be the one with authority. A wife is entirely at the mercy of her husband.'

He drew his brows together as if he were surprised by her choice of words. 'Surely only if the husband is a tyrant?'

'Many men become tyrants when they're allowed so much power.'

'Perhaps, but I would not wish to be one of them. I believe that marriage should be a partnership. I'd like a wife I can share my thoughts with, a woman I can talk to. A true partner.'

'Which is why you'll make a good husband. You should give Lady Cecily time.'

'Time…' He repeated the word thoughtfully. 'How much time is needed to fall in love, do you think? A day? Ten years? Some people even believe in love at first sight.' He paused, his gaze dropping to her lips for a fleeting moment. 'Have you ever thought of marrying again, Pippa?'

'Never!' She gave a startled laugh. 'Unlike Cecily, I'm far too old.'

'You're only a few years older than I am.' He sounded indignant.

'And childless. I've nothing to offer any man now. My failure as a wife is well known.'

'Is that how you see it?' He reached for her hand before she could move it away, folding one of his own around it and sliding his thumb across the inside of her palm, his tone sombre. 'Not all men are the same. Not all want children.'

She held her breath, her pulse quickening. His fingers felt so strong and comforting that she couldn't help but wonder how it would feel to have his arms wrapped around her. For a moment she was actually tempted to find out, to press her body against his chest and burrow her face into his neck. He was right, not all men were the same. He was kind and earnest, the kind of man a woman could talk to, who could make her feel valued and happy, who could help her forget the past, too. If she were only ten years younger or wealthy or if she could bear children…but she was none of those things and it was a foolish daydream. And even if it wasn't, she could never marry again. She would never make the same mistake and surrender her *self* a second time, not to any man.

'Men of title do.' She felt her cheeks flame as she spoke. The words felt too personal, too close to the bone.

'Perhaps, but a good husband also understands that sometimes life does not turn out as we might wish. I'm sure that Sir Nicholas never saw you as a failure.'

'My husband…' It was on the tip if her tongue to agree, to perpetuate the myth of Nicholas as a devoted husband and herself as a grieving widow, but for the first time the words would not come. Instead, she could hear blood roaring in her ears as she answered, 'He was the worst of all.'

Chapter Three

'I should go!' Pippa wrenched her hand away and started up from the bench, her expression aghast. 'I shouldn't have said that.'

'Wait!' Kit stood up, too, reaching an arm out to stop her from running away, though some instinct warned him not to touch her again. She seemed too vulnerable suddenly, one hand clasped to her throat as if she were struggling to contain her emotions. 'Don't go. I didn't mean to upset you.'

'You didn't. I upset myself.' She gave a strangled-sounding laugh. 'Forgive me, I slept badly and I'm not myself this morning. What I just said… I beg you to forget it.'

'If that's what you want…' he inclined his head '…but I'm a good listener, if you wish to talk?'

'I cannot.' She lifted her eyes to his, their expression hesitant and yet pleading somehow, too. 'I've never told anyone.'

'I would never betray any confidence, Pippa, I promise.'

'I believe you. It's just that…all this talk of marriage… mine was not as happy as everyone at court always believed. You see, Nicholas wanted a child, an heir, so badly. So did I, but I could not give him one. It caused…tension… between us.'

'Ah.' He felt a stab of regret for having raised the subject. 'I'm sorry.'

'So am I.' She turned away, hunching her shoulders as if she were withdrawing inside herself. 'I don't know which is worse, living a lie or feeling like a failure every day of your life.'

'You're not a failure.'

'No? That was what my husband called me. I failed to do the one thing he expected. It was no wonder he came to resent me so much.'

'But surely he did not?' Kit came to stand behind her and she turned around again, her eyes bright with a look of hurt.

'You don't believe me?'

'I didn't mean that. I just can't believe that anyone would ever resent you and you and Sir Nicholas always seemed so—'

'Happy?' She grimaced. 'Yes, it was important to him that we seemed so. Appearances meant a great deal to Nicholas.'

Kit drew his brows together. The lack of an heir often caused rifts between husbands and wives—as the country had all-too-frequent proof—but he'd never suspected that the Brays' marriage had been anything less than happy. On the contrary, it had always struck him as an ideal to be emulated. It was hard to believe that a man who'd seemed such an honourable and devoted husband in public could have been so cruel to his wife in private, but then Kit's years as a diplomat had taught him that people were rarely what they appeared. Of course, there was always the chance that she was lying, but he dismissed the suspicion almost as soon as it occurred to him. The pain on her face had been undeniable. Her husband's words had obviously cut deeply—enough to still hurt even a year afterwards. Just the thought of it—of her being in pain and unhappy—made him feel suddenly furious. What kind of a man would say such a thing? What kind of a husband? Although the answer was obvious: the kind who spent most of his time with a king who treated his wives as disposable, that was who.

'I'm truly sorry, Pippa.' He didn't know what else to say.

'Thank you, but it's in the past. It does no good to dwell on it. I don't know why I'm telling you now, except…' She shook her head, looking genuinely confused. 'I don't know why I'm telling you.'

'I'm glad that you did. I'm honoured by your trust.'

'All I want now is to forget. I want peace. That's why Richmond is perfect for me, you see. There are very few husbands. In the eyes of the world, Lady Anne and I are both failed wives.'

'The eyes of the world are often blind. For what it's worth, I think that any man would be fortunate to win the heart of a woman like you.'

'You're a good friend, Kit.' She smiled softly. 'Lady Cecily is a fortunate woman.'

A good friend...

He held on to her gaze, seemingly unable to let go. A bell somewhere close by chimed the hour, warning him to go back inside, but he ignored it. Her eyes looked huge and mesmerising, a rich, hazel-green surrounded by a thin rim of amber, fringed with long lashes that trembled slightly beneath his scrutiny. Funny how he'd never noticed the amber before, but then he'd never had an opportunity to look at her so intimately until now. Nor to stand so close; close enough to see the delicate flutter of her pulse at her throat where her cloak drew together.

Did she *really* see him as just a friend? Her cheeks had flushed several times over the course of their conversation and there had been a brightness in her eyes that had seemed to reflect and respond to his own feelings, which were now substantially *more* than friendly. There had been a wistful, melancholy note in her voice a few moments ago, one that had tempted him to pull her into his arms and show her just how *much* more. It wasn't just that he wanted to comfort her either, although he did. It was desire, too, a feeling that had quickened to life the moment their eyes had met across Lady Anne's chamber the previous evening and that felt all the more potent now.

It was a strange, slightly disorientating sensation. He'd

meant what he'd said about any man being fortunate to win her. He realised now that he'd spent the past ten years unconsciously comparing her to every woman he'd met—comparing and finding them all wanting. She'd been his unattainable ideal and yet now he was drawn to her as a real woman, too, and the real, vulnerable, compassionate woman was even more attractive than the ideal.

How could she say that she had nothing to offer a man? She seemed to think that being unable to bear children made her unattractive somehow, but he'd never felt such a powerful physical reaction, nor such an intensity of feeling for any woman before. When she'd laid her hand on his arm he'd felt as though every nerve in his body had sprung to life. It had been all he could do not to haul her into his arms there and then. In the morning light, hidden from the rest of the world by several feet of yew hedge, she was *more* than just the most beautiful, graceful woman he'd ever met. She was enticing and desirable and, for the first time, attainable, too.

None of which thoughts was a particularly good idea. He had enough problems with George as it was. Telling his brother that he had feelings for an impoverished, thirty-something-year-old widow was unlikely to make him any more sympathetic. If anything, it would only cause him to accelerate his plans. If Kit had any sense, he would leave Pippa and Richmond behind as quickly as possible, before his life became any more complicated. Widowed though she was, it was improper for them to be spending any time alone together, only he hadn't been able to simply walk past her in the avenue. It was potentially incriminating, too, for him to return for the festive celebrations, but he *wanted* to return and for reasons that had little to do with gingerbread. He wanted to see her again, to spend more time with her, and not *just* as a friend.

He swayed closer, encouraged when she didn't move away, bending his head slowly so that he didn't alarm her, breathing in the subtle scent of rosewater that clung to her hair and skin, lowering his lips nearer and nearer…and then spun around abruptly at the sound of a fierce screech, followed by a flash of shimmering blue at the edge of his vision.

'Iratus!' Pippa seemed to jump halfway into the air. 'You scared me!'

'Iratus?' Kit arched an eyebrow at her and then at the peacock.

'Yes, he was a wedding present to Lady Anne and the King. A very grumpy one, too, I'm afraid. My lady named him that because of his bad temper. Come…' She gestured back towards the gap in the hedge, although she seemed to be avoiding his gaze now. 'We should probably leave before he pecks you. I forgot that this is one of his favourite spots and he doesn't like people he doesn't know, men especially.'

'Good to know.' Kit glared at the bird, who twitched its tail and stared back with beady eyes, as if it knew exactly what kind of scene it had just interrupted. 'I'm glad I didn't bump into him earlier. Is there a peahen lurking about, too?'

'Yes, but you rarely see them together. They don't like each other much.'

'A fitting wedding present given the circumstances, then. Who were they from?'

She stopped walking to look back at him, her lips twitching suddenly. 'I believe they were a gift from your brother.'

'George?' Kit gave a shout of laughter. 'Typical! And yet he persists in making alliances.'

'Yes.' The humour in her eyes faded. 'Some people never learn from their mistakes.'

'And some of us don't know how to act in the first place.' He came to stand in front of her. 'You know, in some ways I feel as lost now as I did on that first day you rescued me. Maybe you should rescue me again?'

'I would if I could.'

'You can. Come away with me.'

'What?' Her eyes latched on to his, widening in shock.

'Come away with me.' He repeated the words. In truth, he'd said them on impulse, though now he realised he was being sincere, too. As sincere as he'd ever been about anything. 'We can leave all of this behind and be in Calais by the end of the week.'

'I can imagine what your mother and eldest brother would say to that!'

'All the more reason. By the time they found out, we'd be in Paris, eating mussels beside the Seine.'

'Kit…' Her tone was chiding now. 'I don't think that running away is the answer.'

'I prefer to think of it as a tactical retreat.'

'Your brother is a powerful man. He could ruin your career if he wanted.'

'In England, yes, but I have friends on the Continent, not to mention money of my own and the ability to earn more. I don't want to fail in my duty to my family, but perhaps it would be worth it to be my own man. And with the right woman, too. Think about it, Pippa, I could take you to Venice. We could do all the things you've ever dreamed about.'

'I don't dream.' A guilty expression spread over her face.

'We all have dreams. Why not fulfil them together?'

'This is foolishness.' She laughed, though something about it sounded forced. 'You take courtly love too far, sir, but I appreciate the joke.'

'It's not—'

'Now I should go inside ahead of you.' She jerked her head towards the palace. 'I need to attend to Lady Anne's wardrobe and it would be best if we weren't seen together. I know it sounds absurd to be worried, but—'

'Why?' he interrupted her sharply. 'Why absurd?'

'Because…' She waved a hand in the air. 'I'm sure that nobody would think such a thing about you and me, but people like to gossip.'

'It's not absurd at all. I told you, Pippa, any man would be lucky to win a woman like you, but I do understand about gossip. I'll bid you good morning if that's what you want.' He took a step back from her, though every nerve in his body was screaming at him to do the opposite. 'Until Christmas, then. I look forward to seeing you for the celebrations.'

Chapter Four

'There! What did I tell you? It looks very pretty, does it not?' Lady Anne waved a hand towards the fir tree set in an alcove. The rafters above the hall were hung with boughs of laurel, red berries and mistletoe, giving the strange impression that the world had been turned upside down and that there was a small garden growing on the ceiling, while the trestle tables beneath were decorated with bunches of holly. It was only a small-sized gathering for Christmas Day—just over two dozen people gathered for a feast of pigeon pie, roast boar and venison, followed by sugared almonds and a giant marchpane model of Richmond Palace itself—but the room was buzzing with chatter and the atmosphere was cosy and convivial, making it infinitely preferable, in Kit's opinion, to the more lavish banquet taking place at Hampton Court.

'It looks magnificent, my lady.' Like before, he was sitting in place of honour at Lady Anne's side. 'I think that all homes should have one.'

'If I'd been crowned Queen, then I would have made a royal proclamation.' She laughed and then hastened to correct herself. 'But the King knows best, of course.'

'I'm still sure that nothing at court compares to this.'

'You're an excellent diplomat, Sir Christopher.' Lady Anne smiled her approval. 'You know, in Cleves we tie paper flowers to the branches and then parade the tree through the streets on Christmas Eve. Then there's feasting and dancing and the whole thing is burned, but I couldn't bear to part with this one. It reminds me too much of home.'

'I hear that some people decorate their trees with candles, too?'

'Yes, because of Luther. They say that he looked up at the stars through the branches of a tree one evening and thought to recreate the same effect indoors, but I shouldn't like to take the risk. Richmond Palace, or Sheen as it was, has burned down once at Christmas already and I don't want to be responsible for it happening again.' She sighed. 'You know, the King told me he was here at the time, although he was only a boy. He was carried out in his nurse's arms along with his two sisters.'

'I'm glad that his father had it rebuilt so beautifully. It's a pleasure to be back.'

'And I'm pleased that you chose to come.' Lady Anne raised her goblet of spiced wine. 'Happy Christmas, Sir Christopher.'

'Happy Christmas, my lady.'

'Now, shall we have some dancing?' She sat forward enthusiastically, gesturing to the musicians in the gallery above. 'A pavane to begin with. Will you dance, Sir Christopher? As you can see, men are in somewhat short supply in my household.'

'Of course. I'd be delighted if you'd do me the honour, my lady?'

'Unfortunately, I still haven't mastered the steps. My mother didn't approve of dancing, so I've only recently started to learn, but Lady Philippa loves to dance.' She twisted around to her other side, her expression suspiciously innocent all of a sudden. 'Isn't that so, Pippa?'

'I…yes, my lady.' The woman in question gave a small start from where she was sitting a few places down the table. There had been nothing specifically unfriendly about her manner, but Kit had the feeling that she'd been keeping her distance since his arrival the evening before. There had been no opportunity yet for them to speak alone together, no matter how hard he'd tried to engineer one, and yet every time he looked in her direction, which was often enough, he was struck with the distinct impression that she'd just looked away. 'But I'm sure Sir Christopher would—'

'Sir Christopher could not ask for a more charming partner,' he interrupted, pushing his seat back and bowing to her. 'Will you join me?'

She hesitated for a few seconds before inclining her head and standing up, a wash of pink spreading across her cheeks as they made their way between the trestle tables to the centre of the hall where half-a-dozen other couples were already standing waiting for the music to begin.

'I'm sorry if you felt that you had to dance with me.' She peeped up through her lashes as they stood facing each other. 'There are many other ladies you might have asked.'

'Would you believe me if I said I would have chosen you anyway?' He quirked an eyebrow. 'Or does that sound like something a courtier would say?'

'It does.' Her lips twitched as she sank into a low curtsy.

'But surely it can be true, none the less?' He smiled back, bowing formally as the instruments started to play, a combination of lutes, virginals and drums filling the hall with a rich, harmonious melody. Slowly, they both lifted an arm, raising their hands in the air and pressing their fingers together to form an arch. The dance called for only the lightest of touches, but Kit felt as though a rush of heat passed suddenly between them, shooting through her hand and up his arm before lodging in his chest. He wondered if she felt it, too. It was hard to believe that such a feeling could be entirely one-sided, though she kept her face averted as they took a few swaying steps forward.

'How was court?' she asked after a few moments, though her voice had a slight quaver in it, he noticed.

'Everything I expected. In truth, it's a relief to get away. I'm tired of arguing.'

'You mean with your brother?' She sounded sympathetic. 'I'm sorry to hear it. Did he mind your coming here?'

'At this point, I don't care what George wants. Richmond is exactly what I need right now. Something about this place calms the soul.'

'Yes.' She twisted her head towards him finally, her fingers quivering beneath his. 'That's exactly how I feel about it, too. It's healing.'

He held her gaze as they started to move backwards again, then around each other in a circle, aware that he hadn't been entirely honest. It wasn't Richmond itself that was calming, it was *her*. Even in the two weeks he'd been gone he'd found himself missing her, reliving their conversations over and over in his mind and wondering whether she ever thought about him, too. Now that he was back, her hand touching his, he felt right somehow. Yet her choice of words struck him as odd. Why healing? She'd told him that her husband had resented her, but had there been more to it than that? There had been something else she'd said on his last visit, too, something that had only struck him afterwards, about living a lie. How bad had her marriage truly been? How *much* had she needed to heal? As much as he wanted to know, however, the last thing he wanted to do was spoil the moment by mentioning her husband again.

They continued to dance in silence, moving in perfect symmetry until the pavane ended and the musicians struck up a galliard. It was a more lively dance, filled with hops and kicks, but he had no opportunity to enjoy it properly since the gentleman on his left offered his hand to Pippa and he was obliged to find another partner, contenting himself with watching her out of the corner of his eye instead.

'I think it's time for some singing!' Lady Anne announced as the last notes of the music faded away. 'I've learned a few carols in English especially for the occasion.'

'Pippa…' Kit moved to stand beside her as the rest of

the household started to gather beside the fireplace. 'May we talk?'

'Of course.' Her eyes widened though she didn't object, following him to the alcove containing the fir tree. 'Is something the matter?'

'Nothing at all. I just have something for you.' He reached into his jerkin and pulled out a small leather box. 'I bought it in a market in France last year, though I had no idea why at the time.'

She looked from him to the box and then back again. 'You didn't know *why* you bought it?'

'It struck me as pretty. I just didn't know who to give it to. Now I think that I was simply waiting for the right person, one with the same colour eyes.' He cleared his throat awkwardly. 'Go ahead, open it.'

She did as he asked, unclasping the lid to reveal a small, rose-shaped gold brooch, set with a single emerald.

'Oh.' She let out a small gasp.

'Do you like it?'

'Very much.' She drew a finger over the surface, her gaze admiring. 'It's beautiful, but I cannot accept such a gift.'

'Why not?'

'Because I have nothing for you and...' She glanced across to the singers, her chest rising and falling as if she were short of breath suddenly. 'Other people might not understand. About our being friends, I mean.'

'Or perhaps they might understand perfectly.'

'But if your brother or Lady Cecily were to hear of it...'

'Cecily and I aren't betrothed. I've made no promise to her.'

'Not yet...'

'Not ever.' He clenched his jaw. 'I've told my brother that I won't marry her, duty or not.'

'Oh...' This time she seemed to stop breathing entirely. 'Why?'

'Do you really not know?' He took a step closer towards her. 'Because it would be dishonourable to marry one woman when I care for another.'

'Kit... I don't know what to say.'

'For now, just say that you'll accept my gift.' He drew his brows together, alarmed to find that her eyes looked suspiciously bright all of a sudden. 'Pippa?'

'I'm sorry.' She blinked rapidly, dashing a hand across her cheeks. 'Lady Anne gave me some sleeves and a new gown, but I didn't expect any other gifts. I'm being foolish.'

'I only wish I could give you more. You deserve lots of beautiful things, Pippa...' He reached for the brooch. 'Will you accept?'

'Yes.' She nodded and he pinned it carefully to one side of her collar, the backs of his fingers brushing against the skin of her throat as he did so. 'Thank you.' Her voice was almost a whisper as he moved his hand away again. 'It's the most beautiful gift I've ever been given, but we should rejoin the others or they'll wonder where we are.'

'Very well.' His fingers still tingled where they'd touched her. 'Just know that I don't care what anyone else thinks, Pippa. They would not be mistaken, not on my part anyway.'

'Sir Christopher is a fine dancer.' Lady Anne caught her eye in the mirror as Pippa started to unfasten the laces of her kirtle that night. 'And very pleasing to the eye, too, is he not? Unlike some English gentlemen I can think of.'

'Yes, my lady.' Pippa darted an ironic smile back. It was as close as her mistress had ever come to criticising the aged and overweight King.

'You looked very fine together. I believe he admires you.'

'We're just friends, my lady.' Pippa felt herself blushing again, a tendril of warmth unfurling in her stomach at the memory of their dance. For those few minutes, she'd felt completely, blissfully happy.

'More than that, I think.' Anne laughed softly. 'He hardly took his eyes off you all evening. I might have been offended if I hadn't expected it, but I didn't invite him here for me. Something tells me he didn't accept for the pleasure of my company either.'

'You mean that you invited him here for *me*?' Pippa stared at her mistress in surprise. It seemed so unlikely to think of Anne as a matchmaker.

'I noticed the way he looked at you the last time he was here. And I thought perhaps you liked him, too?'

'I…' Pippa bit her tongue before she could answer truthfully. 'It doesn't matter. His family have a marriage in mind for him.'

'Really? Has a betrothal been announced?'

'No, and he says it won't be, but…'

'Then he's not promised.'

'My lady!' Pippa's mouth fell open in shock. After the way the King had set her aside, Anne was the last woman she would have expected to say such a thing.

'I know.' Anne smiled sadly. 'But I also know the pain of being married to someone who cares for another. I would never wish that on anyone else. If Sir Christopher prefers you, then it's much better for him to say so now.'

'It's impossible.' Pippa shook her head. 'Even if I did like him, his family would never approve. I'm too old, I cannot have children and I have no fortune. I could never make him happy.'

'He seems to disagree and *I* believe that he's a man of good judgement. In general, men leave us in no doubt about what *they* want. The more important question is whether you think you could be happy with *him*?'

Pippa hesitated, touching a hand to the brooch pinned on her collar. She ought not to have accepted such a gift, but she hadn't been able to refuse, overwhelmed by the gesture and what he'd just told her about Lady Cecily. The way that he'd spoken when he'd given it suggested he thought of her as more than just a friend, too—much more—and he'd almost kissed her in the gardens two weeks ago, she definitely hadn't imagined *that*, having relived the moment at least a dozen times in her mind every day since. No, to her amazement, the attraction she felt for him appeared to be mutual. He'd even spoken about running away together, although perhaps he only wanted an affair? She didn't think that he'd act so dishonourably, especially considering her position in Lady Anne's household, yet the alternative seemed so unlikely. Surely there were other, younger women to tempt him? Why would he want her?

'I'm happy living here with you, my lady.'

'And I value having a friend like you, too.' Anne twisted around to grasp hold of her hands. 'This past year has been difficult for both of us, but there can be more to life than friendship. If he admires you and you like him, too, why should you not be together? If nothing else, it would give me hope.'

Pippa squeezed her hands back, feeling a pang of sympathy for her mistress. Anne never indulged in self-pity and rarely spoke about her feelings, but every now and then there were glimpses of sadness behind her dignified façade. How could she feel otherwise? She was neither a spinster, a wife nor a widow. According to the King, she was free to marry again, yet according to the terms of the annulment she was still pre-contracted to the son of the Duke of Lorraine, a man who was soon to marry Princess Christina of Denmark. To all intents and purposes, she was trapped in the role of royal sister for ever.

Whereas she…*she* was free, but how could she consider a future with Kit? There were no advantages for him in an alliance with her, only disadvantages, and there were far too many reasons against it—some she didn't want to think about either. She'd told Kit that she and Nicholas had been unhappy, but his resentment had been only the half of it. Her marriage had been worse than she'd ever told anyone. She could never risk such misery again. Richmond was her home now, her haven, the place where she'd come to heal after the long and miserable years of her life with Nicholas. How could she risk leaving just because of a pair of kind eyes and the feeling of excitement they caused? No matter how much she liked and admired Kit, she couldn't allow herself to be tempted. She might have accepted his gift in a moment of weakness, but it wouldn't happen again. She had to make that clear to both him *and* Lady Anne.

'I'm far too old to even contemplate such a thing, my lady.'

'Very well, if you say so.' Anne sounded faintly disappointed. 'I suppose it would be very different from your first marriage. Your husband was older than you, I believe?'

'He was, my lady.' Pippa couldn't help but stiffen at the words. 'Twelve years older.'

'And a good friend of the King, they tell me.'

'Yes. They were both keen jousters in their youth and… well, they were similar in a lot of ways.'

'Really?' Anne lifted an eyebrow and then shook her head. 'Forgive me, I don't mean to pry—or to push, either. Perhaps you simply think it too soon for you to have another suitor?'

'Ye-es…' Pippa agreed hesitantly. After Nicholas, she'd told herself that for ever would be too soon, although she'd been feeling less and less convinced of that resolve in recent weeks.

'Well then, we won't speak about it any more.' Anne smiled at her kindly. 'I just wanted to give you my blessing, Pippa. What you choose to do with it is up to you.'

Chapter Five

Pippa formed her lips into an O-shape, tipped her head backwards and blew, watching her breath twist and coil upwards as she wandered amid a world of crystal-capped topiary and frozen-looking statues. A sprinkling of snow overnight had made the garden more beautiful than ever, although it wouldn't be long before the sun melted it. A group of stable boys close by, however, were making the most of the weather, scraping up as much as they could into snowballs and hurling them boisterously at each other. There was a tall figure among them, too, she noticed, one whom she recognised instantly as Kit, though he was allowing himself to be pummelled rather than throwing much snow himself.

'Good morning, Sir Christopher,' she called out, wrapping her cloak more tightly around herself like a shield as her treacherous stomach leapt with excitement. 'It's a beautiful morning, is it not?'

'Good mor—'

He didn't finish the greeting as a snowball caught him directly on the jaw.

'Peace!' He chuckled, holding his hands up in a gesture of defeat. 'I surrender.'

'Then you need to pay a forfeit!' one of the smallest boys shouted back.

'A forfeit?' Kit stroked his chin and then reached into a leather pouch at his waist, pulling out a handful of coins and tossing one to each of the boys in turn. 'Will these do instead?'

'Yes, sir!' they all called in chorus, scampering away as if they were afraid he might change his mind.

'Is that how the world of diplomacy works?' Pippa lifted an eyebrow accusingly.

'Most of the time, yes.' Kit brushed the snow from his shoulders and walked towards her, a broad smile splitting his face. 'No matter what the statesmen tell us.'

'I believe you.' She couldn't resist smiling back, although the moment felt bittersweet, too. After another disturbed night, she'd resolved to make matters clear between them and then say goodbye. The thought made her chest feel constricted, as if there were a heavy weight pressing down on it, but at least she could give him something to remember her by first...

'I hoped I would find you here.'

'Really?' His eyes seemed to light up at the words.

'Yes, I wanted to give you some kind of present in exchange for your brooch.' She reached inside her cloak for a small square of fabric. 'It's not much, but... Happy Christmas, Kit.'

'A handkerchief.' His fingers brushed hers as he reached for it, making her chest feel even tighter. 'And you've sewn my initials?'

'Yes, although I confess I had to do them in a hurry last night.'

'I'll treasure it. It's perf— Look out!'

She inhaled sharply as he grabbed hold of her arm, hauling her against him as a snowball flew through the air where her head had just been.

'Sorry, sir.' One of the stable boys looked stricken. 'I wasn't aiming for the lady, I promise. It went higher than I thought.'

'You're lucky the lady is of a forgiving nature.' Kit gave him an admonishing look and then winked. 'Just be more careful from now on.'

'Yes, sir.'

'Thank you.' Pippa gave him a grateful look, acutely conscious of his hand still wrapped around her arm, not to mention the solid pressure of his chest against hers. 'I wouldn't have been so forgiving with a mouthful of snow.'

'I wouldn't blame you.' He loosened his hold, though he still didn't release her. 'Shall we walk? I can shield you from snowballs and you can protect me from Iratus.'

'I think perhaps we ought to talk instead...' She took a step backwards and pressed her lips together nervously. Now that the moment was here, she wasn't sure quite what to say. 'Did you really tell your brother that you wouldn't marry Lady Cecily?'

'I did.' He smiled in a way that made her heart slam hard into her ribcage, so hard that she felt sure it would leave a bruise.

'What did he say?'

'That I was shaming him and the family, that he'd ask the King to remove me from his service, that he'd disown me and...' His lips twitched, though without any mirth. 'A few more things I probably shouldn't repeat to a lady.'

'He threatened to disown you?' The words horrified her. 'But that's terrible!'

'It was nothing I didn't expect. At least now I've made my position clear. What he does next is up to him.'

'But it's your family!'

'My family isn't the same without my father. George and my mother care for nothing that does not advance their ambitions, my sisters are both married and my brother Sidney only wants a quiet life. If they choose to disown me, then I'll be sorry, but it's their decision.'

'You cannot mean that.'

'Why not? I've done my duty to them in every other way, but I won't do this.' He threw a quick look around the garden and then tugged on her arm, drawing her into one of the avenues. 'I wasn't joking when I asked you to run away with me.'

'Kit...'

'Just hear me out, Pippa, please.' He lifted his hands to her face, smoothing his palms gently across her cheeks. 'The first time we met, I thought you were the most perfect woman I'd ever seen, but you were married and so far beyond me that I felt foolish even thinking it. Now I realise that all this time, all these years since, I've been searching for another like you. But there isn't another.' He slid his fingers into the hair beneath her hood, his voice deep and seductive, making her whole body vibrate with longing. 'There's only you. There was only ever you.'

'Me?' Heat flooded her veins, his words making her want to weep and dance for joy at the same time. He looked so handsome, so young and vibrant and tender, too, everything she might ever have wanted in a man, but it was impossible...wasn't it?

She closed her eyes, trying to hold on to some scrap of sanity, but her thoughts were too scattered and his hands were too distracting, cradling the back of her head as he tilted her face upwards. He was standing so close that she could feel the warmth of his breath on her cheek and the fierce beat of his heart beneath his doublet. Her own was pounding violently, too, like a hammer against an anvil, sending out hot sparks to melt her resolve. It was as though her body were waking up after a long sleep, all her nerves springing back to sudden and vibrant life. His lips were barely a hair's breadth away, as if he were waiting for her to close the last remaining distance between them, tempting her to coil her arms up around his neck and surrender... For a moment, she almost did, but it was *only* a moment before sanity returned.

'No.' She twisted her face to one side so that his hands fell to her shoulders. 'I'm not the woman you think I am. You put me on too high a pedestal.'

'I don't want you on a pedestal. I want *you*, the woman in front of me now.'

'No, you don't.' She shook her head adamantly. 'I'm almost ten years older than you. You need a young woman, one who can give you children.'

'Have you never considered that it was because of your husband that you couldn't have children?'

'No.' Her cheeks flamed scarlet. 'Nicholas fathered at least half a dozen that I know of, probably more. I *know* it was my fault.'

'Not fault.' His brows contracted. 'Never call it that. And if not having children is what it costs to be with you, then I don't care.'

'You shouldn't dismiss it so lightly!' She glared angrily at his denial, at the way he made having an heir sound so unimportant. He was too good of a diplomat, telling her the things she wanted to hear, but it had been bad enough to disappoint a man she'd despised. How much worse would it be to disappoint one she cared for?

'You might think that you don't mind about having children now, but one day you might, in a year or two perhaps, and I couldn't bear it. I could never be a disappointment again!'

'What?' He sounded angry this time. 'Pippa, you could never disappoint me.'

'How can a *perfect* woman not be a disappointment in the end? Lady Cecily is far more suitable.'

'Yes.' He moved his hands back to her cheeks, cradling her face between his fingers. 'She's suitable and beautiful and respectable, but when I'm with her I don't *feel* anything. If I married her I could have a place at court, a great manor of my own and a lifetime of boredom. That's not what I want. I want to make my own choices, to travel and live out the rest of my days with the woman I love.'

'Love?' She stiffened beneath his touch. 'You should not say such a thing. How can you love me after so little time?'

'I don't know. All I know is that love doesn't care how

old we both are or how long we've known each other. It doesn't care whether you can have children either. You're the woman I want, the only woman I desire, and if the King no longer wants me in his service then I'll make my own way.' He lowered his head, pressing his forehead against hers as he traced his thumb over the line of her bottom lip. 'We're neither of us bound to anyone else, Pippa, not now, not at this moment. We can make a life together. Come away with me. Marry me.'

Marry! Her mind spun at the word. She couldn't marry him! She had to hold on to that resolve, even though the rest of his words made her feel as if a gaping hole in her chest had suddenly been filled, as if she'd spent a lifetime longing to hear them. He sounded sincere, but *could* he truly love her? Could *she* love him? Incredibly, she felt as if she already did. But it would be selfish of her to say yes, no matter what her heart might suddenly yearn for. She had to say no. In the long run, it would be best for both of them...

Judging by the determined set of his jaw, however, he wasn't about to give up so easily. Which meant that she had to make him and the only way she could think of was to convince him that she didn't care in return. No matter how much it hurt, it was better for him never to guess how tempted she truly was. Far better for him to believe that she still saw him as a boy.

'Pippa...' His lips skimmed lightly across her forehead before moving downwards, grazing her ear and nuzzling the side of her throat. 'I want you. I thought there was something, an attraction between us... Was I mistaken?'

'Yes.' Somehow she found the strength to pull away from him, heat stinging the backs of her eyes. She felt suddenly desperate to get away, to run and hide before the tears could fall in earnest. 'You were always a kind-hearted boy, Kit, but that's what you still are to me, a boy. I'm sorry if I led you to think otherwise.'

'You don't mean that.' His whole body seemed to turn rigid. 'You wanted to kiss me before, I could see it in your eyes.'

'I was curious, that's all, but you speak of love like a child. One day you'll learn better.' She dug her heels into the ground, resisting the urge to fling herself back into his arms and say that she was lying. 'Now you should go back to your brother and Lady Cecily and we should never speak of this again.'

'If that's what you want.' He took a step back from her, his eyes burning with a look of perplexity and hurt as he made a terse bow. 'In that case, thank you for the handkerchief. I will not bother you again.'

Chapter Six

The distance between Richmond Palace and Hampton Court was less than three leagues, but on a rainy afternoon in the very midst of winter, Pippa thought that it was surely twice the distance. Riding on horseback, wrapped up in several layers of fur-lined capes and hoods, the whole household was half-frozen by the time they arrived.

'Pippa?' Lady Anne nudged her horse closer as they rode beneath the red brick archway of the Great Gatehouse and into Base Court beyond. 'Are you feeling unwell? You look pale.'

'Just a little tired, my lady.' Pippa shook her head, touched by Anne's concern. 'I haven't been sleeping well of late.'

'I've noticed.' Anne's brow wrinkled. 'I thought that it would please you to visit Hampton Court again, but it's not too late for you to change your mind. I don't want our visit to upset you.'

'Thank you, my lady, but I'm content to be here.'

'Very well.' Anne gave her a conspiratorial smile. 'I admit that I'm glad to have a friend with me. Hopefully we won't be staying for long.'

Pippa smiled back though she felt her pulse quicken as they drew rein and dismounted, turning their mounts over to the care of the King's grooms. In truth, she'd slept little and eaten less over the past few days and nights, her nerves strung tight. She was acutely aware of how poor she looked, with grey shadows beneath her eyes and gaunt, hollow cheeks. Despite what she'd just told Anne, Hampton Court was not a place she relished visiting again. It held few happy memories and she knew how the people there saw her, too, either pitying her for her failed marriage or holding her in contempt for it—something else that she and Anne had in common. There would be stares and whispers, some more blatant than others, but at least she could steel herself against those. What she couldn't steel herself sufficiently for was seeing Kit. It was only just over a week since he'd left Richmond and the thought of seeing him again made her sick with anxiety.

She'd done her best to put him out of her mind, to *not* remember the intensity in his gaze when he'd asked her to marry him, or the hurt in his eyes when she'd called him a boy, but to no avail. Even if she succeeded, by and large, during the day, she lay awake at night torturing herself with the same recurring question.

What if? What if she changed her mind and told him the truth?

Now she couldn't stop her eyes from searching the courtyard, half-afraid, half-desperate for a glimpse of him.

'Come.' Lady Anne linked an arm through hers. 'Let's get in the warm.'

They made their way through a throng of people to the sumptuous apartments set aside for the King's sister. The court was alive with activity, preparing for the celebrations that evening. It was a stark contrast to the last New Year banquet Pippa had attended at court. That had been three years before, only a few months after the death of Queen Jane, and her loss had cast a pall over the scene. Now it appeared that the new Queen had brought back an atmosphere of merriment and revelry, as if the court had swung from one extreme to the other.

Pippa dressed in a plain deep blue gown and matching hood, then helped her mistress into a cream-coloured kirtle and copper gown, decorated with burgundy ribbons and tiny garnets sewn into the bodice. It perfectly complemented Anne's red hair, making her look modest and pretty—just as she was, Pippa thought defensively—although she had a sense that they were both feeling equally nervous.

Her stomach was alive with butterflies as they made their way to the great hall for the banquet, the sound of minstrels guiding their way. No, butterflies were too delicate, she corrected herself. Whatever it was felt more like a caged animal, scratching and clawing at her insides as it tried to escape. But perhaps she was worrying over nothing, she reassured herself, folding her hands demurely in front of her. There ought to be safety in numbers and, according to the King's Chamberlain, there were currently almost a thousand guests staying at court for the festivities. In such a vast crowd, it was unlikely that she'd even set eyes on Kit. And if she did... Well, after what she'd said the last time they were together, he probably wouldn't want to talk to her again. She could spend the evening in a corner behind Lady Anne, not hiding exactly, but keeping a discreet distance. She would be safe. She would be calm. She would be...

She gasped, her eyes locking on to Kit's the very moment they entered. She hardly knew how it happened, only that her gaze seemed drawn to his as if by some primal instinct. He was standing on the opposite side of the hall, dressed in a silver doublet that intensified the striking paleness of his eyes and made him look even more handsome than she remembered, yet his expression was stern, revealing not the faintest hint of emotion as he stared silently back. It made her heart ache. Worse still, however, was the sight of the woman standing beside him, looking like a vision of loveliness in green velvet. Cecily.

'Pippa.' One of the other ladies gave a sharp whisper. 'You stepped on Lady Anne's train.'

'Oh!' She jumped quickly to one side, keeping her eyes lowered as they crossed the hall to where the King and Queen sat on a raised dais draped with a canopy of gold

and red fabric. A swift glance before they made their obeisance revealed that Henry had gained weight since the last
time he'd visited Richmond in the summer. With his bad
leg propped up on a stool beside him, he looked old and
bloated and tired next to his vivacious young wife, though
there was no mistaking the look of adoration on his face as
Katherine leapt up from her chair to embrace the woman
she'd first served and then replaced.

'Lady Anne.' The new Queen's voice was almost girl-
ishly gleeful, though without any trace of malice. 'We're
so glad that you came.'

'I'm honoured to be here, too, Your Majesty.'

Only once Katherine had led Anne away to another chair
on the dais and Pippa had moved to one side, did she dare
risk turning her head again—and then she wished that she
hadn't. Kit was standing in exactly the same position, still
staring at her, as if he'd been transformed into stone.

'Well done, Brother.'

Kit tensed at the sound of his eldest brother's voice in
his ear. With a twelve-year age difference between them,
they'd never been close, but he was becoming nostalgic for
the days when George had ignored his existence completely.
He wasn't sure what he was being congratulated for either.

'What I have done?' He wrenched his gaze away from
where Pippa was standing against a wall, apparently trying
to disappear into the background.

'I saw you dancing with Lady Cecily a few minutes ago.'
George sounded approving. 'She seems to favour you.'

'Does she?' Kit looked around absently. He'd only just
returned Cecily to the side of the room when he'd seen
Pippa entering and been hit with a wave of longing so painful that he'd promptly forgotten everything, and everyone,
else. 'Where did she go?'

'She's dancing with Hugh Tavistock now.'

'Really? I didn't notice.'

'You might try paying a little more attention.' George clucked his tongue. 'One dance is all very well, but you should do more to secure her. Be charming.'

'I'm not in the mood.'

'So I see. Fortunately Tavistock's not much of a rival. He's already gambled away most of his fortune.'

Kit gritted his teeth. 'George, I said that I'd consider a marriage, that I'd *try* to like her, but I haven't agreed to anything.'

'What is there not to like? She's from a good family and she's biddable. We'll arrange the wedding for the summer.'

'*If* she and I agree.'

'This summer,' George repeated. 'By the way, Mother and I have discussed it and we intend to give you the manor at Easington.'

'The pair of you have already decided my feelings, then?'

'Naturally.' As usual, George was oblivious to irony. He and their mother together were an immovable force. Kit was uncomfortably aware of the duty he owed them, although their ambition had cost him dear, too. There was little doubt that their relentless machinations and striving had sent his mild-mannered father to an early grave. Not that *he'd* done much to help either, he chided himself. Perhaps if he'd stayed in England then things might have been different, but he hadn't truly realised how much pressure his father had been under until afterwards. None the less, he was a Lowell and if Pippa didn't want him then he'd do his duty to the family instead, even if it meant a marriage he didn't want.

'She's already moved on to planning a match for Sidney,' George continued. 'Fortunately, he's somewhat more enthusiastic about the idea than you.'

Kit rolled his eyes. Sidney was four years his junior and happy to do whatever was necessary for a quiet life. He had no desire to travel or to see anything of the world outside

England. The manor at Easington would be perfect for him. As would Lady Cecily for that matter.

'You seem distracted this evening.' George gave him a curious look.

'Do I?' Kit took a sip of wine to guard his expression. He felt more than distracted. When Pippa had entered the room, he'd felt as though all the air had suddenly left it. He was still finding it hard to breathe. Despite the way she'd dismissed him at their last meeting, both his eyes and feet seemed determined to follow her, though fortunately he was managing to restrain the latter. It was akin to torture, watching her from across the room and remembering the humiliation of their last meeting—of declaring his love to a woman who still thought of him as a boy. The stricken expression on her face suggested she wasn't particularly pleased to see him either.

'What is it?' George followed his gaze and smirked. 'Don't tell me you've been struck speechless by the Lady Anne's beauty?'

'She's a fine lady.' Kit directed a glare at him.

'Not fine enough for the King. Even if she weren't so plain, he would have lost interest in her soon enough. She couldn't sing or dance or even play cards when she first arrived in England.'

'She's intelligent and kind. I would have thought those were more important qualities in a wife.'

'Spoken like a bachelor.' George snorted. 'Now Lady Cecily's a different kettle of fish. She's a beautiful girl.'

Kit sighed. That was undeniably true. He almost wished he *could* be drawn to Cecily. It would make his life a great deal easier. In truth, he wished he could find solace in *any* other woman's arms, but there was only one woman he wanted.

'Beauty isn't everything and certainly not an indicator of a happy marriage.' He paused meaningfully. 'How *is* Elizabeth, by the way?'

'Quite well, as far as I know.' George's gaze narrowed. The antipathy between him and his own beautiful wife was legendary. 'You know that she prefers living in the country to being at court.'

'So it's not because you don't allow her a choice, then?' Kit lifted an eyebrow provocatively. 'Well then, forget that I spoke.'

'Of course, maybe it isn't Lady Anne herself that you're staring at?' George's expression seemed far too pointed all of a sudden. Kit could almost see his mind searching for alternatives.

'Or maybe I was just wondering why the King invited her?'

'He's in a good mood—for obvious reasons.' George jerked his head subtly in the direction of the new Queen. 'And no doubt he wants Lady Anne to send a good report of his behaviour back to her brother.'

'No doubt.'

'You know it was an honour that he sent you to Richmond with the invitation.' George swilled the wine inside his cup thoughtfully. 'I think the King likes you. He was talking about appointing new ambassadors the other day. You know, if we talk to him together, we might…'

'No more scheming for tonight, thank you, Brother.' Kit put his cup down before George could say anything else. 'I need some air.'

'What?' George sounded aggrieved. 'It's still early. You should dance with Cecily again!'

'I've danced enough. Now I'm going for a walk.'

'The new Queen has a great deal of energy, does she not?' Anne murmured as they climbed the stairs back to her chambers that night. 'The court seems very lively these days.'

'Yes, my lady,' Pippa agreed cautiously, knowing that Anne probably couldn't help but compare herself. 'Although,

I confess, it's a little *too* lively for me, not to mention the King. He retired to bed after the Masque.'

'I wish I could have done the same. It's been a long day.' Anne sighed as Pippa closed the door to her bedchamber behind them. 'But the Queen is a kind lady. The King gave her a present of a ruby ring and she handed it straight to me. I believe that she's trying to make me feel welcome as a sister.'

'I think that you're right, my lady.'

'I noticed Sir Christopher across the room, too.' Anne gave her a surreptitious glance. 'I thought that he might come and speak to us, but he left quickly.'

'Yes, my lady, I noticed that as well.' She swallowed, trying not to remember how incredibly handsome he'd looked. Seeing him again, even from across a crowded room, had been even more painful than she'd expected. Seeing him side by side with Lady Cecily, looking like a pair of golden swans, had made her feel as though she'd been kicked hard in the ribs. She'd done her best not to look at him again afterwards, yet she'd been aware of his every gesture and movement, including his terse exchange with his brother.

'Pippa.' Anne sounded hesitant. 'I know it's none of my business, but have the two of you quarrelled?'

'Not exactly, but I told him…' Pippa pursed her lips… 'That is, when he visited at Christmas, I made it clear that an alliance between the two of us would be impossible.'

'Ah. You're certain of that, then?'

'Yes. I made sure that he believed it, too.'

'Well, then…you go to bed. Hansi will undress me tonight.'

'Thank you, my lady, but if you don't mind, I think perhaps I might take a walk outside instead. I'd like to clear my head after all the noise. I'm afraid I've become used to the peace and quiet of Richmond.'

'Of course.' Anne's smile suggested that she understood perfectly. 'Only don't go too far and don't stay out in the cold too long either. I'll see you in the morning.'

Chapter Seven

Pippa swung a cloak around her shoulders and hurried back down the staircase, through a warren of large corridors and then smaller ones until she found a side door out on to a courtyard, relieved to be out in the fresh air and on her own again. The moon and stars were obscured by cloud, but the small knot garden within the palace was illuminated by torches, creating pools of light amid the shadows.

She stopped just outside the doorway and breathed in several lungfuls of air, listening to the distant sound of drunken revellers and wishing that she were back at Richmond. Hard as it had been to see Kit back with Lady Cecily, at least now she could congratulate herself on doing the right thing—the *best* thing for his future. She ought to be proud of her actions, especially since she had no intention of ever marrying again herself. She *ought* to let him go and be happy...

She tipped her head back against the wall and let her eyelids drift closed, only dimly aware of footsteps approaching, then stopping abruptly beside her.

'Lady Philippa?'

She jumped and opened her eyes again, muffling a startled exclamation at the sound of her name. There was no doubting who the speaker was, though the face before her was like that of a stranger, steelier and harder somehow, with a furrowed brow and eyes that looked uncannily like those of his brother, more like granite than smoke. And he was calling her Lady Philippa again, she noticed.

'Kit?' She put a hand to her chest, trying to calm the suddenly frantic pounding of her heartbeat.

'What are you doing out here?' His tone was faintly accusatory. 'Did Lady Anne send you on an errand?'

'No, I just wanted some air.'

'It's not safe outside on your own, especially at this hour of the night.' He folded his arms, a shadow of suspicion crossing his face. 'Unless you're waiting for someone?'

She stared back into his eyes for a moment, wondering whether to be offended or to burst into peals of laughter. How could he think that she was there for an assignation? She supposed it was a compliment of sorts that he thought she had other suitors, although it hurt, too, that he believed her feelings to be so fickle. But then he didn't know that she had any feelings for him…because she'd told him she hadn't.

She pulled her shoulders back, adopting a look of offended dignity. 'As I said, I came outside for the air.'

'Ah.' He unfolded his arms, his frown easing slightly. 'How was your journey from Richmond?'

'Cold and slow. The roads are heavily rutted.'

'And how is Lady Anne finding being back at court?'

'I believe that she's enjoying herself, but we're only here for a few days. We'll be returning to Richmond before the week's end.'

'Indeed.' He glanced away and then back again. 'I didn't think I would see you here.'

She stiffened at the implication. 'I serve Lady Anne. That means I travel where she travels.'

'I still thought you might have found an excuse. You told me once that you didn't like court.'

'Ah, I thought you meant…' She bit her tongue. 'That is, I thought…'

'You thought I meant because of me?' His expression turned sardonic. 'I wouldn't presume to have such importance in your thoughts.'

'Kit…' She started to speak and then stopped herself, her

throat tightening around the words. What could she say? That he rarely left her thoughts?

'You and Cecily look well matched,' she said instead.

'So I've been told.' A muscle tensed in his jaw. 'I'm doing my duty to my family as you suggested.'

'Yes.' She paused awkwardly. 'I saw your brother.'

'Quite. It's hard to escape George, but I won't keep you any longer.' He started to move away and then stopped, his tone softening slightly. 'Goodnight, Lady Philippa. If our paths don't cross again before you leave, I wish you good fortune.'

'Wait!' she called out as he moved on. 'Can we not remain friends?'

'We *are* friends.'

'You know what I mean. As we were.'

'As we were was based on a misunderstanding on my part.' He looked back over his shoulder, his voice hardening again. 'You made your feelings about me clear the other day.'

'No, I didn't.'

'I told you that I loved you and you told me I was just a boy. Or am I misremembering the details?'

'No, but I didn't mean it like that. I meant...' She stopped mid-sentence. It would be foolish of her to say any more. As much as she wanted for them to part on good terms, she was already dangerously close to revealing too much.

'Then what did you mean?'

'Nothing.' She shook her head. 'Only that I never meant to hurt or offend you.'

'Pippa?' He turned around slowly to face her, one eyebrow raised in a way that made her feel suddenly apprehensive.

'Goodnight.' She whirled about, hastening towards the safety of the doorway. 'I wish you good fortune, too.'

'Pippa!' He reached a hand out, catching her around the

waist and twisting her back towards him. '*What* did you mean? Either you see me as a boy or you don't.'

'I already told you!' She swallowed, glad of the darkness concealing the heat she could feel spreading across her neck and cheeks.

'Tell me again.'

'You're a boy!' She lifted her chin, trying to brazen it out. 'Just a boy!'

He stared down at her for a few seconds, his eyes boring into hers so intently that she was afraid he could tell she was lying. They looked like his own eyes again, she realised, not like those of his brother any more, only with an added glimmer of suspicion. She tensed, acutely aware of the pressure of his hand on her waist and the sound of her own breathing. It was too fast, too guilty sounding. For some reason, it made him smile, too.

'I don't believe you.'

'You can believe what you wish.' She strove to make herself sound convincing. 'It doesn't matter anyway.'

'Of course it matters.'

'No, it doesn't! There are far too many obstacles between us. We could never be together, and if we could…you'd only come to regret it.'

'You think that I know my own mind so little?' His grip on her waist tightened. 'Because I'm *just* a boy?'

'*No!*' she protested and then stiffened, realising what she'd just said.

'Then I'm not?' His smile widened, both of his hands around her waist now.

'Kit…' She felt as though her stomach were tying itself in knots. 'I should go.'

'Just tell me the truth. If you still think of me as a boy, then I'll let you go and never speak of this again, but if I'm not, if I'm more than that, if you care for me at all, as a man…' he lowered his head, brushing his lips softly against the side of her mouth in a way that made her neck arch in-stinctively '…tell me.'

She lifted her hands and pressed them against the hard expanse of his chest, every part of her body tingling. 'How I feel isn't important.'

'It's important to me. I love you, Pippa. Nothing about that has changed. You don't have to say that you feel the same way, but if you think that you could, if there's hope, then tell me before it's too late.'

She caught her breath as he pressed his mouth against her throat, desperately trying to remember all of her reasons for pushing him away, but his lips were moving against her skin, tracing the line of her collarbone, and it was hard to remember anything, let alone to be rational.

'Come away with me. We'll overcome whatever obsta-cles there are together.' The rough edge to his voice caused a quivering sensation in her stomach. 'We'll go wherever you want, see all the places you want to see. We'll go to the far ends of the earth, if that's what you want. Just say that you'll marry me and we'll find a way. I'll never resent you, I swear it.'

'But you could!' She wrenched her neck to one side. 'When Nicholas died, I told myself that I'd never allow any man so much power over me again. It's not important how I feel because I'll never marry again! I *cannot*!'

He didn't say anything for a few moments, his chest heaving beneath her fingertips, before he slid his hands upwards, clasping her own between them.

'Tell me.' To her relief, his voice sounded tender. 'It was more than resentment, wasn't it? Tell me what happened to you.'

She licked her lips, her skin burning in all the places he'd touched her. 'He was a good husband at first, or at least I thought he was, but I was so young and I didn't know any better. It was only after a few years, when it became obvi-ous that I couldn't have children, that he started to become cold and distant and then…unfaithfulness was the least of his faults. He wanted to be a perfect knight, you see, and that meant having an heir.' She let out a sob, feeling as if the words were being wrenched from her chest. 'He came to hate me and I loathed him in return. The last ten years of my marriage were a living hell. Everyone thought he was such a good husband, so charming and gallant and handsome, but it was all a lie. He was a monster.'

'Did he hurt you?' Kit's voice sounded tense.

'Not physically. He never struck or beat me, but he revelled in coldness and cruelty, in making me feel worthless. Sometimes I would look at him across the dinner table and know that he was inventing new ways to humiliate and punish me for ruining his life. That was what he called me—the woman who ruined his life. He kept his mistresses in our house, flaunting and comparing them in front of me and hurling insults in front of our servants. He was still always the best of husbands in public, but he made sure that everyone in our home knew of my failure. He sucked all the joy and happiness out of life until I hated myself. I think that was what he wanted, to break my spirit completely. Sometimes I wondered if he was trying to drive me mad.'

'Pippa…' Kit released her hands and wrapped his arms around her shoulders, pulling her close. 'I'm sorry.'

'When the King divorced Queen Catherine, I was actually hopeful. I thought that maybe Nicholas might ask for a divorce, too, so that we could both be free, but he never did. Either that or the King refused. Then Nicholas caught the Sweat and…' she lowered her forehead against his shoulder '… I nursed him, but I felt so guilty.'

'Why guilty?'

'Because I was glad that he couldn't hurt or humiliate me any more! I did my best to save him, truly, but when he died, I couldn't grieve and then I felt doubly guilty, as if I'd caused it by not caring enough. People thought that I was such a convincing widow, but my tears at his funeral were ones of shame, not grief. Because I was free and that was what I'd wanted—my freedom restored to me.'

'No one could blame you for that.' He moved his hands over her shoulders in slow circles, caressing and soothing.

'But freedom wasn't what I'd imagined either.' She lifted her head again with a sob. 'I still felt wretched. Even now, whenever I think of Nicholas, I feel wicked and weak, as if there's a shadow hanging over me. Sometimes I think I'll never feel sunshine again.'

Kit pressed his lips into her hair, tightening his hold as Pippa sobbed quietly against his shoulder. He couldn't blame her. His heart ached to think of how much she'd suffered alone and for so long. It was no wonder that she'd hidden herself away at Richmond afterwards. Her damaged soul had needed time and space to heal.

'I'm sorry, Pippa. I had no idea.'

'No one did.' Her voice sounded muffled. 'No one outside our home.'

'If I'd known…' He clenched his jaw, visualising all the ways he might have *punished* Nicholas Bray in return.

'Even if you had, he was my husband. He had every right to treat me as he wanted. There was nothing anyone could have done.'

'Don't be so sure.' He gritted his teeth. 'I would have found a way. And you can't blame yourself. You didn't cause his death and you can't help how you feel either. He doesn't deserve your grief and you're not weak. To go through all that and still be the person you are makes you one of the strongest people I've ever met.'

'No, I'm not.' She shook her head. 'If it hadn't been for Lady Anne and Richmond, I don't know what I would have done. It's taken me all this time to feel some sense of peace again, to think that maybe one day I might be free of his shadow.'

'You can be. Come with me and start a new life. You

don't have to push me away.' He pulled her closer to prove it. 'I asked you to rescue me once. Let's rescue each other.'

'It's not so easy.'

'It can be...' He lifted one of her arms and pressed his lips to the inside of her wrist. 'Pippa, I can't pretend to know how I'll feel about children in five or ten years, but I know how I'll feel about *you* and, if it's just the two of us, then I'll still be happy. Tell me how to prove it to you and I will. If you think you can care for me?'

'Of course I care, but...'

'Then give us a chance.'

He bent his head and kissed her, slowly and tenderly at first, then more deeply, nudging her lips apart until he possessed the whole of her mouth. For one terrible, heart-stopping moment, he thought she might push him away, but instead she sagged against him, her body softening and her lips moving against his with an equal fervour that sent heat rushing straight to his groin.

'You're all I want.' He growled the words as they came apart briefly. 'Just you.'

'I want you, too.' She gave a low moan, her fingers touching the side of his neck as she curled her arms around him.

'Then say yes.' He slid his hands lower, over her bottom and hips, relishing every curve and contour of her body. It seemed so incredible that she was in his arms and that he was finally kissing her, yet it wasn't the way that he'd imagined either. It was different. Better. Perfect. 'Say that you'll be my wife.'

'No!' She stiffened and then pulled away from him, pressing a hand to her swollen lips as her eyes clouded with a look of pain. 'This is wrong.'

'What?' He felt genuinely confused. How *could* it be wrong when it felt so utterly and completely right?

'Because I told you, I can't marry again, not ever.'

'I'm not like your husband. I would never resent or humiliate or dishonour you. You can trust me.'

'I know.' She lifted a hand to his face, gently trailing it along the edge of his jaw, her eyes glistening with unshed tears. 'I know you wouldn't. If I could marry any man, it would be you, but if I did then you'd have power over me and I'd always be waiting for you to wield it.' She let her hand fall again. 'I'm sorry, Kit, but I cannot. It's already too late for us. It was too late ten years ago.'

Chapter Eight

'How was it, my lady?' Pippa laid aside her embroidery as Anne walked back into the chamber the next morning. She'd woken with a pounding headache and begged to be excused from the scheduled activities, although being alone with her thoughts hadn't made her feel particularly better. She was still feeling shaken from the night before.

'Unfortunately, my archery is roughly on a level with my dancing…' Anne smiled ruefully '…but the Queen was very proficient. Much to the King's delight.'

'I can imagine.'

'It would be nice to find one thing I excelled at…' Anne sighed '…but I suppose there's no help for it. Here, drink some spiced wine with me.' She poured out two cups and handed one to her. 'How are you feeling now? Is your head any better?'

'A little.'

'Have you dabbed it with lavender?'

'Yes, my lady, but I'm afraid it's not that kind of headache.'

'No, I thought not.' Anne sat down on the daybed beside her. 'You've been crying.'

'Only a little.' Pippa took a mouthful of wine, relishing the warmth as it slid down her throat. 'I had an important decision to make and I made it. It's just going to take some getting used to.'

'Very well, but I hate to see you upset. You know that I think of you as a friend.'

'Thank you, my lady. I'm very grateful for your friendship. If it wasn't for that, I don't think…' She bit her tongue as tears welled in her eyes again. 'I'm sorry.'

'Don't be. Is it about Sir Christopher?'

'Yes. We met outside by chance last night. He asked me to marry him and I…' She sucked in a deep breath and then let it out again in a rush. 'I wanted to say yes so badly.'

'But you refused?'

'I *had* to. He could have a great future if he marries Lady Cecily.'

'Perhaps. Perhaps not. Look at my marriage. That was supposed to be a great union, bringing together England and the German Duchies, but even the best-laid plans have a way of not working out in the way we expect.'

'He said we could go to Europe together.' Pippa smiled weakly. 'To Cleves perhaps.'

'Ah, now you make me jealous.'

'It cannot happen. Even if it weren't for everything else, it would mean breaking with his family and the end of his career if his brother turned the King against him. He could lose everything.'

'But he would have you and he seems to think you're worth all the obstacles, as well as the risk. That's his choice to make, is it not? Besides, his brother might be powerful, but I still have some influence—and the Queen even more. I could ask her to put in a word if that was what you wanted?'

'I can't. I'm scared of making another mistake, my lady.'

'Another?' Anne tipped her head to one side quizzically. 'What was the first?'

'My marriage. It wasn't as happy as some people might have told you. I married Nicholas the day after my sixteenth birthday and it became worse every year afterwards. I didn't realise it at the time, but I gave my whole *self* away, and when it turned out that I couldn't have children, he blamed me.'

'Ah, Pippa.' Anna laid a hand on her shoulder. 'I'm sorry.'

'I always found it too difficult to speak of, my lady, but when he died, I promised myself that I'd never remarry and allow any man to have so much power over me again, no matter who he was or how honourable he might seem. Being a widow gives me the freedom to make my own choices.'

'Yes.' Anne nodded thoughtfully. 'You're right, marriage is unfair to women. It gives husbands rights over our bodies, our fortunes and even our actions. The only thing it doesn't give them power over is our minds and then only because they have not yet found a way.'

'My husband tried. He almost succeeded. Now I know that I'm safer this way.'

'Safety is good. When the King divorced me I thought that at least I was safe, unlike his other wives. He treated me well by comparison, but my life can still feel empty. Perhaps…' Anne leaned sideways, nudging her shoulder lightly against her '…forgive me for saying so, but perhaps your husband is still exerting his power over you.'

'What do you mean?' Pippa stiffened immediately.

'You're letting your past decide your future. Understandably, I might add, but perhaps you're so afraid of making the same mistake again that you're making a different one instead. You're letting love go.' She smiled sadly. 'It might not come back again another time. I think, if I had a second chance at a happy marriage, then I would take the chance and grasp it.'

'So afraid of making the same mistake again that you're making a different one instead…'

Pippa held her breath, the words echoing in her mind as a wave of longing rushed through her veins like quicksilver. Anne was right, she was so determined to protect her heart that she was in danger of breaking it completely. It all seemed so obvious now. She loved Kit. She trusted Kit. She *knew* that he would never treat her the way Nicholas had done. And as for the rest, who was she to say how he ought to live his life? It was his choice—*and* hers. *Theirs*. It was a choice—and a risk—they would take together.

'My lady.' She jumped up, reaching for one of Anne's hands and squeezing it tight. 'Never say that you do not excel at anything. I doubt all the other Queens in the world could have given me such good advice. You'll always be the greatest of them to me.'

'You can't leave.' George's face was puce-coloured. 'I'm head of this family and I forbid it.'

'I've already spoken to the King and he's given me permission.' Kit held into his brother's gaze for a long moment before gathering up his reins.

'Then *I'll* speak to him next and summon you back again.'

'If you can find me.' He sighed. 'George, I've always done my best to bring honour to the family, but I won't marry Lady Cecily. It's too much to ask and it's not fair on either of us.'

'This is because of *her*, isn't it?' George's expression turned waspish. 'Philippa Bray? She was the one you were staring at last night? I saw her face as you left.'

'Yes.' He supposed there was no point in denying it now.

'Kit.' George put a hand on his arm. 'I don't care who you dally with. Keep her as your mistress if you want, but marry Cecily.'

'It's not *just* a dalliance.'

'Surely you don't care for her?' George looked shocked. 'She's a childless widow with her best years behind her.'

'She's a beautiful, intelligent, kind-hearted woman and her best years are still to come. Or at least I hope they are. She deserves to be happy.' He glanced up at the windows of Lady Anne's apartments. Tempted as he was to make one last attempt to persuade Pippa to run away with him, he knew it would only bring more heartache. He didn't want to open up any more old wounds for her either, especially when she'd been so definite last night. If peace and calm were what she wanted, then they were the least he could give her. 'I love her, George, and that means I won't marry anyone else. Not ever.'

'Love?' George sounded scornful. 'What does love have to do with marriage? Only peasants marry for love.'

'Or kings. The King loves his new Queen.'

'He's infatuated with Katherine Howard, that's all.' George's temper made him incautious for once. 'And not for the first time. Remember her cousin and how that ended? This will pass, too.'

'You shouldn't say such a thing.'

'It's only the truth. They've been married for six months and there's still no sign of a child.'

'If he loves her, that won't matter.'

'Exactly.' George sneered. *'If.'*

Kit put his foot in the stirrup, filled with an uncomfortable sense of foreboding. 'You won't stop me believing in love, Brother, but if you want an alliance with the Actons so badly, you should marry Cecily to Sidney.'

'He's a third son. She'd never take him.' George's expression turned calculating. 'Not unless I cut you out of the family completely.'

'If that's what you need to do, then go ahead with my blessing. I don't suppose Mother will object.' Kit shrugged and hauled himself into the saddle. 'It's your choice, Brother. I can earn my own living.'

'So that's it? You're just going to leave? What about your Bray woman?'

'She doesn't want me and England isn't the same for me without Father.'

A flicker of something like regret passed over George's face. 'You know, I told him to stay at home and let me deal with affairs at court, but he always insisted on joining me. He went over everything I ever did, too. If he'd only let me take care of everything...but he thought I was too ambitious, just as you do.'

'I'm not condemning you, George. I should have been here, too.'

'Why? He arranged for you to go. He was happy for you.'

'Yes, but if I'd stayed then maybe I could have helped him. Maybe *that* was my real duty, but I failed him.' He sighed. 'That's a weight I need to carry on my conscience.'

For a fleeting moment, George looked as if he were about to say something sympathetic, then changed his mind, sounding aggrieved instead. 'Then make it up to your family by staying and doing your duty now!'

'I'm sorry, Brother, but honour is more important.' He turned his horse towards the gatehouse and gestured to a groom already mounted nearby. 'Farewell, George. I'll send the groom back with the horse later.'

'Kit!' Pippa called out as she ran through the courtyard, clutching her skirts around her knees, heedless of the scandalised expressions of several startled grooms. She'd been on her way to the great hall when she'd heard rumours of his departure and come racing outside. *'Kit!'*

'You're too late.' George Lowell's voice came from close to her ear. 'He's gone.'

'Gone?' Her heart plummeted to her stomach as she spun around, surprised to find Kit's brother already standing beside her. 'What do you mean?'

'I mean that he's broken with Cecily Acton and his family as a result.' George's silver eyes flickered and turned accusing. 'I understand that I have you to thank?'

She drew herself upright, trying to look dignified despite the fact that she was still panting for breath. 'I *told* him to marry Lady Cecily.'

'Indeed? Then apparently he doesn't listen to either of us. We've both lost.'

'This isn't a game.'

'No.' His lips curved. 'I'm usually better at winning those.'

'Where has he gone?'

'I wish that I knew. Somewhere on the Continent, presumably. He says that England isn't the same for him any more.'

'But why has he left so soon? We only spoke last night!'

'I get the impression that he didn't think there was any point in staying. But since you're here now...' George's gaze travelled from her head to her feet and then back again. 'Did you change your mind about something?'

'Yes!' She looked around for a horse, but there were none saddled. 'I have to go after him!'

'I've no idea which road he took. Or where he intends to sail from.'

'But you must have some idea!'

'None at all, he made sure of it.' George studied his fingernails absently and then squinted up at the sky. 'Do you know, I'm afraid it's going to snow again.'

'I need a horse!' Pippa started towards one of the grooms.

'By the way, I was acquainted with your husband.'

'What?' She froze mid-step. 'You were friends with Nicholas?'

'Oh, I wouldn't say that.' George gave a tight laugh. 'We were far too similar, although I like to think that I'm less of a hypocrite. I never bother to hide my true nature.'

She felt as though he'd just reached out and slapped her. Obviously at least one person had known the truth about her marriage. 'I don't want your pity.'

'Good, since I rarely bestow it, but I presume you *do* want my help. You can hardly go searching the docks on your own.'

'You mean you'll help me find Kit?' She caught her breath in surprise. 'I wouldn't have thought you wanted me anywhere near him.'

'I don't. I did my best to persuade him against you as it

happens, but since he won't listen and he's determined to leave...' He arched an eyebrow. 'Or do you think I don't care a fig for my brother's happiness?'

'I don't think you've given much sign of it so far.'

'No, well...perhaps I haven't, but I do know when I'm beaten. Besides, even a man like me is prone to a twinge of conscience occasionally, especially when he hasn't been entirely honest.'

'What do you mean?' It was her turn to sound accusing. 'Have you lied to Kit?'

'Not lied—*withheld information*. There's a difference. The question is, what to do about it—and you—now.' He tapped his foot and then sighed. 'First things first: you go and pack your belongings and I'll arrange a barge.'

'A barge?'

'Yes. We can hardly search every wharf from here to Gravesend on foot. I wouldn't gamble on our chances of finding him, but in case we do, you ought to be ready.'

Chapter Nine

The *Amber Lady* was a medium-sized merchant vessel with three masts and a mermaid figurehead at the bow. It was also, Kit thought, a sight for sore eyes, especially after a snail-paced journey into London, made even slower by the abysmal state of the winter roads. More importantly, it was loaded and ready to set sail to the Low Countries as soon as the tide of the river turned.

Fortunately, the dour-faced Captain accepted his coins without question, allowing him to go straight below deck to a tiny cabin and fling himself into a hammock with a weary sigh. All he wanted now was to escape England as quickly as possible. For one thing, because he didn't trust George not to send an order from the King summoning him back, for another because he wanted to place some distance between him and Pippa. It was the only way he could think of to put his emotions behind him.

He must have been more exhausted than he'd realised because the next thing he knew, he was being jolted awake by raised voices outside. Judging by the lack of creaking timbers or any discernible swaying, they hadn't departed yet, which meant that it was likely some dispute with a trader or another passenger haggling over their fare. Whoever it was, the argument was getting more and more heated. If he wasn't mistaken, there was a woman's voice, too. It sounded familiar, but it couldn't be, not unless… He rolled over, squeezing his eyes shut at the thought. Now he was really letting his imagination get the better of him. Pippa was back at Hampton Court, probably relieved to hear of his departure and already packing to return to Richmond Palace. The last place she would be was on a wharf by the Thames.

On the other hand... He opened his eyes again, curiosity and hope triumphing over despair as he swung his legs to the floor, climbed out of the hammock and made his way up to the deck. It was already dark and the evening air was bitingly cold, blustery and swirling with snowflakes, though all of those facts faded into insignificance at the spectacle before him.

A barge was moored alongside the merchant vessel and there on the harbourside were two familiar figures, though he'd never thought to see them in the same place, let alone working together. The sight was so shocking that for a few stunned seconds, he actually wondered if he were still asleep and dreaming.

'Kit!' It was the woman who looked up and saw him first.

'Pippa?' His heart stalled in his chest. 'What are you doing here?'

'I've changed my mind!' She started towards the gangplank, but the Captain barred her way.

'You haven't paid.'

'Oh, for pity's sake.' George shoved his way forward angrily. 'We can see he's on board now so there's no point in haggling over information any longer. Here.' He held out a leather pouch. 'That's all you'll get so you might as well let her on board. Unless you'd prefer an inspection from the King's customs men?'

The Captain muttered something indistinguishable, eyeballing George for another few seconds before lifting his arm and letting Pippa hurry past.

'Kit!' She met him at the top of the gangplank, her cheeks red and glowing with cold, looking wild and stunningly dishevelled. Even her hat had fallen to one side so that her hair billowed in loose strands over and around her face. 'I want to come with you. If you'll still take me?'

'You want...?' He was too amazed to take in the words. 'How did you find me?'

'*I* didn't. Your brother sent his men out to find which vessels were departing this evening and to ask if they had any passengers. Then he commandeered a barge for us. I was so afraid that we might have missed you or that you'd ridden to Dover. We must have been out on the river for hours.'

'But how did you convince George to help you? He wants me to stay and marry Lady Cecily.'

'I know!' She laughed incredulously. 'He told me all that, but then he said that if you were going to throw your future away then you might as well do it properly. And with your father's blessing, too.' She lifted a hand and placed it on his chest, over his heart. 'He said that this is what your father wanted, for you to be free to choose your own path.'

'And my brother just *forgot* to tell me?' Kit clenched his jaw as George made his way up the gangplank behind her. 'Is this true, about Father's wishes?'

'Yes, he mentioned it a few times, pointing out the obvious, that we were cut from a *very* different cloth, and advising me to let you be. Only I thought I knew better.' He arched an eyebrow. 'Perhaps, on this one occasion, I was mistaken. Perhaps I was even a little jealous. Father wanted you to have the life he would have chosen for himself if he hadn't been born a first son. It's not a position suited to everyone. We inherit the money and houses, but we have fewer choices, too. A second son, on the other hand, is more... dispensable.'

Kit felt a slow smile spread over his face. 'You've no idea how happy I am to hear that.'

'So you can let your conscience be clear. And to alleviate mine, I won't cut you off completely. Easington Manor will have to go to Sidney, naturally, but you'll still be part of the family should you ever choose to come back.' George looked between the two of them enquiringly. 'Now can I consider matters satisfactorily resolved? I'd hate to have wasted an afternoon *and* destroyed a woman's reputation for nothing.'

'My reputation doesn't matter,' Pippa interjected, moving her hand away from his chest. 'If it's too late for us, Kit, then I'll understand, but Lady Anne made me realise that I was still living in shadow, letting Nicholas cast a pall over my future as well as my past. I don't want to do that any more. I want to live in the sunshine with you.'

'Then what are we waiting for?' He caught hold of her waist, pulling her the rest of the way up the gangplank and into his arms, capturing her lips and kissing her with an intensity that took both of their breaths away.

'Well, thank goodness for that.' George rolled his eyes when they came apart finally. 'Now if you'll excuse me from this tender scene, I'd like to go somewhere warm.'

'Wait!' Kit put a hand on George's shoulder as he turned to leave. 'Thank you, Brother. I'm in your debt.'

'Good. In that case, I'll find some way for you to be useful to me in Europe.'

'I'm sure you will.' Kit smiled ironically, looking down at Pippa's bag as one of George's men deposited it on the deck beside them. 'Do you have everything you need? Because if you want to return to Richmond first…'

'No.' She shook her head quickly. 'I'm leaving the past behind. You're all I need—and this…' She reached into her jacket and drew out a folded piece of parchment. 'Lady Anne wrote a letter to her brother while I was packing. It asks him to give us a home in Cleves if we ever want one.'

'Lady Anne gave you that?'

'Yes, when I told her how much I loved you, on condition that I send regular reports from her homeland.'

He tightened his arms around her waist, tugging her even closer. 'That sounds like an excellent arrangement to me, but Cleves can wait. First I want to show you Venice.'

'Truly?'

'As soon as the weather improves enough for us to travel, but perhaps we'll take rooms in Bruges for a few months first. Then we can take some time to really get to know each other.' He pressed a kiss to her forehead. 'I won't ask you to marry me until you're ready.'

'I think we might not have a choice.' She gave a ragged laugh. 'Your brother's right, my reputation's already ruined.'

'Only in England. As for anywhere else, who's to know? I won't rush you, Pippa. Tell me when you're ready, but until then, it's enough for me just to be with you.'

'I'm ready now.' She tilted her head back, lifting her lips to his as a pair of sailors pulled up the gangplank behind them. 'After ten years, I don't want to waste another moment.'

* * * * *

Author Note

When my editor first suggested the idea of a Tudor novella I was a little uncertain. The sixteenth century wasn't an era I'd ever considered writing about before, mainly because it wasn't one I associated with romance—and definitely not with happy marriages! I did, however, associate it with strong, often notorious women, whose names are still part of our national consciousness half a millennium later, so I decided to use one of those as a secondary character.

After some research—and a difficult choice between Anne of Cleves and Katherine Parr—I eventually settled on Anne, the fourth wife of Henry VIII, whom he set aside after six months. I've never been sure whether to see her as the cruelly used victim of a tyrant husband or a woman who had a lucky escape, but she outlived all his other wives and is the only one to be buried in Westminster Abbey, so I veer towards the latter.

Anne's image was famously immortalised in a painting and, although it's extremely likely that Thomas Cromwell asked Hans Holbein to exaggerate her attractiveness in order to promote an English alliance with the Protestant German states, historians are divided on the degree of exaggeration. Some insist that she was 'plain', even adding that she had a strong body odour, yet others claim that, while she was tall for a woman and had strong features, Henry's dislike was based largely on a bad first meeting—he horrified her by charging into her rooms in disguise at Arundel Castle—and the fact that he'd already met Katherine Howard.

I've chosen largely to ignore the stereotype of the plain Queen because I prefer a different portrayal—the one in the 1933 film *The Private Life of Henry VIII*, in which Anne deliberately makes herself unattractive in order to get an annulment and be reunited with her true love.

I couldn't go that far in my story, since there's no historical basis for the theory—that I know of—but I hope I have at least made her a heroine.

HIS MISTLETOE LADY

Amanda McCabe

Dear Reader,

I hope you love spending Christmastime with Catherine and Diego as much as I did! I've always enjoyed this time of year so much—the music, the lights, the food, the laughter, spending special time with loved ones. And the Tudors certainly did Christmas in a big way! They spent not one day but several dancing, feasting, masquing, wearing their finery, flirting under kissing boughs. (I recently watched the wonderful documentary *Lucy Worsley's Twelve Days of Tudor Christmas*, and it brought the time period to vivid life!) My grandmother also loved this time of year, and she was a wonderful cook. She taught me some of her recipes, including one that would be very at home in the 1550s—mince pies.

Amanda McCabe

Chapter One

December 1554

"'To prevent us from being overrun by strangers, who know not our religion and ways and would make England but a Spanish servant, we do raise arms to beseech our Queen to take an English husband...'"

Catherine Greaves read the smudged, printed words of the pamphlet that had once been nailed to a tree, but had now, months after the failed Wyatt Rebellion, blown loose and landed on the snowy ground. She had found it when their litter had paused for a rest on the journey from Kent to London.

'Throw that away, Catalina, it belongs on the night-soil cart,' her mother said.

Elena Martinez, Lady Greaves, sat across from Catherine in the swaying litter, bundled in furs as she lay back against the cushions. Her heart-shaped face was pale, the black hair beneath the edge of her headdress turning grey from all she had been through that endless year.

Catherine glanced back down at the pamphlet and remembered the reason for this uncomfortable winter journey from their home at Greaves Manor. Her father, Sir Walter Greaves, languished in the Tower for his part in last spring's rebellion against the Queen. When word had come that Queen Mary intended to marry Prince Philip of Spain rather than an Englishman such as Edward Courtenay, the Greaves's neighbour, Sir Thomas Wyatt, and some of his cohorts, including poor Lady Jane Grey's father, the Duke of Suffolk, rose up to overthrow the Queen and set Princess Elizabeth and Courtenay on the throne instead.

The rebellion had reached as far as the banks of the Thames beyond London Bridge before they were driven back by the royal forces. The Queen had indeed married Philip and they were now expecting a child and heir.

Catherine's father had escaped Wyatt's fate on the block, but he was still locked away. Her mother had written letter after letter to the Queen for months, begging to be allowed to see her, to plead her husband's case. After all, Elena had come from Spain with the Queen's own mother, Queen Catherine of Aragon, when they were both barely more than children. She had served the old Queen faithfully, until her marriage to Sir Walter, and it was said Queen Mary treated all her mother's old servants very well. That she was merciful.

At last a reply had come, just in time. Their estate had not been seized, but their funds grew meagre. The fires could not always be lit in the bitter winter. The very worst was her father's absence. In every corner, Catherine remembered him.

Then that prayed-for letter came. They were invited to Whitehall for Christmas, to celebrate the heir who would be born in the spring. It was the chance for their salvation.

The uncertain future made Catherine's stomach seize with nerves. Yet she also had to admit that she felt just the tiniest bit—excited. She hadn't been to Court except for one visit when she was a child, when her mother went to visit Princess Mary. That small glimpse had fuelled her daydreams for years, images of beautiful gowns, dancing, laughter. The thought that one day she, too, would dance and sing, marry a handsome suitor and have her own home…

Now she was only nineteen, yet her future seemed a shadow. She tore the pamphlet into tiny shreds and tossed it out.

'How could your father have done this to us?' her mother whispered. 'We've been married for so many years. I thought I knew his heart.'

Catherine squeezed her mother's gloved hand. She knew her parents loved one another. Had she not grown up on tales of that great love, born the instant they saw each other?

Once, she had dreamed of such a love for herself. Now she trusted in marriage not at all.

'All will be well, *mi madre*, once you talk to Queen Mary,' Catherine said. 'She knows your loyalty, she'll help us.'

'And your father? Will she help him? He is not a young man, Catalina, and the damp of the Tower cannot be good for him.'

Catherine nodded sadly. Her father wasn't the only one whose health she worried over. Her mother, never robust, had been growing thinner, more delicate, by the week. Catherine found a flask of wine in the basket and pressed it into her mother's hand. 'Here, *Madre*, drink this, it will warm you. It cannot be far to London now.'

As her mother sipped at the wine, they fell back into heavy silence. Catherine opened her prayer book on her lap and ran her fingertip over the faded scene of Holy Mary in a garden. The book had once been her Spanish grandmother's, sent to England with Elena, and they found much comfort in its images. Today her mind wouldn't be distracted. What would happen once they reached London?

'Nearly to the city gates, mistress,' their driver called.

Catherine parted the curtains and peered out. They really had left the countryside behind and entered the crowded, noisy world of London. As they passed through Aldgate, they joined a vast flow of humanity. So much *life* after all those empty months!

Their progress was slow through narrow lanes, the faint sunlight made even dimmer by the tall, close-packed buildings. The peaked roof lines nearly touched high above the streets, while at Catherine's eye level the shop windows were open and counters spread with fine, tempting wares—ribbons, embroidered gloves, gold and silver. Leather-bound books enticed her most of all.

And the smell! Catherine pressed the edge of her cloak to her nose, her eyes watering as she took a deep breath and held it. The cold wind helped; the latrine ditch along the middle of the street was almost frozen over, a noxious stew of frost and waste.

The dangers of the rebellion, the Queen's marriage, the coming royal baby—it all seemed to affect the business of the city not at all.

A few ragged beggars pressed towards the litter, but the outriders pushed them back.

'Stand away, varlets!' the driver shouted. 'These ladies are the Queen's own guests.'

The Queen's own guests—who might well end up as beggars themselves, if her mother's pleas were turned away.

Her mother sat up and tried to smooth her velvet sleeves. Catherine took a small looking glass from where it hung from her sash. Her hair, a reddish chestnut-brown as her father's had been before he turned silver, straggled from under its netted caul. Her cheeks were red with cold, her eyes purple-shadowed from the long nights of worry. She tidied her hair and reached for her velvet hat. She rubbed at a smudge on the edge of her wool and velvet doublet, but it wouldn't be banished.

She had barely straightened her green woollen skirt when the driver announced they had reached Whitehall at last and the litter lurched to a halt.

Catherine took a deep breath and stepped down to stare up at the blank wall before her. Most of the vast maze of the palace was hidden from view, tucked away behind those high walls and long galleries whose glinting, blank windows held all its secrets. But Catherine knew what lay behind them—large banquet halls, palatial chambers, beautiful gardens. Gossiping courtiers.

A door somewhere above opened and there was the patter of footsteps. Catherine glanced up to see a lady coming towards them. It could be no mere maidservant. This lady's fine red-wool gown, embroidered with gold, was too fashionable. Her round, pink-cheeked face peered out at them from beneath a fur-edged headdress and she smiled, her eyes crinkling at the edges.

'Lady Greaves—Elena,' the lady said, her smile widening. 'Perhaps you don't remember me, I was once Susan White.'

'Susan Clarencius, of course,' Elena said with a smile. 'I remember you. You sang the loveliest songs to keep us entertained.'

'I've served the Queen for many years now,' Susan said, rattling the keys at her sash to emphasise her high position of royal trust. She beckoned them to follow her up the stairs. 'We'll keep you very busy, I'm afraid, with the Christmas season upon us and so much to celebrate! Queen Mary has ordered the season to be especially merry.'

They made their quick way along the gallery, the tall windows looking out on the city beyond. It was empty and silent at that hour.

'We're happy to be here,' Elena said. 'Her Majesty has been most kind.'

'She remembers the friends who were loyal to her blessed mother,' Susan said. 'I have orders to take you to her right away. She's eager to greet you.'

Elena gave Catherine an alarmed glance and Catherine almost squealed with dismay. They were so road-worn. What if they couldn't make the very best impression to the Queen? 'Right now?'

'Oh, aye. She has talked of little else lately but seeing her old friend again. She wants to share her joy with all,' Susan said.

They crossed high over the lane through the crenel-lated Holbein Gate and found themselves in the Great Gallery, a long, wide passage that ran the length of the palace. Windows of Venetian glass looked down at the river. A shimmering, blue and gold ceiling arched overhead, and tapestries covered the opposite wall, warming the space.

Groups of people gathered there, impossibly beautiful in their velvets and satins, their plumed hats and gleaming pearls. The Spanish courtiers were easy to spot, clad in more sombre colours of black and deep amethyst. They all watched Catherine walk past, their whispers like the low hiss of snakes.

Near the window, she glimpsed someone who struck her as even more beautiful than the rest. More beautiful than anyone she had ever imagined.

He was dressed simply compared to the people around him, especially the lovely golden-haired lady in sea-green silk who held on to his arm and laughed up at him. He wore a doublet of black velvet embroidered with silver on the sleeves, a narrow frill of silver at the throat, and his only jewel was a single pearl drop in one ear. But he had no need of any adornment.

He was very tall and lean, the long, lithe lines of his body set off by the black garments, the faint sunlight behind him that turned him gilded. His hair, waving slightly, was the glossy black of a raven's wing. He pushed it back from his brow in an impatient gesture, revealing high, sharply carved cheekbones and dark eyes set off by sooty lashes that no man should possess. He seemed to sense her watching him and turned his head. A small smile touched his sensual lips and he gave her a nod.

Flustered, Catherine looked away. Was he laughing at her, at the country mouse newcomer, the daughter of a traitor? But she had no time to stand about gaping at handsome strangers as if she was indeed a country milkmaid. Mistress Clarencius led them along another corridor and the man was lost from sight. They passed a row of closed doors, where all was quiet.

'Some of the Queen's ladies sleep there,' Mistress Clarencius said, 'and the dormitory of the maids of honour. It is all crowded at the moment; good Catholic families have had no proper place to send their daughters for many years. But Queen Mary will see that you have a chamber of your own.'

'How kind of her,' Elena murmured and Catherine wondered at such generous treatment from the Queen.

'These are Her Majesty's own apartments, as I am sure you remember, Elena,' Mistress Clarencius said. 'The Queen keeps her father's apartments, while King Philip is lodged in the old Queen's wing, along with his closest advisers.'

They went through a crowded chamber, dominated by a pair of gilded velvet thrones on a dais beneath the Cloth of Estate. Courtiers played cards and gossiped there, just as they had in the gallery, and Catherine couldn't help but notice that the English and Spanish seemed to stay separate.

'The Presence Chamber,' Mistress Clarencius said. 'If Queen Mary asks for a message to be brought to anyone, you will probably find them here.'

Catherine held her mother's hand as they followed Susan through the crowd, who quickly cleared a path for her. They made their way through a small chamber filled with fine musical instruments, a lute and a beautiful set of virginals; it was said Queen Mary, like her father, was a talented musician. Then at last they were at the innermost sanctum, the royal bedchamber.

Catherine was surprised to see that it was not very large and there were only a few windows to let in the winter light. A fire blazed in the richly carved fireplace, crackling and snapping as it tried to warm the space. Silver oil burners in the corners gave off rich scents of rose and lemon to rival the ladies' perfumes.

The room was dominated by a grand bed, set high on a dais that would have dwarfed her entire room at Greaves

Manor. A great, carved edifice with vines, fruits and flowers, shimmering with gilt, twisting up its posts and on to the headboard. The initials M and P entwined beneath coronets gleamed on the footboard and it was draped in green brocade.

A dressing table in the corner glittered with Venetian glass bottles and a carved chest spilled out ropes of creamy pearls and chains studded with rubies and emeralds. A *prie-dieu* with a scarlet-velvet cushioned kneeler was in the corner and the rest of the chamber was scattered with clothes chests and cushions for the ladies, where they sat sewing and reading, lapdogs cavorting around them.

Catherine glimpsed a lady writing at a table by the windows and realised it must be the Queen herself, for she looked much like the portrait displayed at Greaves Manor, with her white skin and auburn hair, deep-set dark eyes and slight figure. She was thirty-seven now, yet looked rather older, short and thin, her hair touched faintly with silver, braided on top of her head with pearl pins. Her cheeks glowed pink, not as pale as she had been rumoured to be with ill health for years, and she narrowed her short-sighted brown eyes as she peered up from her work.

'Is that my Elena at last?' she said, her voice surprisingly deep and rough.

'Indeed, Your Majesty,' Susan Clarencius said, with a curtsy. Catherine and her mother hurried to do the same.

'Our prayers are answered with your safe arrival,' Queen Mary said. She rose from her desk and her loose blue brocade surcoat, trimmed with sable, fell open over her swollen belly. She laid a protective hand, glittering with jewelled rings, over her child nestled there.

She hurried across to raise Elena up, kissing both her cheeks. 'My dear old friend. How lovely you look. You were always the prettiest of my mother's ladies.'

Elena smiled. 'Indeed I was not. In my memory, Lady

Willoughby got all the attention. The French ambassador could not take his eyes from her.'

The Queen laughed huskily as she turned to Catherine and studied her closely. 'And this must be your Catherine. She looks very like you.'

'Aye, this is my daughter,' Elena answered.

'We welcome you most heartily in this blessed season.' The Queen waved to her other ladies. 'I am sure you do remember Cecily Barnes, Elena, as well as Friedswide Strelly, who have been such loyal friends to me for so long. And this is my youngest lady, Jane Dormer. I think she is near your age, Catherine, and I hope you'll be friends.'

Jane Dormer, who was small, elfin, golden-haired, gave Catherine a sweet smile, and curtsied. 'You are welcome indeed, Mistress Greaves.'

'Perhaps, dear Jane, you could show Catherine to her chamber? I hope you will join us for Evensong, Elena? There is so much to be thankful for now.' Her expression turned solemn. 'And perhaps we must speak of some business, as well.'

'Of course, Your Majesty,' Elena replied.

'But such solemnities must be for later,' Queen Mary said, taking Elena's hand in hers. 'Tomorrow is Christmas Eve! Tell me, Catherine, have you come prepared to enjoy yourself? You are so young!'

'I...' Catherine, flustered, started to reply.

'And perhaps you wish to find a good husband while you are here?' the Queen said teasingly. 'I do assure you, from my own blessed experience, it is a lady's finest state. We must look about for someone suitable! Yes, Elena?'

'I've always wished my daughter to be well settled,' Elena said carefully.

'Of course. Go now, my dear, with Jane. Elena, tell me all your news of Kent.'

Jane smiled at Catherine and led her to the chamber door. Catherine glanced back at her mother, but Elena looked better than she had for months, chatting with the Queen in Spanish.

Mistress Dormer took Catherine's arm as they made their way back to the crowded gallery and gave a shy smile. Catherine couldn't help but like her, despite her enviable beauty and fashionable gown.

'How glad I am you've come to Court, Mistress Greaves,' Jane said. She nodded to people they passed, who gave her smiles and curtsies. More than a few gentlemen watched her avidly as she walked by, but she ignored them. 'Her Majesty is all that is good to my family and her ladies are kind. But everyone is so—well, they are rather older than I am, except for the Maids. I'm happy to have someone to be friends with at last.'

Friends? It had been a long time since Catherine could call anyone that. She felt a touch of excitement, and also nervousness. 'Is your family not nearby then, Mistress Dormer?'

'Nay, my mother died many years ago and my father lives in Buckinghamshire. I was raised mostly by my grandmother.' They stopped near one of the windows. 'What of you, Mistress Greaves? Or may I call you Catherine?'

'Oh, yes, please do.'

'And you must call me Jane. Do you have no siblings?'

'None. I was born rather late to my mother, I think she had quite given up hope. And my father, well—' She broke off, flustered. What could she say about her father? Who was he, really? The man she had loved so much, or the traitor who had joined with Wyatt?

Jane gave her a sympathetic smile. 'We cannot be accountable for some of our relatives, I fear. My mother's family had a great love for the heretical new faith. But I'm sure your father has been unjustly accused and the Queen will soon set all to rights.'

'I hope so, Mistress Dormer—Jane.'

Jane's smile brightened. 'It's Christmastime, the month

of miracles! All is brightness here in England after so long in darkness.'

Catherine thought of the Christmases of her childhood, the music and laughter. 'I confess I've always loved this time of year the best of all.'

Jane took her arm again and they continued on their way down the gallery. Near the tapestried wall, she glimpsed the man she'd noticed earlier, the one who was so handsome her eyes were dazzled just to see him. And he watched *her*, a small smile quirking his lips.

Blushing, she glanced away, but then couldn't help but peek back, just for an instant.

'That man there is Don Ruy Gomez,' Jane said, gesturing to an older man who stood with the handsome god. Gomez, in contrast to the taller man's plain garb of black velvet and leather, was richly dressed in deep purple brocade, his pointed beard carefully shaped and oiled. 'He is the King's closest adviser, be wary of him. And with him——' She broke off, her cheeks turning as pink as Catherine feared her own were. She pointed at another man who was talking quietly with Catherine's object of fascination, a younger man almost as handsome. He seemed to be the one Jane blushed over.

And he seemed just as fascinated by Jane, his gaze never leaving her face.

'Who is that, then?' Catherine asked.

'The Count of Feria. One of King Philip's oldest friends.'

'Is he your sweetheart?' Catherine whispered teasingly. How lovely it felt to giggle with a friend again!

Jane's blush deepened. 'Not at all. He is just—well, quite charming. All the King's Spanish courtiers are so cultured. Not like some young Englishmen, who have forgotten how to behave in a chivalrous manner.'

Catherine peeked again at the man in black, his sculpted features and dark eyes. Was *he* chivalrous, too? 'Who is the other man with them?'

'Don Diego de Vasquez. One of the wealthiest men in

Spain, they say. He has only just arrived, but already so well known. Even Mistress Clarencius blushes when he is near!'

As they strolled to where a staircase led back to the narrower corridors of the palace, Catherine dared to glance over her shoulder. Don Diego gave her a bow and she spun back around, her stomach churning. Luckily they soon passed out of sight and went down a staircase.

'When shall we see King Philip?' Catherine asked. 'We've heard tales of his fine looks and good manners.'

'At tomorrow's feast. He wakes at dawn and after Mass works all hours, just as the Queen does. They are never ceasing in their tasks.'

They turned down another corridor and passed yet another group of courtiers, who played at dice near a window. One of the men was tall and very thin, his hair so fair it was nearly white though he was clearly young. He would surely be considered good looking, but something in his pale blue eyes made Catherine feel unsure. He watched her very closely as they passed.

'Who is that man?' she whispered to Jane. 'The very fair one?'

Jane followed her gesture, and frowned. 'Master Andrew Loades. His brother is in the Tower. But no suspicion attaches to Master Andrew.'

In the Tower? For rebellion? Perhaps that was why he watched her so closely, he knew who her father was. She did not like it at all. But Jane still led her onwards, chatting happily, distracting her.

Jane opened the last door of the corridor and led Catherine inside.

'It's small, I know, and the Queen wishes she could offer you something grander, but with the Spanish courtiers here, every corner is filled,' Jane said.

Catherine untied her cloak as she studied the chamber. It *was* small, tucked under the eaves with a sloping ceiling overhead, but cosy, with a fireplace where a blaze was already lit. A double bed was hung with blue-wool hangings and spread with embroidered quilts. Their trunks were waiting.

'It's lovely,' Catherine said. 'We're happy to have anywhere to lay our heads after such a journey!'

'You must be tired, poor Catherine,' Jane said. 'I'll have a page send up some ale and some warm water for washing. Is your maid with you? There's a truckle bed for her, as well.'

Catherine remembered their straits and nervously fidgeted with her twice-turned wool skirt. 'Nay, we—we brought no one.'

Jane looked stricken. 'Oh, you must have left your home in such a hurry! You'll borrow my maid, she's a marvel with the latest fashions in hair.' She took Catherine's hand with a smile. 'I'm truly glad you've come to Whitehall this Christmas, Catherine Greaves. All will be well, you'll see.'

She left, softly closing the door behind her, and Catherine was alone. She sat down on the edge of the bed, staring into the fire. She suddenly felt very tired.

She closed her eyes and imagined the handsome man she'd seen in the gallery, his dark beauty, the way he smiled at her. He was like something in one of the old Spanish poems of knights and crusades that her mother had told her about, something romantic and dashing and unreal. Smiling at handsome gentlemen, the kindness of Jane, the welcome of the Queen—it was as if her old, wonderful life was there again, just for a moment.

Catherine laid down against the velvet bolsters and closed her eyes, trying not to cry. Jane was right—it was Christmas and they were at Court at last. It was a time for wishes to come true, if she could only find that hope inside herself again.

Elena felt her smile slip, her steps grow heavy, as she followed the page to her bedchamber and tiptoed inside. In front of Queen Mary she could never let her smile fade.

She'd learned that lesson long ago, as a girl in Spain. She was a Mendoza, chosen to accompany the Infanta Catalina to England when they were barely more than children. Her family was an old and noble one, and she had to be always perfectly correct. She never forgot that, even after years of life in England. Even though she would probably never see her beautiful Spain again.

Except once, when she fell in love and forgot all else. Walter was so handsome, so charming, always making her laugh. Always kind. She never regretted their marriage. He was her love and, when Catherine came along, their happiness seemed perfect. They always had each other, even in the dark days of poor Queen Catherine's downfall.

Then he'd betrayed her. She alone had to fight for Catherine.

But—what if he had not been guilty of such treason? She held tight to that tiny piece of hope that she held in her secret heart. Queen Mary had said Elena might visit Walter in the Tower, had promised to look for a suitable husband for Catherine. Someone to take care of her, protect her. Not as grand a marriage as they once could have hoped for, but something.

But even if she *did* see Walter, what would they say to each other now?

Elena saw her daughter was already asleep, collapsed over the bed still in her travelling clothes. Elena sat down beside her and gently smoothed a rumpled curl of chestnut hair back from her daughter's brow. How young she looked when she slept, as she had when she was a child and Elena would sit for hours watching her, marvelling at her child's beauty and sweetness.

'*Querida mia,*' she whispered. 'All will be well now. I will make it so, I promise you.'

It was a vow she would never break, no matter what dangers they faced. Her daughter's happiness was all that mattered now.

Chapter Two

Two days earlier

Diego de Vasquez studied the banks of the river Thames as the barge wound its way from Gravesend, where his ship had docked, towards London. It had still been warm in Spain when he left. The sky a clear turquoise-blue above the white walls of his home, the air scented with lemon and orange groves.

And that sun had shimmered on his little daughter Isabella's golden hair as she kissed him goodbye. As she held his face between her little hands and stared at him with her sapphire-blue eyes.

Even at six, she knew that sometimes his duty lay far from home, that he had to do his work for Spain and the King, as one day she would have to. She had a calm dignity far beyond her years and Diego knew the family motto gilded on their coat of arms, I Serve, suited her, as it did him. Yet they had been all to each other since Isabella's mother, Diego's wife Juana, died five years ago.

He'd never gone as far away from her as England before and he wasn't sure when he would return. King Philip, it was said, had no desire to stay long in England. Perhaps he would leave when the Queen's babe was born and send his Spanish household home at last. But Diego's task was a delicate one, not to be rushed. He had to find out all the information the King required.

So he kissed his daughter's warm cheek and closed his

eyes as he inhaled her sweet scent. 'I shall write you every day, *mija*, and tell you about the strange land of England,' he said. 'And you must write and tell me how you progress with your lute. And I think you will keep an eye on the fields for me, won't you? And Pedro.' He nodded at the new puppy who gambolled at her feet.

Isabella nodded solemnly. 'I shall, *padre mio*. Every week. I'll work so very hard at my Latin and my dancing. You won't know me when you come home, I'll be such a grand lady.'

That was what he feared. 'Not *too* grand, I hope. Now, go to your *abuela* and be very obedient to her while I'm gone. Remember how much I love you.'

'And I love you. And maybe…' She glanced away.

'Maybe what, *querida*?'

She smiled mischievously. 'Maybe you might even bring me a mama when you come home? I wouldn't mind an English one.'

Diego laughed. He knew he needed to marry again, to provide an heir for his family, but what had happened with Juana had left such a scar. And what sort of Englishwoman could understand his life in Spain? 'We shall see.'

Isabella kissed him once more, before she took up Pedro's lead and skipped across the garden to take her grandmother's hand.

'Safe travels, *hijo*,' his mother said, blowing him a kiss. 'All will be well here, I promise. You must only do your task and bring honour to us, as I know you shall.'

Isabella gave him one more wave and a sad smile before walking away towards the house. She was a veritable angel, his girl, but had she been forced into a solemnity beyond her years in their vast estate, surrounded always by adults? Perhaps she needed a bit of merriment, a bit of lightness.

Perhaps he did, too. His life had been one of only work for so long. Maybe Isabella did need a mother?

Yet he knew he was unlikely to find someone suitable,

or any merriment, in England. He studied the river now from his barge. The high tides of winter made the waters thick and muddy, choppy with the bitter wind, choked in places with dead fish.

Diego shuddered and drew his cloak closer.

'Was it a terrible journey?' Ruy Gomez asked. He was one of the King's closest advisers and it was a great honour he had been sent to fetch Diego to London, but the man was also rather dour.

'It was faster than I would have expected in winter, and the river seems orderly,' Diego answered, gesturing to the vessels that flowed past them. Barges, smaller boats, fishing trawlers.

'You're fortunate to traverse the Thames now and not a few years ago, when it was most wild. The rowers were often thieves,' Gomez said with a laugh. 'The King and Queen passed an act declaring that ferrymen must be certified with Parliament. Just one example of the good order that is being set in place here at last.'

Diego nodded. He had read all Ruy Gomez's reports on the journey from Spain. The information he was to gather himself could aid in that 'good order'.

'And what is Queen Mary like? One does hear such reports in Madrid.'

Gomez frowned. 'She is a perfect saint who hears Mass several times a day—and dresses very badly. You must prepare yourself, Don Diego, for these Englishwomen do not have the elegance of our Spanish ladies. Their dresses are gaudy and when they dance they trot about in a most undignified manner.'

Diego tried not to laugh aloud at the image of tinselled ladies hopping up and down. Surely Gomez exaggerated. 'They say that the King and Queen seem fond of each other. Even in love.'

'King Philip knows his duty and he treats the Queen with every respect. This coming child shall one day inherit the

English throne and the Low Countries and, if it's a prince, Spain and Portugal as well, and the lands of the New World. We must make certain this England is a fit place for the new little Prince.'

Diego studied the peaceful-looking hamlets. 'Is there still much danger of rebellion? After Wyatt was executed, and the marriage arranged, Emperor Charles was hopeful of his son's safety.'

Gomez nodded warily. 'Since the news of the child, there has been much rejoicing. But there have been troubles between our own people and the English in the streets and the inns. We've often been robbed and chased, and serving the King here means our own families and estates are neglected. Once the babe is here and the King can leave to see to his duties in the Low Countries, he will take us with him and many of us will be quite relieved. But what if the Queen were to die in childbirth?' He crossed himself. 'The King would be needed here again.'

Diego remembered his own wife, who had lost her life just so, along with the child. The child he had known wasn't his. He and Juana had never been devoted to one another as a husband and wife truly should be, but he still felt her loss. 'It is always a grave risk.'

'King Philip would be named regent, if the baby survives. All of this is of vital importance. Sir Walter Greaves is a friend to us, a very good contact. Queen Mary is merciful; some might say *too* merciful. She spared the lives of many of the Wyatt rebels and sent them to the Tower, even in comfortable lodgings. Her heart might be too kind, but we have people like Sir Walter who has the chance to befriend some of them, win their confidence. He hears much of the privy conversation in the Tower, so we may be forewarned.'

Diego nodded. It was a clever plan, if trustworthy spies could be found. 'What sort of man is Sir Walter?'

'An Englishman, but of a good Catholic family in Kent, where the rebellion arose. His wife is Spanish by birth, who came to the country with Queen Catherine of blessed memory. They have one daughter, as yet unmarried, and are at Court to wait on Queen Mary.'

Diego remembered his own Isabella as she kissed him goodbye, her eyes shining with trust. Had Sir Walter parted with his own child thus? 'Do they know of Sir Walter's work in the Tower?'

Gomez frowned again, but he looked compassionate this time rather than contemptuous. 'They don't. As far as they, or anyone, can know, Sir Walter was truly part of the rebellion. The King thought the fewer people who know such a secret, the more secure it is. That is why the Queen has asked them to come to Court for Christmas, in the hopes they can be reassured by her favour and that all will be finished soon, and Sir Walter may be released.'

Diego nodded. It was the best plan, to keep such a secret, but still he felt for Lady Greaves and her daughter, to be so cast down at Christmas.

'My own wife would murder me herself if she believed me to be a traitor to my monarch,' Gomez said. 'I feel for the Greaves ladies. But they'll understand one day and be proud of their family's service. The new baby Prince must be completely safe. Your uncle dealt well with Sir Walter, we were sorry when he left, but you're here now. The King speaks of your bravery in the Low Countries.'

'My uncle made a good end, the warm sun seemed to do him some good.'

Gomez sighed. 'If only we could be in the sun of Spain again. So many of the younger, more poetic of the King's attendants thought they were coming to the land of King Arthur and his chivalric knights. Instead we have mud and terrible music. But the King needs us, so here we must be for now.'

'Indeed.'

Gomez laughed and clapped him on the shoulder. 'All is not quite so grievous, Don Diego. The Queen has ordered a merry Christmas Court, there is much to celebrate! And not *every* lady at Court is old and ill dressed.'

The barge turned a corner towards the towering chimneys and steeples of London and Diego glimpsed the notorious gallows at Wapping, where rebels were hanged to rot. They'd been taken down for Christmas, along with the heads on pikes high above London Bridge. Yet the light of the festive season seemed far away.

After another turn of the boatmen's oars, Gomez pointed out the stone walls of the Tower, glaring white in the misty day. Much of Diego's work would be done there. It looked so silent, so peaceful from the water, almost empty, but who knew what lurked behind those walls.

There wasn't time to say anything more, for the barge arrived at the water steps of Whitehall. A knot of people waited on the wooden landing stage, bundled in furs against the biting wind. Diego waved at his old friend, Suarez, the Count of Feria. He'd been in England ever since the King arrived and Diego was glad of a familiar face. Next to him was Diego's own cousin, Manuelita de Chavez, who waved and smiled as she bounced on her toes.

Ruy Gomez smiled. 'Ah, you see, Don Diego, how eager we all are for news of home?'

Diego nodded, thinking again as he did of Isabella. 'Then it's fortunate I bear so many letters…'

'Tell me, Diego, what do you think of England?' Manuelita asked him two days later, as they walked the length of the Privy Gallery. Manuelita was one of the few Spanish ladies who'd accompanied her husband to England and she seemed to be one of the centres of the lonely group of exiles moored in a strange land.

Diego glanced around at the crowded gallery. Gomez had been right that most of the ladies didn't dress as well as they did at home; Manuelita's simple amber-velvet gown with sable sleeves was in contrast to the bright brocades and sparkling trim of the English ladies. But everyone had been very welcoming to him.

'I fear, Cousin, I haven't been long enough at Whitehall to be certain. And I've not seen much of the city.'

'We must do something about that! Men such as you and my husband, and the King—it is all work, work work. It's Christmas! And we're far from home.' She stopped next to the window and faced him with a smile. 'I've have heard talk of a masque, of acrobats and dancing. I must warn you, though—these English dances are not like our own.'

Diego laughed. 'Gomez tells me it is merely hopping about?'

Manuelita laughed, too, and Diego remembered when they used to learn dancing together as children, all the dignified gliding and spinning. 'Something of the sort.'

'I doubt I could find anyone as lovely as you to partner me,' he said gallantly.

Manuelita waved his words away. '*Tonta!* Every lady here will be standing in line to be your partner, as they always have. You were always a most handsome devil. Let me see—what of Lady Waldegrave over there? Or Mistress Barnes? Mistress Dormer *is* the prettiest of the Queen's ladies, but she only dances with our friend Feria. But Lady Frances, the woman in blue velvet there by the fire, she is not so bad, I think.'

'I told you, Manuelita, I can only dance with you,' Diego said.

'An old married lady like me? No, you deserve a young beauty. Juana has been gone for so long.'

Diego shook his head. Manuelita was only a year older than him and had had many suitors before she married Chavez. 'You *are* a young beauty.'

'You have your pretty little *niña*. She needs a mother and you need a son.' She studied the room with the same narrowed, matchmaking eyes he had seen too often with his mother. 'My husband does have a sister in Valladolid...'

'I cannot think of marrying again until I leave England.'

'Perhaps not.' Manuelita sighed. 'It does feel as if all our lives are frozen for a time. But we can still make merry at Christmas!' A new group appeared in the doorway, two pretty ladies.

'Ah, there is Mistress Dormer now,' Manuelita said. 'You can see why Suarez is so besotted! It must be almost time for the Queen to process to Mass.'

Diego glanced at the petite, golden-haired Mistress Dormer. She was indeed pretty, but it was the lady beside her who captured his attention. She didn't wear the fine gowns of the others, but a travelling skirt and doublet of green wool, the sleeves slightly shabby, her gleaming chestnut hair escaping from a netted caul to lay against her white neck. She was small and slim, with a pointed little chin and shimmering, jewel-bright green eyes. She bit her lip as she studied the crowd, as if she was shy, and hung back a bit behind Mistress Dormer.

Suddenly, her gaze met his and her eyes widened. Her cheeks turned bright pink and she turned away—only to glance back again, like a delicate, frightened, lovely little fawn.

'Who is that lady with Mistress Dormer?' he asked Manuelita, watching the mystery lady. She peeked at him again, making him smile.

Manuelita's gaze sharpened, as if she was interested by his interest. He knew he could give nothing of his thoughts away or she would be writing to his mother about his imminent betrothal to a lady he hadn't even yet met. 'I don't know. She must be new to Court. She's pretty, isn't she, despite that ghastly skirt.' She turned to one of the men near them. 'Don Pablo, do you know that lady with Mistress Dormer?'

Don Pablo, a notorious old connoisseur of female beauty, rubbed at his silver beard as he examined the lady. 'I believe I did hear something of her this afternoon. Her name is Catherine Greaves. Her mother is Spanish, but her father is a great scandal, locked in the Tower. I'm not sure why Queen Mary now has her close. But she must have her royal reasons, I suppose. Keep one's enemies closest…'

Greaves. The daughter of Diego's secret contact in the Tower. Tasting the bitter tang of disappointment, he turned away from her pretty face and stared out at the grey river. The one lady who had intrigued him in years—and she was the very one he couldn't draw close to at all.

Chapter Three

Catherine studied herself in the looking glass, wondering
if she looked well enough for the banquet, or if she would
be whispered about as a little country mouse, a scandal's
daughter. In Kent, when her father was still at home, they
often had banquets for neighbours in their own great hall.
But those were small gatherings with people she'd known
all her life.

Whitehall was different. Everyone at Court was so elegant.

Catherine remembered the man she'd glimpsed in the
gallery. Don Diego de Vasquez, Jane said. Newly arrived,
as Catherine was herself, yet she saw not a trace of her own
awkward uncertainty in him. He'd looked so tall and commanding, like a knight in one of those Andalusian poems.

She had to admit that she had looked for him again as she
followed Jane around the palace, but she hadn't glimpsed
him. Jane had whispered a bit more about him as they made
their way through the corridors and chambers, morsels of
gossip such as she served about everyone around them.
Like the King himself, Don Diego was a young widower,
the owner of vast estates in Spain, of an ancient family.
His uncle had been one of the King's original attendants to
come with him from Spain, but then he had taken ill and
Don Diego had sailed to England to replace him. All the
ladies were in raptures over him.

Catherine studied herself a little more carefully. She
wished she was taller, had a more generous bosom and a

nose that didn't turn up at the tip, but those were old complaints she rarely noticed any longer. Not until now, when she might want to catch someone's eye. Surely a Spanish don, a man of old family and great wealth, a widower already, and so very, very handsome, wouldn't look twice at her.

Catherine patted her hair and gave herself a smile. Even if he paid *her* no attention, that didn't mean *she* couldn't look. After the long months alone in Kent, a little colour, a little life, a little fantasy, might be nice.

'How lovely you look, *mija*,' her mother said, smiling at Catherine as their borrowed maidservant finished lacing up her gown. Elena was still too thin, Catherine noticed, but her cheeks were pinker, her dark eyes shining. Being with the Queen seemed to have done her good.

Catherine smoothed the ribbon edging of her partlet. 'Thanks to you and your magical needle, *mi madre*.' When they heard they were to be allowed at Court, there'd been frantic activity to put together a suitable wardrobe from every available scrap of fabric. Catherine's gown was made of an old one of her mother's, an overskirt and sleeves worn when Queen Catherine herself was on the throne and a bodice and forepart made of old draperies. The silver brocade and white satin had been taken apart and remade into the square-necked French style the Queen liked. A partlet of sheer muslin trimmed with ribbon meant she didn't need a necklace and the sleeves were edged with glass beads that shimmered.

A length of the blue ribbon had been made into a sort of floral wreath for her hair, which the maid had brushed until it gleamed like mahogany in the torchlight and then pinned into elaborate plaits.

Her mother shook her head. 'Nay, it is only you. You bring the beauty here, *mi dulce*, and you will surely shine like a star, as I always knew you would.' She waved away the maid and went to the small table, her smile turning sad.

She opened the box there and took something from it, holding it carefully against her heart for a moment.

'Here,' Elena said, turning to her daughter. 'You must wear these, Catalina. They will go well with that brocade.' She held out a pair of pearl-drop earrings, suspended from cabochon sapphires.

Catherine stared at them in astonishment. 'But—those were your wedding gift from Father.' She'd so often stared at those earrings as her mother dressed for banquets, had loved hearing the story of when her father gave them to her and told her she was his 'pearl of the world'. Catherine had never even touched them. She'd thought them sold with so many other things in the last months.

'So they were, *mija*. And now I have no use for them. You must wear them.' Elena pressed them into Catherine's palm and folded her fingers over them. The pearls were cool on her skin. 'We still have our pride, never forget that. We cannot look shabby in front of the Queen.'

Catherine slid them into her earlobes and studied them in the glass. The sapphires winked and shone, the pearls lay creamy against her dark hair. What would someone like Don Diego think of them? Of her, in her cobbled-together finery?

Her mother gently kissed her cheek. 'Come, Catalina, we should go. Don't worry now. All will be well.'

Catherine smiled at her mother and nodded, but deep inside she wasn't sure anything would be well again.

Catherine followed her mother as they joined the crowd taking their places in the Great Hall. The towering double doors opened and, as they stepped inside with the rest of the courtiers, she was dazzled. Outside, the night was freezing, deepest black, but the Hall looked like something out of an old tale of kings and knights and fair maidens.

The Hall was more than a hundred feet long, with the floor polished to look like marble and glowing in the light of thousands of candles. Soaring overhead, the arched ceiling, held aloft with carved and gilded timbers, was decorated with painted Tudor roses and entwined M and P initials. And the people sparkled just like the Hall.

Catherine peeked at a group of Spanish courtiers near one of the windows, which included the beautiful and stylish Dona de Chavez in purple velvet banded with gold satin. Their dark colours and furs, cut simply but perfectly, seemed the richest of them all and made Catherine fidget nervously with her skirt.

'Catherine! Come and sit with us,' she heard Jane call and she turned to see her new friend waving at her from a table near the front of the hall. She, too, wore white, trimmed with deep blue velvet that set off her golden curls. Catherine was sure she would hate Jane, if she wasn't so sweet and welcoming.

'Go with your friends, *mija*,' her mother said with a smile. 'I see Mistress Clarencius over there and long to reminisce with her a bit more. We would bore you young ladies with tales of so long ago!'

Catherine bit her lip, unsure if she should really leave her mother. 'Are you sure, *Madre*?'

'Of course! You deserve to make merry and I deserve a warm seat by the fire. Go, go, enjoy yourself!'

Catherine kissed her mother's cheek and made her way to Jane's table. The seats for the ladies-in-waiting were just below the crimson-draped royal dais. Its gilded chairs, beneath the royal Cloth of Estate, sat empty as the other tables around them filled quickly. Musicians played a lively tune high up in their hidden gallery, but it could barely be heard over the loud chatter. She looked around for Diego, but he was nowhere to be seen.

She slid on to the end of the bench next to Jane, across from Cecily Barnes. Catherine stared at the tables before her, marvelling at the luxury. The long tables were spread with spotless white-damask cloths, woven with roses and pomegranates. The benches were lined not with hard planks, but with gold-velvet cushions. At the centre of the table was a silver salt cellar and each place had its own small silver salt bowl and a loaf of fine, white manchet bread wrapped in linen, along with a silver goblet.

'If London is so grand, what must it be like in Spain itself?' Catherine whispered to Jane.

Jane laughed. 'I hear it's all gold and rubies everywhere! And sunny all the time. Can you imagine? Lemon trees and vast gilded cathedrals.'

Catherine could just imagine it from her mother's tales. But she'd never known those lemon orchards and golden cathedrals were peopled by men like Diego de Vasquez.

Pages clad in green-and-white Tudor livery appeared bearing platters of the first course—venison, capons, partridges, eels with precious Seville oranges, sallots of vegetables dressed in vinegar and silver ewers of richly spiced red wine.

At one of the Spanish tables across the room, the Count of Feria appeared and all the ladies whispered teasingly to Jane, who blushed bright red and begged them to be quiet. He *was* handsome, Catherine thought, with his finely trimmed dark beard and gold-satin doublet, and he and Jane would look well together. But there was no one quite like the mysterious Don Diego.

A fanfare of trumpets heralded the opening of the doors again and the royal couple appeared at last, everyone leaping to their feet to bow and curtsy. Queen Mary was so small that Catherine could barely glimpse her over the heads of the crowd, but the swell of her belly under her loosened red and gold brocade gown was most evident, as was her radiant smile as she took her husband's arm. The giant table diamond pinned at her neckline, from which dangled an astonishing pearl-drop pendant, could not compete with her brightness.

Catherine hadn't seen King Philip since she'd arrived at Whitehall and she studied him curiously. He wasn't very tall, but was well made with fine legs, his golden hair and beard shimmering like the jewelled chain over the shoulders of his white-satin doublet. He smiled politely at his wife and nodded at her words, but he seemed distracted.

Behind them was Cardinal Pole, the papal legate come to reconcile England with Rome. Portly, he sailed along in his vast red robes, overwhelming the petite royal couple.

The Cardinal joined them on the dais and the Queen smiled and waved. 'Please, my dear friends, eat, eat!' she said, her deep voice full of merriment. 'We've so much to celebrate, do we not? We'll have dancing later.'

The royal couple were served with the most delicate of the dishes, while another course was passed between all the tables. As the wine flowed, the gossip grew louder, the laughter more raucous.

But Catherine felt a tiny, tingling prickle on the back of her neck as she listened to some tale of Cecily Barnes's telling and she turned to see what it could be. She was shocked to find that one pair of eyes did *not* watch the royal couple at all. Instead they stared directly at her. And they were the midnight-dark eyes of Don Diego, who sat across the room with Feria and Dona de Chavez and her husband.

Don Diego had been beautiful when she first saw him in the Great Gallery, but here, in the glow of candles, he looked as if he must surely be a dream and not a real man at all. His hair, glossy black, was brushed back from the sharply carved angles of his face. His sharp cheekbones, the blade of his nose, his smooth olive skin set off by the black satin of his doublet—he looked like a painting. When last she saw him, he had been laughing with Dona de Chavez, his sensual lips curved in delight.

He didn't laugh now. He looked questioning, solemn, as he watched her, the corners of those tempting lips turned down ever so slightly. Did he know of her, had he heard the gossip about her father? It made her want to cry to think of him considering ill of her, which was silly. Surely he was just a stranger?

Yet he didn't seem like one. He seemed like someone she had known before and had somehow just found again, as fanciful as that sounded.

Her new bodice seemed to tighten like a vice, pressing in on her along with the heat of the room until she couldn't draw breath. Her hand shook as she reached for her wine and took a deep swallow.

She closed her eyes and reminded herself of who she was. A Greaves and a Mendoza. She had to overcome scandal. Rise above it all. Even with Don Diego. She opened her eyes and forced herself to lift her chin, turning her gaze to look at him once more. Slowly, ever so slowly, those beautiful lips of his lifted in a smile, revealing a quick flash of white teeth. It transformed the starkly elegant planes of his face, making him seem more like that man of laughter and sunlight she had glimpsed so briefly in the gallery.

She found herself smiling back. She could no more keep herself from doing it than she could stop herself from breathing—his smile really was like the sunshine itself. But then his own smile suddenly dimmed and he glanced away, and she was left feeling even more confused, flustered and flushed.

She faced the table again and pretended to nibble at a bit of manchet bread, wondering if he still watched her. She dared not look.

'How is so much eaten every night?' she asked, prodding at a piece of venison with her eating knife. 'I'm sure to burst!'

'Oh, this is naught!' Cecily said. 'Wait until the Christmas banquet. There will be dozens and dozens of removes. Even plum cakes, my favourites!'

'What is left is given to the poor,' Jane said. 'They gather at the gates every night.'

'And *some* people steal unbroken meats even when they

are not meant to,' another of the ladies said with a giggle. As there was more gossip about who took which privileges they should not, sweet wafers stamped with Tudor roses were passed around and even more wine poured. Catherine found herself giggling much too loudly, just like everyone else, the wine going straight to her head. At home it was always well watered; here at Court, it wasn't diluted at all.

'Z'wounds, but look who is walking over here!' Cecily hissed and all the ladies froze as they glanced over their shoulders.

It was the Count of Feria—and Don Diego. Catherine, who was sure she was already flushed rosy-red from wine and laughter, felt her cheeks burning even hotter. She scarcely knew where to look and hoped no one else could hear the way her heart pounded, so loud in her ears she could barely hear anything else. In those poems of Spanish knights and ladies her mother so loved, the maidens fair were always serene and composed and perfect. How did they know what to say to their perfect knights at all?

She twisted her damask napkin between her fingers and stared down at the mangled fabric.

'Ah, Mistress Dormer,' the Count said, bowing low over Jane's hand. She smiled up at him, dimpling prettily, and Catherine wished Jane would teach *her* how to do that. 'It's wondrous to see you again and on such a happy evening.'

''Tis true we haven't seen you for a day or two, Count,' Jane answered. 'I did wonder if you had grown bored with us!'

The Count clasped his hand over his heart. 'Never! I can easily say that these days in England have been the most astonishing I have ever known, thanks to all the fair friends we've made here. I had to show your city to my friend, who is newly arrived from Spain and cannot accustom himself to the cold winds yet.' He turned to Don Diego, waving him forward. As he stepped close into their circle of candlelight, a smile touching his lips, Catherine realised he was even more handsome than she had imagined from a distance. 'May I present Don Diego de Vasquez? We were once squires together as boys, at the home of the Duke of Abeyta.'

'I'm honoured to join your Court in such a merry season,' Don Diego said with a bow. He brushed close to Catherine and she could smell his delicious, lemony cologne, like a summer day in the midst of winter. 'And in such delightful company.'

All the ladies giggled and Catherine was most glad she wasn't the only one suddenly overcome with girlish silliness.

'Diego, may I present formally Mistress Jane Dormer, one of the Queen's chief ladies?' Feria said. 'And Mistress Strelly, Mistress Barnes, and…' He glanced at Catherine and laughed. 'And this lovely lady, who I don't think I have the honour of knowing yet.'

'This is Mistress Greaves, who has just arrived at Court with her mother and thus as new to Whitehall as yourself, Don Diego,' Jane said. 'Her mother was once lady-in-waiting to Queen Catherine and came here from Spain.'

'Ah, a Spanish lady!' Feria said in Spanish. 'No wonder you show such refinement, Señorita Greaves.'

Catherine laughed at his teasing and answered in her own faltering Spanish, asking about what the gentlemen liked best of the Court so far. She tried *not* to stare at Diego, but she was constantly aware of his presence, his warmth, his smile.

The pages finished clearing the dishes from the tables and pushed the benches back to make a long, wide aisle up the middle of the chamber. The musicians struck up another lively tune as couples took hands and moved into patterns for the dancing.

'We must have an Almain,' Queen Mary said, clapping her hands in delight. 'Something lively. I know it may seem old-fashioned, but I remember it well from when I was a girl.'

'Mistress Dormer, would you do me the great honour of being my partner?' Feria asked. 'I do know your English dances so little and I know your kind heart will always forgive my missteps.'

'Thank you, Count,' Jane said, her cheeks turning pink, and she took his hand to let him lead her away.

'Would you favour me, Mistress Greaves?' Diego asked, bowing to her. For a moment, Catherine wondered if she had heard him aright. Had he just asked *her* to dance? But his smile told her she *had* heard him correctly. 'I fear I am like my friend, I'm out of practice dancing, but I enjoy what I've heard of your English music.'

'Oh,' Catherine breathed, her heart beating even faster with longing, her toes already tapping beneath her hem. She did love to dance, the music and movement, but it had been months since she'd practised. What if she forgot, what if she tripped—in front of *him*? She glanced at the other ladies and Cecily frantically waved her towards the dance floor.

'I—I'm not sure I know this particular dance well, either, Don Diego,' she said, praying her voice sounded steady, normal, that she didn't tremble under his gaze.

'Perhaps we could learn together?' he suggested.

He held out his hand and she could resist no longer. She carefully slid her fingers against his. His hands were long, lean, strong, elegantly manicured, but surprisingly calloused along the edge of his palm, as if he was used to riding and swordplay. He gently led her into their place.

Catherine smoothed her skirt. Across the hall, she caught a glimpse of her mother, talking with the Queen herself. Elena smiled, but her brow was puckered, as if she worried about something. Catherine tried to smile to reassure her, but her attention was caught by the music.

'My mother told me they often used to dance the Almain at Christmastime when she was lady-in-waiting,' Catherine said. 'She once taught it to me and hopefully I remember enough to guide our steps. I'll try not to step on your fine shoes!'

Diego laughed and his whole face seemed to glow with it. How Catherine longed to make him laugh again! 'I'm most content to put myself, and my shoes, in your fair hands, Señorita Greaves. As we're both newcomers to your English Court, we shall stumble through together, yes?'

'Yes,' Catherine said, with far more confidence than she felt.

'Though you must not be such a newcomer as all that, if your mother served the Queen,' he said. 'Were you named for her?'

'Aye, she was my godmother, though of course I remember nothing of those days. My mother left courtly service when she married my father and then...'

Diego nodded. Certainly he would know of those dark days when Queen Catherine was exiled, though he couldn't be much older than herself. 'But the light shines again, *si*?'

The musicians launched into the tune, a quicker melody than Catherine expected, especially in her flustered state. She wanted so much for him to admire her, or at least not think her silly; but how could she impress a man such as him?

But her feet, which had yearned for so long to dance again, started to tap and twirl, and carry her back into happier days. Music and dance and laughter always did that for her. She spun around and smiled at him in delight. He smiled back and his fingers closed tightly over hers when they met in the centre of the line and danced closely, shoulder to shoulder. He was so much taller than her, she had to tilt back her head to glance at him. To her joy, he seemed carried away by the fun of it all, too.

They stepped off with the others in their pattern—right, left, right, left, glide, glide, jump, twirl. She laughed when the leaping cadence somehow came off perfectly, their steps matched as if by magic. His hands came around her waist to spin her, his touch so warm and strong, safe.

It had been a very long time since she had felt safe.

For just a moment, she forgot she was in the middle of a royal Court, dancing with the most handsome man there. She enjoyed the quick, light movements, spinning with Diego as if they had always moved just so together. She let herself be guided by his deft, light touch and they moved in perfect unison, jumping, twirling again, skipping between the intertwined lines of dancers. She laughed with utter delight and spun around to see that he was laughing again, too. How young he looked when he forgot himself thus, like an angel in a fresco, singing with the joy of heaven.

Yet there was a naughtiness in that smile, too, one that could hardly be called *angelic*. It made her blush all over again.

All too soon, the music ended with a flourish and Catherine had to stand still, to let the wild blur of colour around her cease. The Queen applauded and Catherine stepped back to curtsy to Diego.

'I think we did rather well, don't you, Don Diego?' she said.

He smiled at her gently. 'Very well, *señorita*. Or rather, *you* did very well, I managed to not embarrass myself.' The people around them shifted. 'Would you care to walk with me around the hall for a moment? I've learned so little of this English life and I have many questions.'

Catherine found she *did* want to walk with him, more than she had ever wanted to do anything. Even her earlier nervousness seemed to have melted away in their dance and she found only a warm pleasure in his smile.

'Of course. Yet I may be of little help, being so new to London myself. My life in Kent is very quiet,' she said.

He held out his arm and she laid her hand on top of his velvet sleeve, feeling the taut muscles beneath, the heat of him. As they strolled along the edge of the hall, she noticed the other ladies watching them, whispering. A cluster of Spanish courtiers, who clearly did not realise she spoke the language, were complaining about the awkward jumping of 'crude English dances', making her laugh.

'You must forgive my countrymen, Señorita Greaves,' Diego said. 'They obviously have not had the benefit of a good dance teacher, as I have this evening.'

'I do think an Almain rather merry,' she said.

He laughed. 'I fear some people are sadly resistant to enjoyment, even during the festive season,' he whispered in her ear. 'Pity them.'

Catherine smiled shyly. What would he do if she gave in to temptation right now and rested her cheek against his velvet-clad shoulder, inhaling deeply of that lemon tartness? He would probably run away, as sure as his fellow Spaniards that they had come to a land of barbarians. 'But you aren't one of them, Don Diego? A resister of enjoyment?'

'Never. I shouldn't say nay to a dance. My work too often keeps me from such things.'

Catherine remembered the gossip about his vast estates in Spain. 'You must have a great deal to occupy your hours in Spain, with your duties at Court and your own estates.'

He sighed and smiled teasingly. 'Ah, so I have been a subject of courtly talk already?'

Catherine felt herself blushing again and glanced away. 'I should think you are most accustomed to that. Handsome young gentlemen of ancient estate are always of much interest—even in Madrid?'

He laughed again, as if delighted by her words, and he laid his free hand over hers on top of his arm. Catherine suddenly wondered why the Spanish had such a reputation for sombreness. She could have listened to his laughter for hours. 'Indeed you're right, Señorita Greaves. I'm too busy to listen to chatter as well, so I am never as well informed as I would wish. It is why we men rely on our womenfolk at Court to bring us such important information. You are right, my family has long been servants to the Court and our lands demand much attention. As does my daughter.'

'Oh.' Catherine had forgotten, in her golden dream of walking with him, laughing with him, that he'd once been married, he was a father. He was much more worldly than she. Had he loved his wife? Did he miss her terribly? 'You have a daughter?'

'*Si*, Isabella. She's six now and with my mother at the present, who spoils her greatly.' His smile turned proud, his gaze distant as if he missed his faraway daughter so much. Catherine's heart ached for him and for wee Isabella, too. Did *she* miss her father as Catherine did hers?

'And you don't spoil her at all, I'm sure,' she teased.

'Ah, you doubt me, Señorita Greaves, and you are right to do so. Isabella is so pretty, so full of bright chatter, I cannot help but be indulgent. Though I sometimes fear she must miss the influence of a mother. She'll grow up soon, much too quickly, and it will be time for her to marry and have her own household.'

'Has your wife been long departed, then?' Catherine asked carefully.

A frown flickered over his face, and he looked away. 'Nearly five years. Isabella does not remember her.'

And no doubt such a beautiful daughter had had a beautiful mother, one no doubt intelligent, adept at gathering Courtly gossip, devout, charming. Not like Catherine herself. 'You must have married quite young, then.'

'Indeed. We were always intended for each other. Our families' lands are very near.'

Catherine nodded with a sigh. How he must have loved her! 'And I am past an age to wed, I fear. I shall have to sit in that corner with a bit of lace-making and an old gable hood on my head, clucking out my disapproval of how the young people do hop and gambol about so when they dance.'

He laughed again and those clouds vanished. How

changeable he was! How frighteningly fascinating. 'Surely you have your pick of suitors here at Court. I confess I was told that Queen Mary's English ladies weren't very stylish or with very pretty faces, but I've found that to be not true at all.'

Was he saying *she* was pretty? Catherine bit back a delighted smile and wished she could tell him how beautiful *she* thought *him*. But if he thought she could easily find a husband here at Court, he must not have heard the tale of her father yet. Then he wouldn't tease and flirt with her again.

She would have to take full enjoyment from this moment while it lasted.

'I haven't yet met anyone I would care to wed,' she said. 'We are so quiet at my home in Kent, but my mother told me marvellous tales of her girlhood in Spain. How sunny it is, how the air smells of oranges and wine, how the churches glitter. Is it truly like that?'

They turned the corner at the end of the Great Hall and found themselves in the gallery, with the moonlight streaming through the windows. It was quieter there, only a few couples whispering as they watched the river.

'In some places, like my own home of Andalusia and in the provinces near the sea, it's bright and warm. But there are also mountains and places where it snows and the wind howls in the winter, just like here. Our cities are beautiful, with art and cathedrals, but crowded, too. My estate has groves of orange and lemon trees, olive gardens and vineyards where we make our own wine. The sky is so very blue, the light so piercing in the summer, you can barely look at it. And in Barcelona, you can walk by the sea. When I was a boy, I would travel there with my father to work on some of his shipping concerns. I would stand there on the seawall and look out, imagining the strange places that lay far beyond those waves. If I had not been born a Vasquez, I think I should have liked to be a sailor and see all those places for myself.'

Catherine was enthralled with the images his words created. 'If I was not a Greaves, and a girl, I often imagined being a diplomat, so that I could visit distant lands myself.'

Diego leaned back against the windowsill, crossing his arms over his velvet-covered chest. The moonlight created a halo around his glossy black hair. 'And where would you go?'

'Paris, I think,' Catherine said, conjuring up old girlhood dreams she hadn't dared think of in ages. 'And Venice! Imagine—a city built all on water. But most of all, I have wanted to see my mother's home in Valencia.'

'It is beautiful there.' He glanced out of the window at the tiltyard below. 'Yet I am sure that this land, too, has its lovely things.'

'Yes. The park at our estate is as green as Queen Mary's emerald in the summer! And this palace is a marvel, to me, anyway. But so much of its beauty is hidden by this winter weather, I fear,' Catherine said with a sigh, as she saw snowflakes drifting down from the black sky again. 'That frozen, muddy river…'

'But what of the way the moonlight shimmers on the water? Just there, see? Like a pearl.' He leaned close to her to gesture to the view out of the windows, his velvet sleeve brushing the bare skin of her neck. It made her shiver. 'You cannot see the brown of the river now, or the crowds on the streets. None of that. Life can have its rare beauties, I find, even in the strangest of moments.'

'Yes,' Catherine whispered. For *this* moment was certainly beautiful. Maybe one of the finest she had ever known. The realities of life seemed far away. 'It does look very different from this maze of a palace.'

'Where we scurry about like mice?' He smiled down at her. 'I have discovered a walkway just beyond this tiltyard, with a view along the river, a glimpse of all of London. I intend to make it a regular stroll. Perhaps I might see you there one day?'

Catherine swallowed hard, a longing sweeping over her as if it would carry her away down that river. To walk with him again, talk to him like this, watch him… 'Perhaps so, Don Diego.'

'Catalina,' said a soft but firm voice from behind her. 'There you are. I've been looking for you.'

Catherine spun around and smiled at her mother. Elena did not smile back, but stood there with her head high, watching them. '*Madre*. I am sorry, I just needed a—a breath of air. This is Don Diego de Vasquez.'

'Lady Greaves,' Diego said, making a low bow. 'Your daughter has honoured me with a few words of advice on life here at the English Court, as I've just arrived to serve His Majesty.'

'I've heard of your family, *señor*. I would think far more experienced courtiers than my Catalina could be of assistance to you,' she said sternly. But then she smiled, the indulgent smile Catherine had seen so many times. 'Though few could have such amusing viewpoints, I think.'

'I've enjoyed our conversation very much, Lady Greaves,' he answered. 'And I've heard of your family, as well. The Mendozas are much renowned.'

Catherine's mother inclined her head and held out her hand. 'I'm glad we're remembered. And I'm glad you enjoyed my daughter's company. Yet now I must take her from you, for it's time for me to retire. I bid you good evening.'

Elena turned to leave and Catherine made a quick curtsy to Diego before she hurried after. At the door, she glanced back, only to find him vanished.

Her mother took her hand tightly as they made their way back along the winding corridors and staircases, yet she was quiet, her expression unreadable.

'Don Diego is very charming,' Catherine ventured.

'I'm sure he is, *mija*, and such a handsome face, too.' She shook her head. 'You must be wary of men such as him.'

'Wary?' Catherine said, confused. She knew well that

men could prove false, too well. But someone like Don Diego? She couldn't quite fathom it. 'I thought the Spanish courtiers were said to be of the highest morals.'

'I've heard nothing ill of his reputation.'

'Then of his family?'

'Not at all. The Vasquez family have been servants of the royal Court since Don Diego's forefather helped King Ferdinand and Queen Isabella themselves to form their secret marriage. They have been richly rewarded for their service.'

'Then what is it, *Madre*?'

Elena stopped and laid her hand gently on Catherine's cheek, her smile sad. 'He is a powerful man and we must be careful. Your father...'

Catherine sucked in a sharp breath. How could she have forgotten even for a moment why they were really in London? She couldn't add to her mother's worries. 'Of course. I'll be careful, *madre mia*, I promise.'

'Oh, *mi dulce*. You are so young. You deserve to enjoy yourself, to make merry, to have friends, maybe even a little romance. If we were in Spain, or even if your father was—well, a gentleman as he was before—I promise you I would move all the heavens to make such a splendid match as a Vasquez for you. But...'

'But that is not our life now,' Catherine whispered sadly. 'I do understand.'

Elena squeezed her hand and turned towards their chamber. Catherine knew that was all that needed to be said between them. The real world fell upon her again and the wistful dream she knew as she stood in the moonlight with Diego vanished like a wisp of fog on the river.

Diego stood for a few more long moments in the hidden shadows of the gallery, watching that moonlight on the London river from behind the velvet curtains. The merriment still went on beyond him in the Hall, but he imagined he heard only the rush of the tide swirling in and out, reminding him of his constant duty.

Yet he also heard something else—the memory of a lady's joyful laughter, bringing a light into his life he hadn't known in so long. He looked down at his hand and remembered how hers felt in his grasp, how she leaned into him as they danced. Startlingly green eyes staring up at him as if she was just as fascinated by the moment as he was. Just as surprised by how it all felt.

He curled his hand into a fist and pressed it to the chilly glass of the window. There was no respite from what a man of his name had to do, the secret tasks he was in London to perform.

In Spain, he'd looked at Isabella's solemn little face and wondered what it would be like in their world if they could find a spot of joy in their shadowed lives. For an instant, as he danced with Catherine, he saw what that life might be like.

That was all it could be, though, a moment.

Chapter Four

Catherine watched the teeming shores of the Thames slide past as their boat made its way from Whitehall to the Tower. The wind whipped past, catching at the hood of her cloak with icy sharp fingers as she huddled on the hard seat next to her mother. The life of the city swirled around them, careless of the sad errand the two Greaves ladies found themselves on, but Catherine tried to forget the looming grey walls that waited just ahead by daydreaming about that brightly lit hall, all music and candlelight.

And dancing with Diego.

She drew her hood closer to hide a secret smile. Even though she had been so tired after the banquet, she'd lain awake long into the night, remembering the wine, the music, the sparkle of the jewels. Diego's dark eyes, eyes that were as bright as the diamond the Queen wore, as he looked down at her in the moonlight, talking of how beauty could be found everywhere. She wanted to know so much more about him.

Yet she knew that, despite her dreams, she was scarcely likely to ever know him better, ever find his secrets. How could she compete with his first, Spanish, wife, a lady always meant for him? The mother of his child.

She would just have to control herself when they danced, *if* he ever danced with her again. That one dance had so filled her heart with light and merriment, when she thought all such things were gone from her life for ever. It was no small thing and would have to suffice.

Their boat gave a jolt and she glanced up to see that they had arrived at the lower water steps of the Tower.

'Come, Catalina, we must not be late,' her mother said. She looked very pale against her black fur-edged hood.

The boatman helped them out and up on to the wooden pier, where a man waited to escort them through the gates. He wore a dark russet woollen doublet and cloak, no uniform or sword, yet Catherine found the complete lack of expression on his bearded face fearsome enough. He glanced them up and down, as if he was a man accustomed to making quick judgements.

'I'm Master Thornton, secretary to Sir Thomas Bridges, Governor of the Tower,' the man said abruptly. 'I've been sent to fetch you to him.'

Elena and Catherine exchanged an uncertain glance, but Catherine took her mother's hand in a reassuring grasp and they hurried to follow Master Thornton. Once through two sets of iron gates, they found themselves on a green. Despite the ominous walls outside, inside it all seemed like an ordinary village. Maidservants with laundry, children dashing about. In the distance she glimpsed the looming spires of the White Tower, the dark square of the Church of St Peter ad Vincula, but there were no gallows. It all seemed quite ordinary. Which made Catherine feel even more unsettled.

'This way, if you please, Lady Greaves,' Master Thornton said. They turned past a row of two-storey half-timbered cottages. Ladies in fine brown and green woollen gowns paused in their gossip to watch them go by, pity on their faces.

'The families of the chief officers live here,' Master Thornton said. 'Your father's lodgings are just beyond this wall.'

Catherine wondered where they would end up. Some grim little stone cell? She held tighter to her mother's arm and felt so very cold.

They were taken not to a dungeon, but a freshly plastered house set in a neat row of them near the far wall. A rectangle of garden stretched before them and smoke curled invitingly out of the chimneys.

'Is this where my husband is lodged?' her mother asked, her voice cautiously hopeful. But her accent was stronger, which Catherine knew meant she was anxious.

'Indeed, Lady Greaves.' Master Thornton gestured to a substantial brick home on the other side of the garden. 'The rest of the Wyatt group is in that building just beyond, past the hedges. Much the same.'

Elena looked to Catherine again and in her mother's dark eyes she read her own relief and confusion. They followed Master Thornton through the door and found themselves in a parlour. The walls were warmed with painted cloths; the chairs, a chest, a long table, were plain but substantial. Books were piled on the table along with platters of delicacies and pitchers of wine.

A man waited by the fire and turned to greet them. He was older, stout, red-cheeked, with a sparse, pale beard and kind smile. 'Ah, Lady Greaves. And this must be your daughter? I see why she has caused such a stir at Court! I'm Sir Thomas Bridges, Governor here. Her Majesty did write to me to expect you, but I'm afraid the letter arrived rather late with the winter tide and Sir Walter is with another caller. He shouldn't be long, though, if you'd care to wait in here? Lady Bridges has sent ginger cakes and wine.'

'That is kind of you, Sir Thomas,' Elena said warily. 'But, are you not to guard us while we're here?' She and Catherine had been sure their conversation would be chaperoned and recorded.

'I fear I have business elsewhere. But please do ring for the servants if they can bring you anything at all. I have a new volume of poetry from Paris just there on the table, Mistress Catherine, if you might care to peruse it? Your father tells me you enjoy reading.'

With one more bow, he left them alone in the parlour,

closing the stout door behind him. Catherine wondered if it was locked, but when she tested the latch it turned easily. She glanced back at her mother, who sat huddled in the armchair by the fire.

'Are all prisoners treated thus?' Catherine asked.

'I should imagine not,' her mother said tautly, and Catherine knew she remembered the terrible tales they had heard in Kent. Torture, cold stone cells. 'Though they did say the rest of the Wyatt band is in the house just beyond, which looks most similar. And who is visiting your father besides us? But come, Catherine, drink some of Lady Bridges's fine wine and warm yourself.'

Catherine took off her cloak before she went to pour out goblets of wine and choose some cakes for her mother. She found she couldn't sit still, so she went to look out of the window that opened to the pathway in front of the house. A few flakes of snow were falling now, landing in the garden just beyond.

The moments had ticked past, marked by the fine clock on the table. At last, after what felt like hours, but according to the clock had only been thirty minutes, she heard a door open somewhere in the house, the murmur of voices, footsteps moving down a staircase, the creak of the front door. Catherine turned back to the window and saw a man emerge to be met by Sir Thomas in the garden. He wore a hooded cloak of black wool, his face hidden, but he was quite tall and moved with a quick, lithe grace.

He half-turned to look at the house and Catherine saw to her shock that it was Diego. Diego de Vasquez had been her father's caller! What was he, a friend to King Philip himself, doing in her father's lodgings? Had the King set her father up in some way to be blamed for something in the Rebellion? Had Diego danced with her to find out about her father?

Catherine pressed her hand hard to her mouth, to hold back a gasp.

'What is it, *mija*?' her mother said. 'What do you see?'

'Nothing, *Madre*.' She could say nothing to her mother, not until she knew more about what was happening.

There were more footsteps, a burst of laughter, then the door flew open and her father stood there. Catherine shoved away her fears and ran to embrace him.

'Papa!' she cried. She'd feared to find him starved, broken, yet he felt just as her father always had in her arms. Tall, strong, a bit portly in the belly now, smelling of cloves, his beard tickling her cheek when he kissed her.

She stood back to look at him. He'd gained a bit of weight, his skin pale under his beard, which had once been as chestnut as her own hair, but was now greying. He wore a warm robe of deep brown velvet, a cap on his balding head.

'My little cabbage,' he said and touched her cheek. 'How beautiful you're growing!'

'I've missed you,' was all Catherine could say, all that stood in for the fears and hopes and worries of the past months.

'And I you. So very much.' He turned to her mother, his smile turning down at the edges. 'Elena.'

Catherine saw that her mother had risen from her chair, but Elena didn't move closer. She looked much as she had as she watched Diego in the gallery, her face serene, smooth, serious, giving nothing away. 'Walter. You are well?'

'Well enough, as you see. Becoming a bit too stout, I fear, but I am promised more exercise when the weather warms. Bridges is a gentleman, and I've had time to read more, as you've always urged me, even *El Cid*.'

Elena shook her head. 'I'm surprised you should wish to read it, if you did agree with Master Wyatt that the Spanish should stay away from England.'

Catherine glanced between them, worried about what Diego had been doing there, worried about—well, everything. She wasn't sure what to do. Strangely, the person she wished to be beside her, the person she wished she could talk to, ask for advice, was Diego himself. She'd felt so close to him there in the moonlight! But she was alone.

She took her father's hand and smiled up at him, trying to ease some of the tension between her parents. No matter what had happened before, they were together now, if only for a few moments.

'Come, Papa, have some wine, and we'll tell you all about what's happening at home,' she said, drawing him to the fire. Her mother said nothing, but she sat down again, her hands folded in her lap.

Catherine poured out the wine, chattering about the harvest, gossip of neighbours at home, the fashions at Court. She had so many questions, so many doubts—but for that hour, it all had to wait.

Chapter Five

Christmas Eve

'Holly and ivy, box and bay, put in the house for Christmas Eve! Fa-la-la-la...'

Catherine smiled at the familiar song. It reminded her of Christmases past at home, when she and her father would gather greenery from the park and she and her mother would tie them into wreaths and swags. It distracted her from her own brooding doubts since the Tower.

All the Queen's young Maids of Honour were assigned to decorate the Great Hall for the Christmas Eve feast. Long tables were covered with piles of holly, ivy, mistletoe and boughs of sweetly scented evergreen, along with every colour of ribbon and spangle.

They were supposed to work together efficiently to turn them into wreaths, but *efficiency* didn't seem to be the order of the day. Most of the ladies sang out of tune as they worked, often leaping up to do a dance or twirl with their ribbons like Morris dancers at a country fair.

Catherine laughed at their antics. She glanced over at her mother, who sat sewing by the fire with Queen Mary and Mistress Clarencius while the Queen's dogs played about their feet. Even her mother smiled at the music, and seemed content, though Catherine had heard her crying and praying over her rosary in the darkest of the night.

Catherine tied a bow on the wreath she had just finished and had a memory of her mother leaning over when she was a child, helping her clumsy infant hands with the slippery fabric as they both laughed.

She also remembered once glimpsing her parents standing in a close embrace under a kissing bough. How they had leaned into each other, smiling into each other's eyes before her mother reached up on tiptoe for a kiss.

Catherine felt a sad pang at remembering that tender moment and to know that once she had dreamed of such a thing for herself, too.

'Is that a kissing bough you're making, Jane?' Cecily asked.

Jane held up her handiwork, a delicate sphere of greenery. 'My grandmother taught me how to fashion one at our house in Buckinghamshire. She said that when she was a girl, it was rumoured that if you stood under such a bough with a gentleman at Christmas, you would be in love always.'

Catherine had a flashing image in her mind of Diego, smiling down at her as they held hands under a kissing bough. It was much too alluring and she shook it quickly away.

'And we do know who would like to be with *Jane* under the bough this year!' another Maid teased.

Jane blushed, and turned away to reach for more ribbon. ''Tis merely an old tale.'

The doors at the far end of the Hall opened and King Philip appeared with a crowd of attendants, all of them clad in warm clothes for the frosty day outside. He laughed with Ruy Gomez and just behind him were the Count of Feria, Manuelita de Chavez and her husband, and Master Andrew Loades, the pale-haired gentleman whose brother was in the Tower. For some reason Catherine felt uneasy whenever she saw him.

Diego stood just behind them, his dark hair brushed back from his brow beneath a plumed cap, a pair of gloves slapping against his thigh as if he was eager to be outside. He didn't smile, but his eyes seemed warm as he surveyed the gathering.

Catherine looked away before she could do something as silly as jump up and run to him. To take his hand, or to demand to know what he was doing at the Tower, she wasn't sure which. She glanced at Jane's kissing bough and imagined him standing beneath the green sphere, her gazing up at him, at his beautiful lips, longing to know what they would feel like on hers. She imagined her hands on his shoulders, those powerful muscles beneath softest velvet, so warm and strong and alive, sliding her palms down his chest as his lips lowered to hers...

Master Andrew stopped at the table to examine their work. He pinched Cecily's cheek, making her giggle, and reached for a sprig of dark green holly. 'They say if the holly leaves are rounded, the lady shall rule the house. If barbed, then 'tis the lord.'

'And which is this?' Jane asked.

Master Andrew ran his thumb over the glossy leaf. 'Barbed, of course, as is the natural way.'

'I doubt the Queen would agree with that,' Jane retorted.

The King knelt beside the Queen. 'My dear wife,' he said in Spanish. He kissed his wife on her cheek, making her blush like a girl. 'It's a sunny enough day outside at last and I am venturing out to the countryside to find a fine Yule log, and to give my advisers an afternoon free. You should join me. The little one needs fresh air to help him grow strong. Is that not so, Mistress Clarencius? Lady Greaves?'

Queen Mary gave her deep laugh. 'Would you call for a sleigh, Husband?'

'Your Majesty, you must not!' Mistress Clarencius said sternly. 'It's much too cold. You catch a chill so easily.'

Queen Mary sighed. 'Perhaps you are right, my wise Susan. But you must go, my dear Jane! You need to be outside, in the sun, having some fun while you are so young. And you can make sure the Yule log is a pretty one.'

Catherine glanced up just in time to see Diego walking towards the gallery. He was obviously also venturing outside. She remembered he said he sometimes strolled on the walkways above the river, and on a whim she decided to follow him.

'I won't go out today, Jane, I have some sewing to do this afternoon,' she said. 'But I will get a bit of fresh air.' She dashed outside before anyone could say anything else.

But when she reached the walkway, he had vanished. Her heart sank in cold disappointment and she strolled towards the gallery to find a quiet moment alone. Outside the window, she caught a glimpse of him again—climbing into a boat that turned down the river towards the Tower.

'What then doth make the elements so bright? The heavens are come down upon earth to live!'

A dozen of the Queen's strongest men carried the Yule log into the Great Hall. It was as large and stout as the gilded ceiling beams high overhead. Greenery and garlands bound up with red ribbons adorned the wood, which would be lowered into the largest fireplace to burn until Twelfth Night.

Catherine wondered what her own fate would be after Christmas. Would she and her mother return to their lonely home, without her father?

Yet there was no time for gloomy thoughts that night. Catherine laughed as she watched the log paraded around the cheering crowd, its bright streamers waving merrily, until it came before the King and Queen, who sat in their velvet-cushioned chairs near the fire, holding hands.

Catherine glimpsed Diego standing behind the King, his face aglow with laughter, and she caught her breath. She couldn't help but stare at him there in the firelight, but she turned away before he could catch her gaping like a country maid.

'Who has the embers from last year to set the light?' Lord Rochester, the Queen's comptroller, called. A pageboy stepped forward with a glowing torch. 'I do now command those of you whom Queen Mary calls upon to tell your favourite Christmas memory.'

The Queen laughed happily, her cheeks pink in the firelight. She looked ten years younger that night. 'Who do you command should go first, my lord?'

He bowed. 'Why, Your Majesty must favour us yourself, of course.'

The Queen laughed and told a story of when she was a very little girl and the Venetian ambassador had visited her father's Court. 'And I did love the tunes of his Italian musicians so very much that I broke away from my nurse and ran back to the lute player, begging him to play just one more song! My mother indulged me and let me stay there long after I should have been abed.'

'Thus you still love music,' her husband said.

'So I do,' Queen Mary said with a laugh. 'But tell us, Husband, your own favourite Yule tale.'

King Philip related a story of his own childhood, of his long-dead mother's garden and a choir of nuns who would sing beneath her window at night until the hour of the Christ child's own birth, when he and his sisters would toss them sweetmeats and oranges. 'But Don Diego's home was in Andalusia, the land of the finest feast days,' King Philip finished. 'Perhaps he may tell us more.'

'I recall a game even my grandfather's generation enjoyed in their youth,' Diego said. 'El Tio—simple but lively, with a hollowed-out log filled with sweets. The children knock it about, energetically and noisily, until it breaks and spills out all its treasures. My grandfather said it taught us well how to hit a target with a sword, but my grandmother would declare he only wanted to share in the sweets.'

Queen Mary laughed with everyone else and laid her hand on her belly as she so often did, as if she imagined her own child playing such a game. 'I dare say you excelled at this game, Don Diego.'

'I hit my mark often enough, Your Majesty, but I think my daughter may surpass me this year. Her aim last year was remarkable.' His smile turned wistful, as if he missed her so much in that moment, and Catherine longed to go and take his hand.

'My cousin's daughter is quite the prettiest child ever seen, Your Majesty,' Manuelita said.

'She must come to England as soon as she is old enough, then, and tell me of all the traditions of a Spanish childhood,' Queen Mary said. 'I must incorporate some into my own nursery, would you not say so, my dear?' She smiled at her husband, who squeezed her hand as more of the courtiers told their favourite Yule tales.

Catherine looked for Diego after the storytelling, as everyone chatted and laughed together while the pages passed around goblets of wine.

'Mistress Greaves,' someone said and she turned to find Andrew Loades smiling at her.

'Master Loades,' she said warily.

'So you do remember me? We were neighbours in Kent, though it was my brother Robert who was mostly at your house.'

'Of course,' she said. She did remember Robert Loades, he was in the Tower with her father now, his house just beyond the garden of her father's. Though their family had never been so close to the Greaveses before.

'I know you haven't been at Whitehall long,' he said quietly, stepping close to her. Too close. 'But I feel, for your father's sake, I must warn you.'

'Warn me?'

'Court ways now are not the ways of true Englishmen and women. There are many elements to be careful of here.' He looked over at Diego and the Count of Feria. 'The way matters stand today may not be as they are tomorrow. A delicate lady such as yourself naturally must wish to see the best in all people...'

'Are we not all God's children, Master Loades?' Catherine said sharply, fearing he trod perilously close to treasonous talk now. She had learned indeed from her father; she wanted nothing to do with such things.

His smile turned gentle. 'Perhaps—not all? I only wish to make sure you are on your guard. As an old neighbour, and one who admires your father.'

Catherine nodded brusquely. 'That is indeed kind. I shall take your words under great advisement.' She curtsied as he bowed, then turned and hurried away as quickly as she could.

Chapter Six

'How are you faring, then, Sir Walter?' Diego asked Catherine's father as they strolled the walkway on top of the walls of the Tower, the river far below. He thought that Sir Walter, despite the warm cloak he wore, seemed tired. He carried a walking stick today, his gloved fingers tight on the carved handle.

'I'm well enough, Don Diego,' Sir Walter said with a laugh. 'I have a warm fire at all hours and the Bridges's cook has a fine touch with herbs. I dine often with Master Loades and the others. I shall grow fat soon and my Elena will never want to kiss me again.'

His smile turned sad and Diego remembered well that Catherine and her mother couldn't yet know what was going on. How he longed to help Catherine, to hold her close and tell her the truth! To banish those shadows of sadness from her green eyes. 'The Queen shows your wife much favour, she has such gratitude for your work.'

Sir Walter waved this away. 'Elena and Catherine gather all the royal favour by their own endeavours. My Catherine is growing into a beauty, don't you think?'

Diego smiled, remembering how Catherine's face glowed when she laughed at the dancing. 'She is indeed.'

Sir Walter reached out and caught a drift of snow on his palm. ''Tis days like this I think most of my dear wife's tales of Spain. The warmth of the sun, the bright blue skies. Is it truly like that, Don Diego?'

'We do have orchards and vineyards, and wide balconies to enjoy the warm evenings.'

'You sound as if you miss it.'

'I do. But mostly I miss my daughter.'

Sir Walter sighed sadly. 'As do I, Don Diego. And how I should love to see my wife's homeland! For her to see it again. We've had a happy life together and I do thank Providence every day for bringing her to me. But I know she has been homesick.'

'Would you like to see it, Sir Walter? I'm sure King Philip could arrange for you to travel there, once this sad business is finished. My own mother would be most honoured to host you.'

Sir Walter smiled and clapped Diego's shoulder. 'You do paint a tempting picture, Don Diego. Yet I fear our business may never be finished. Elena must concentrate on Catherine now, find her a match—if she can.'

Diego felt a sharp pang at the thought of Catherine married to some Englishman. 'That will surely be only the work of a moment. Your daughter is very charming and with the Queen's assistance…'

Sir Walter's smile brightened. 'You think her charming, Don Diego? What a flatterer you are, knowing where best a compliment might touch me.'

Diego laughed. 'I speak only the truth, Sir Walter.' And indeed he did. But he could tell no one how beautiful, how bright and lovely, he really thought her.

'You're a good man, Don Diego. If only those Wyatt fools had actually met some Spaniards…'

'They have met us now and they seem to like us no better.'

'Aye. Like I said. Fools.' Sir Walter stared out over the river. 'I have made such interesting friends here at the Tower, Don Diego. One of them, that Master Robert Loades, is a good chess player and quite the talker.'

'Not as good a talker as you, I would warrant.'

Sir Walter chuckled wryly. 'Far better, or at least more voluble. Especially when he is in his cups, which he is often enough. His brother, Master Andrew, sends him Malmsey from Court.'

Diego recalled Master Andrew Loades and his attentions to Catherine. 'Master Robert was one of the Wyatt plotters, but nothing was found about his brother?'

'Not as yet, so he's allowed to stay at Whitehall. He also helps his brother stay informed about the outside world, just as we hoped he would. Better informed than I am at times and I think I have discovered why. His brother puts messages into those wine flasks.'

Diego stood up straight, a bolt of alarm shooting through him at the thought that Catherine might be in danger if Master Andrew pursued her. 'A spy in the midst of Court?'

'One of many, for that's the way of Courts, you know.'

'I know that indeed,' Diego said grimly. He knew how to navigate every dark corner; but would Catherine?

'I think Wyatt's friends who were spared do hope to gather their supporters again, the ones who fled England or who remain in hiding in the country. Robert Loades thinks his brother will be able to find these men and let them know of new plans after the New Year. They mean to strike before the new Prince is born.'

'That is only a few months away. They say the babe will come in May.'

Sir Walter nodded. 'I have no great expectation of the success of such a plan. The Queen repelled them before and with the coming heir she is more popular than ever. But mayhap if a courtier who is close to the Queen is a traitor, in fact, he could find a way to harm her or the child.'

'And you don't know who Andrew Loades works with at Court yet?'

'That is my task now. I am to dine with Master Robert tonight for Christmas. There is sure to be a great deal of Malmsey, Don Diego. Persistence and wine shall win the day, I vow! He rambles on about plans to kidnap the Queen and tonight he will surely tell me all the details.'

Diego did like Sir Walter. He could see Catherine's positive, sunny nature in his, despite their travails. 'That sounds a dismal way to spend the holy holiday.'

'It must be done, Don Diego, and I'm happy to serve the Queen however I can.' Sir Walter shook his head. 'I confess I miss my family, though, and our own hall. My Elena would not even touch my hand when she and Catherine visited me here.'

Diego knew well that duty could be a cold thing. 'When this sad business is over and she knows the truth, she will surely shower you with kisses.'

Sir Walter laughed. 'Will she indeed? Or will the hurt be too deep? Once we were as one mind and heart, our lives full of laughter. We can only hope, Don Diego, to find such a gift again.'

Diego's own marriage had never been thus. He couldn't understand Juana, nor she him. Theirs had been only duty and in the end not even that. He envied the Greaveses and their happiness. 'Is there any service I may do for you at Court, Sir Walter?'

Sir Walter reached into the pouch at his belt. 'Can you see that my daughter is given this?' He handed Diego a small package.

'Of course.' He took it and tucked it into his own purse. He would do anything that might brighten Catherine's day a bit.

'You must be returning to Whitehall now. But you have my thanks, Don Diego, for everything.' He looked up at the sky, which was beginning to spill damp flakes of snow again. 'I think I shall be dreaming of your Spanish orchards tonight...'

'Tonight, my dear friends, we shall dance a candle bransle, which my good husband tells me is a favourite of

the Spanish Court in this festive season,' Queen Mary said.
The Great Hall was cleared of tables after that night's feast
and the King and Queen sat at their cushioned thrones by
the fire. Catherine could see no glimpse of Diego and she
wondered if he hadn't yet returned from his river voyage.
Had he truly been to the Tower again? To what purpose?
Catherine was most puzzled.

The Queen laughed and waved an imperious hand. The
gold hoop of her wedding ring gleamed. 'And I say we all
must dance!' She took her husband's hand and rose from her
chair to stroll into the crowd, matching up partners herself.
Catherine smiled to see Jane take Feria's arm.

'Mistress Greaves, would you do me the honour of this
dance?' said a voice behind her—that deep, velvet-warm,
musical Spanish voice she had hoped, and feared, to hear.

Catherine squeezed her eyes shut for an instant and tried
to breathe deeply to calm her nervous trembling. It was always thus when she was with Diego—she thought about
him, longed for him, too much.

She turned and smiled at him. He wore purple brocade
tonight, dark and mysterious, his eyes gleaming. 'Thank
you, Don Diego, I would be most pleased.' He held out his
arm and she slid her palm on to his sleeve, feeling that finally she was anchored into a place, a place where she could
belong. She knew it was an illusion, but still she longed
for it.

They found their position in line and maidservants
handed each man a candle in a silver holder. The musicians launched into the dignified tune of the old dance and
Catherine was glad her mother had once taught her the steps
for that dance one Christmas in Kent. She remembered her
parents dancing it, the slow, gliding steps, hands touching
and parting, the gleam of the light.

And most of the slow, intricate steps began with the line
of men and she could follow along easily enough. The gentlemen of each couple, his lighted candle held high in one

hand, stepped towards his lady, a series of complicated steps that ended before her in a low bow. The ladies then curtsied and danced to meet him, their skirts swaying in a blur of colours like the birds Catherine had earlier imagined them.

Diego met her with a bow and a teasing smile, and she laughed in turn as she curtsied. They spun around each other, the candlelight flickering on the sharp angles of his face, making him look even more handsome and mysterious.

'Do be careful, Don Diego,' she teased as they moved through the stately steps. 'Don't they say if you let the candle go out it will be a year of terrible fortune?'

He laughed. 'Not for me, Mistress Greaves. So far this has been a most lucky time indeed.'

She laughed, too. For was it *not* fortunate that they were together now, hands clasped as they moved down the line? No matter what happened tomorrow, they were here now, together.

All too soon, they had to change partners, candles exchanged between the men. She danced with the Count of Feria and an elderly knight who must surely have been alive when the first Tudor Henry reigned. Catherine had to hold him upright to keep him from setting his beard afire.

The next in line was Master Andrew Loades. He took her hand and smiled down at her, just as her other partners had, but there was something in his eyes that spoke to her of ice, as cold as the wind that howled outside the windows.

'How does your father fare in this cold weather, Mistress Greaves?' he said.

Catherine longed to snatch her hand back. 'Well enough, thank you.'

'He would want me to warn you to be careful. A royal Court like this is no fit place for the child of a good man like him.'

Catherine didn't like something in his tone, or his tight touch. She was most relieved when he let go of her hand and she spun away, but that cold feeling persisted. She stumbled out of the pattern of the dance and fled the hot, perfumed press of the crowd. She wanted to run, to be alone, but she didn't know where she could go.

She quickly ducked behind one of the tapestries and wedged herself into the small, quiet space just between the wooden wall and the thick cloth. She closed her eyes and breathed deeply, letting the muffled silence wash over her.

She thought of her father, alone tonight, and their old life in Kent, when her parents would dance and laugh at Christmas. How secure their life had been then, how sure she was of it all. Now she was sure of nothing.

Suddenly, a flash of light and noise intruded again for an instant as the tapestry was eased aside. Her eyes flew open and she spun around, her stomach tight as she feared it was Master Andrew. She glimpsed a tall figure outlined in the torchlight, before the cloth dropped behind him and they were alone in their own dark little world. She knew then it was Diego. No one smelled like him, felt like him. No one made *her* feel as he did, warm and strong, a rock between her and the dangers of the world.

'Catherine,' he said gently. 'Are you ill?'

'Nay, I just…' She swayed dizzily. 'It was just so crowded, I needed a breath of air.'

'I, too, miss the quiet evenings of home,' he said gently. 'With the windows open and a breeze smelling of lemon filling the rooms, my mother playing her lute…'

'I do love to hear these little glimpses of your home,' she said. She wondered if he felt lonely, as she did.

She glanced up to see Jane's kissing bough hanging over them. She thought of what they said—if a person stood under such a bough with a man at Christmas, they would be in love for ever. She feared she might indeed be falling in love with Diego, but it would make her heart ache when he left.

His arms came around her, drawing her close to him,

and she felt truly safe—even if she wondered if he was the one she should fear most.

She rested her forehead against the soft brocade of his doublet and closed her eyes. For just an instant, she could pretend they were all alone. She felt him kiss the top of her head, and she tilted her face up to his. His face was all sharp angles in the shadows, his eyes like the night.

'See the kissing bough?' he whispered and she laughed softly. His lips skimmed warmly over her cheek, so light, so sweet, it made her crave yet more and more.

At last, his lips touched hers and it was so wondrous—hot and cold all at once, as caressing as a wave of the sea washing over her and carrying her away. And then his kiss deepened, grew harder, hungry, and her lips parted on a delighted gasp.

That small sound against his lips made him groan and he pulled her closer until there didn't seem to be even a breath between them. Catherine went up on the tips of her toes, clinging to him. His tongue lightly, shockingly, touched hers, tasting, testing, before his kiss deepened and he was all she knew in the world.

She wound her arms around his neck, feeling the soft silk of his hair between her fingers, holding on to him tight as if he would fly away from her. Fly all the way back to Spain. Their kiss turned desperate, blurry and warm, full of a frantic need she hadn't even known was hidden inside of her.

That raw need frightened her, yet she also desperately hoped for more and yet more of it. More of *him.*

'Diego,' she gasped. 'Wh-what is happening?'

'I don't know, my Catalina,' he said roughly, holding her close, his breath ragged in her ear, answering the rhythm of her own. 'I only know it will not go away.'

Did he feel as she did, then? Lying awake in the darkest hours, trying to push the feelings out of her heart. They could come to nothing, yet she couldn't let go of him now.

It had been thus ever since she saw him. Even the poems and songs could not have prepared her for such feelings.

Beyond their little sanctuary, she heard the music end and Diego stepped away from her. His touch fell away and she shivered with the sudden cold. He was still there, still close to her, yet he suddenly seemed so far away. As if the kiss had been just a dream and now she had to wake. This separation was the reality.

'I should go,' she whispered. 'My mother will look for me.'

He looked down at her, his face filled with an anguish that made her want to weep. 'Catherine—I...'

She held up her hand. She could not bear it if he said he was *sorry* for their kiss. She wanted to dream just a little longer.

'Christmas is a time out of real time, is it not?' she said. She tried to smile at him and gently touched his cheek, memorising the way he felt under her fingertips.

She spun around and ducked past the tapestry, letting herself into the real world again. She straightened her shoulders, smoothed her hair back and smiled.

'Catherine!' Jane called. 'Do come and try this gingerbread, it is delicious.'

'Of course,' Catherine answered and hurried to join her friends before she could glimpse Diego and lose her composure again.

Before she went to bed, as her mother was brushing her hair and chatting of Court gossip, Catherine found a small linen package under her pillow. When she unwrapped it, she found a small ruby ring she recognised as one her father often wore on his small finger. There was a small scrawled note.

The happiest of Christmases to my darling Cat. May next year bring us all we can desire. Have faith.

She smiled and hugged the ring close. She knew her father's words were only a fantasy, but they brought her comfort none the less. Where had it come from? Who had cared enough to bring it to her? She remembered seeing Diego go into the boat and dared think for a moment that he was her messenger of hope.

She silently blessed whoever had been kind enough to bring it to her and closed her eyes to dream of happier times indeed.

Chapter Seven

'Catalina, hurry! The Queen's hunt will ride out soon!' Catherine's mother called from her bath behind the screen at the fireplace.

'I am already dressed, *Madre*,' she answered and smoothed her hair under her new riding hat. She did look forward to riding again after so long in the crowded palace. She glanced out of the small window and glimpsed a familiar figure hurrying across the courtyard towards the river walkways. *Diego*. No one was as tall as him, walked with his confident stride.

On a whim, she decided to follow him. 'I'll be right back, *Madre*,' she called.

'Catalina…' her mother said, but Catherine made her escape. She dashed down the back stairs until she found him in the garden.

'Catherine,' he said with a bright, welcoming smile and held out his hand. She ran to take it.

She leaned against his shoulder, drawing in a deep breath. He smelled so warm, so delicious. She could feel her heart pounding in rhythm with his. He seemed a part of that day, the freedom and excitement, the wild winter beauty. All the reasons she had thought she couldn't be with him seemed so far away, there was only him and that moment.

She noticed a small pendant surrounded by pearls that hung from his neck on a thin gold chain, sparkling in the pale light. It must have escaped the high collar of his doublet. It was obvious he wore it often, for the enamel backing was worn. Curious, she studied it closer. It was a portrait, a little girl with golden curls and wide, dark eyes.

'Your daughter?' she asked.

He examined it with a tender little smile. 'Aye, my Isabella.'

'How very pretty she is.' Catherine traced her fingertip along the painted lines of the tiny face. 'She has your eyes and your smile. Is she also much like her mother?'

The smile faded. 'A bit. Mostly she looks like my own mother, with her fair hair. They adore each other. Isabella was beside herself with happiness at being told she would stay with her *abuela* while I was away.'

Catherine's heart ached at the sadness she heard in his voice. 'You miss her.'

'Very much.'

'And I know she must miss you. It's hard for a father and daughter to be parted, especially at Christmas.' She laid her hand over her own secret token, her father's ring she wore on a ribbon beneath her partlet. Was it, could it be, Diego, who had brought it to her? She dared not ask him, but she did hope.

Diego gently touched her cheek and she leaned into the comfort he offered. 'So it is. But look at how beautiful this day is! I've never known anything like it.' He held out his hand to catch a flake of snow on his gloved palm, laughing at its silvery magic.

Catherine had never seen anything like *him*. She tilted back her head to stare up at him in wonder.

He looked down at her and, as if his thoughts matched hers, his expression turned serious, intent. She wrapped her arms around his shoulders and held him close.

He kissed her just as she longed for, his mouth taking hers hungrily as they clung together in the cold. His hands at her waist dragged her even closer, until nothing was between them. She wanted more, wanted everything of him. All else was forgotten.

Her lips parted, welcoming the touch of his tongue to hers, the heated rush of desire that warmed the chilly day.

She went up on her toes and slide her fingers up into his hair and his kiss deepened even more, his lips slanting over hers. Their kiss seemed perfect, as if it just *fitted*, as if they had always known each other's movements and tastes, the way they moved together. He knew just how to touch her to make the world go away.

Suddenly, the magical spell was torn by the sound of voices nearby. Diego drew away from her, resting his forehead against hers as they tried to breathe.

Catherine hardly dared to move even a whisper. Her heart pounded in her ears, an erratic pattern that drowned out everything else. Slowly, slowly, she floated back down to earth.

She blinked her eyes open and stepped back, almost stumbling her legs were shaking so much. She peeked up at Diego and he was watching her carefully, his own thoughts unreadable to her now. Only a moment ago it had almost felt they were one.

Her gaze caught on the pendant and she remembered who they were. Their duties and obligations, and what they had to do.

'The hunt will be leaving soon,' she said quietly.

Diego nodded, not saying anything. She wasn't sure she could bear it if he did. She did not want to know regrets yet. She dared to touch just the tips of her fingers to the rough silk of his hair. He flashed a smile at her and she knew she should not look at him. When he did that, she wanted to never leave his side at all.

She spun around and ran back to the castle—away from the confusions of her own heart.

Chapter Eight

Bringing in the Boar Day

'The boar's head in hand bear I, bedecked with bays and rosemary! I pray you all now, be merry, be merry…'

The company gathered in the Great Hall cheered as the pages carried in the roasted boar on a large silver platter, adorned with garlands of herbs and candied fruits, a whole polished apple propped in its mouth, its tusks gilded in gold leaf. Queen Mary laughed, her cheeks as rosy as a girl's.

Catherine cheered with everyone else, yet all the time she was achingly aware of Diego just across the room from her and she could not forget what they talked of before the hunt. About the sadness she longed to erase from his life.

Maidservants poured more wine into the goblets. As Catherine took a sip, she realised she would have to be careful. She already felt giddy with everything, with Christmas and Diego. She didn't need to be cup-shot as well.

She took one more sip, just as the doors flew open and a company of acrobats tumbled down the aisle in a blur of colour and music. Catherine laughed with everyone else, delighting in that moment of distraction. The uncertain world waited out there beyond the palace walls. But in here all was light and plenty. Diego was just across the room, not over the seas in Spain. It was enough. It had to be.

She smiled at him, putting all she couldn't say into that smile, and his answering, beautiful smile lit up the vast hall for her.

How very dark his eyes were, she thought, so full of secret depths. She was sure she could fall into them and be lost, like plunging deep into the icy river. A place of such wondrous beauty, it would be worth the danger.

She was torn away from her dreams when the players scattered among the company, drawing them into the wild swirl of their dance. Catherine laughed as a masked acrobat seized her hand and pulled her from her seat. She lost sight of Diego as the crowd closed around her, blurry in the twirling dance of ribbons and bells.

Someone grabbed her around her waist, too hard, and spun her around until she was almost lifted from her feet. She saw it was Master Andrew Loades, drawing her up against him. His hands were so damp she felt it through her gown and she longed to wriggle away.

'Remember what I warned you of, Mistress Greaves?' he whispered. 'You must be careful. Your father is not here to protect you from the Spaniards, is he? Let me be your friend.'

'I don't know what you mean,' she gasped and pulled away from him to search desperately for another partner. She didn't know what it was about Master Andrew, but he always awakened such disquiet inside of her.

He finally let her go and she spun away. Breathless from the whirl, Catherine fell out of step and leaned against the wall just past the tapestry where she and Diego had first kissed. It felt like a refuge of sorts and like the most dangerous place of all. Who *should* she beware of here at Court?

Someone touched her hand and she gasped in surprise. Was Master Andrew back? She turned and saw with a rush of warm relief that it was Diego. He gave her a worried frown and she wished she was better at hiding her emotions. She would never get ahead at Court without learning to dissemble.

But she feared she could never hide from him.

'Are you well, *querida*?' he asked softly.

'I—someone just said something about my father. I felt so lost suddenly.'

He smiled gently, almost sadly, and held out his hand. 'Come with me.'

Catherine took his hand. She well knew now the feeling of his skin against hers, the warmth and strength of it. He led her to their secret spot, in that darkened, tiny space between the tapestry and the wall, below the kissing bough.

Catherine leaned against him, felt his strength and was suddenly sure that, there, in that place, she was truly safe.

'All is well now,' he said, pressing a kiss to her brow, his lips soft.

'I know,' she whispered, and in that moment she truly believed it. With Diego's arms around her, nothing could harm her.

'Catalina,' he murmured. He reached out to touch her cheek, his long, elegant fingers stroking through her hair, loosened by the dance. Slowly, slowly, moving still in that dream, he cupped his palm to the back of her neck and drew her closer.

Her eyes closed tightly as he kissed her, their lips meeting hungrily. He tasted of wine and sugared fruit, and that darkness that was only him. The kiss was slow, gentle and so very sweet, as if they could have all the time in the world. As if they could have more than these precious stolen moments.

She leaned her palms against his chest and felt the steady rhythm of his heart moving into her. He took her face between his hands, as gently as if she was a precious pearl. She wanted always to remember that very moment, every sensation, store them up for the cold days when such moments had flown.

She slid her palms up to curl over his shoulders, holding on to him, her one still, strong point, as the earth tilted beneath them. She leaned into him as their kiss deepened and turned hungry. Tasting, touching, *knowing*.

With a sigh, she finally drew away and leaned her forehead against his shoulder, feeling his breathing as rough as hers. She clung to him as if he might vanish from her like so much mist, as he would all too soon in truth.

He'd never spoken of the future and nor had she. They couldn't. Yet there, alone with him, everything felt so right. If it was all she had, then she would savour it, make it a glowing memory she could hold on to for uncertain years to come.

She tilted her head back to stare up at him. His face seemed etched deeply in the shadows, his smile as bitter-sweet as she felt. She smoothed back the lock of his hair she had disarranged and traced her fingers over his cheek-bones, the blade of his nose, the edge of his jaw above his velvet collar. He watched her intently, not moving, his eyes pools of night.

'Some day, when I am an old, grey lady shivering by my fire, I'll remember this moment,' she said, trying to laugh.

But he didn't smile. He took her hands tightly between his. 'What will you remember?' he said roughly, in Spanish.

'How alive I feel with you. How I feel I could burst into flames I'm so alive! Like I could fly higher and higher, like a bird in the summer sky, above Whitehall and London and Kent, everything, and find a place where there is always sunshine. And always happiness.'

'Where there's a true home,' he said.

'*Si*,' she said, amazed and yet unsurprised he understood her so well. 'Surely when someone finds such a place, they must hold on to it with all their strength, even if only in dreams.'

He wrapped his arms around her and held her so very, very close, as if they could never be parted. Suddenly weary of everything, the Court, her father, her worries, weary of being strong for so long, she rested her head against his chest and let herself cry out the fears of months. She knew her tears were safe with him.

For a long moment, he held her in silence. A burst of

music just outside their sanctuary made him kiss her forehead and step away. Catherine shivered with the cold. 'Meet me at the river steps tomorrow morning, early, Catherine,' he said. 'I'll show you something that might help.'

Catherine was confused. 'Show me what? What do you mean?'

The music grew louder. 'We cannot speak now. Will you trust me?'

Catherine knew that if she was wise, she would not. She couldn't afford to trust anyone, especially a king's man. One who went to the Tower on mysterious errands. And yet— this was Diego. 'Yes, I will.'

He kissed her once more, a swift, hard, deep caress that spoke of something like—hope. Fragile and elusive, but so sweet. Maybe it was a futile hope, but Catherine clung to it. It was all she had.

Chapter Nine

Catherine slipped out of the back door of the palace, the hood of her cloak drawn close. It was early in the morning, but her mother was sewing with Queen Mary and the other ladies, for a quantity of embroidered baby clothes was needed and they would surely be busy for hours.

Catherine had never crept away to meet a man before and she smiled at how daring and wicked she felt. But she glanced back over her shoulder, wondering if, to be wise, she should turn back. She remembered her resolve to seize every moment she had with Diego and turn them into memories and rushed forward. Soon, it would be New Year's, and then Twelfth Night, and she and her mother would leave Court. She had to seize what she longed for.

She rushed down the outdoor stairs. Catherine felt as if someone was watching her, closely; she felt the prickle of it on the back of her neck. But when she glanced back, there was no one. Trembling, she turned towards the water landing. The river looked brown and choppy, breaking against the pier, slushed with ice. Diego waited for her, next to a boat.

Catherine's heart stuttered at the sight of him, tall and austere in his black doublet and fur-edged cloak, his face half-shadowed by his hat. She ran to him and took his hand between hers. 'Where are we going?'

He gave her a wry twist of a smile. 'And good morn to you, too, Mistress Catherine. It's almost New Year, and I will venture to guess you haven't found all your gifts.'

Catherine gasped at the thought. She *was* behind arrangements! 'I have not! Z'wounds, but I did want to find my mother something lovely, she's had such a difficult year.'

'I have great faith that this New Year will find her merrier,' he said, with that mysterious smile. 'And it will start with the New Year's banquet!'

He helped her into the waiting boat and sat down close by her side on the narrow wooden seat, giving the ferrymen directions. How warm and cosy it was to be pressed against him this cold day, how exciting to be exploring the city at last!

'I've consulted all the Queen's ladies, especially your friend Mistress Dormer, who the Count of Feria says is considered most elegant in her taste,' Diego said, 'and they've told me some of their favourite merchants.'

'I doubt I could ever afford what Jane considers truly elegant.'

Diego squeezed her gloved hand in his. 'Do not worry about such things, *dulce*. Choose what you like and send the shopkeepers to me.'

'Oh, nay!' she cried. 'Diego, you are too, too kind, but I must not take advantage...'

'Hush, Catalina.' He held one of his fingers to her lips. 'I owe you so much. More than you can know. You've brightened my days here, made me laugh. Let me do this. It would give me such pleasure to shop for a lady again, as I do for my mother and daughter.'

Catherine sat back in her seat, still uncomfortable. She could never say no to something that would bring him a bit of Christmas joy. And joy to herself, as well. 'I did hear tell of a fine toymaker in Cheapside,' she said. 'There should be lovely dolls there, mayhap a hoop or drum Isabella might like.'

'That sounds marvellous.'

'What will your family be doing now for the festive season, Diego? Have you brothers and sisters to give your Isabella cousins to make merry with?'

Diego shook his head. 'My only living brother is one of the King's governors in the New World, we haven't heard from him in a long time. But Isabella is so busy with her tutors now. She will surpass me in learning very soon, and she's already a finer dancer!'

Catherine could hear the pride in his voice as he spoke of his daughter and the loneliness, too. 'I was an only child, but I don't remember feeling lonely at Christmas. We would go skating and sledding, gather in the greenery. And, in those times when our Mass was against the law, we would slip out at night to a neighbour who had a visiting priest. I found it most thrilling at the time. Now I see how frightened I should have been.'

Diego took her hand. 'I'm sorry you had to do that, Catherine. But your parents sound like wonderful people, to give you such a family.' His smile looked wistful as he glanced down at their joined hands. Catherine wondered how his own youth had been—as the heir to a grand family, he'd have felt a great duty. Had he anything that was as warm and cosy and safe as her own home?

'They were wonderful. They *are*. I always felt so loved, so safe.' Until her father left. She glanced away to hide the prickle of tears in her eyes, the houses along the riverbanks grown blurry.

Diego squeezed her hand again. 'What our families do is not who we are, Catalina.'

'Oh, but it is!' Catherine saw the great spire of St Paul's in the distance, austere, eternal, judging. 'We *are* our families.'

Diego raised her hand to his lips and pressed a kiss to her gloved fingertips. 'This is a season of faith, *querida*. Soon all will be well in ways we cannot imagine now. It's a complicated world we live in, this world of crowns. We must be strong, as I know you always are.'

Catherine so often did *not* feel strong at all. But when

Diego looked at her like that, she did feel like herself again. Like the Catherine who laughed and danced and trusted, and ran forward no matter what.

She smiled and leaned against his shoulder, feeling suddenly warm. 'I do feel I could be, Diego, when I'm with you. Right now, I just want to think about *today*. About our delightful errand. What should we buy for your daughter's gift, then? What does she enjoy?'

He smiled, an easy, open grin, and wrapped his arm around her shoulders as they watched the river slip past. 'I fear I know not what a growing girl likes. What gifts were your favourites as a child?'

Catherine told him about her dolls and their clothes, embroidered by herself, the tiny pans for making tiny cakes, the balls on sticks she would chase around the kitchen garden for hours. Before them now were streets of silversmiths, bookshops, importers of cloth from Venice and Lyon, laces and velvet dancing shoes. She took Diego's arm and let him lead her along the lanes.

The air smelled of sweetmeats and spices, the crispness of fine brocade, the scent of French perfume. Her eyes wide, Catherine stopped to peek in windows and stare at lengths of ribbons in all colours, the glitter of bracelets and brooches, piles of leather-bound books.

'Where shall we visit first?' Diego asked. 'This merchant, they say, has a new shipment of velvets from Florence. Or perhaps the goldsmith?'

'This one,' Catherine whispered, stopping in front of the bookshop. The scent of leather, parchment and glue was dusty and delicious through the door.

Diego smiled as he watched her enchantment with the piles of gilt-edged volumes in the window. 'Of course.'

The bells above the door tolled their entrance and the shopkeeper glanced up from the crates he was unpacking. 'Good day to you, gentles! How may I assist today?'

'The lady enjoys poetry,' Diego said. 'May we see your latest volumes?'

The man frowned a bit at the sound of Diego's accent and Catherine remembered hearing that many shopkeepers in the city did not like to serve the Spanish courtiers. But Diego discreetly jangled the heavy purse at his belt and the man smiled. 'Aye, I do have this one, a volume of poetry from Seville, by a writer named Herrera. Does the lady read Spanish?'

'I do, a bit,' Catherine said. 'I've heard of this Herrera.' She took the book from the man, studying the fine red-leather bindings, the gold lettering and lovely illuminated illustrations. She knew the price would be too dear for her and sadly handed it back, choosing instead a smaller volume of plays for her mother, bound in cheaper paper.

In other shops, Catherine decided on a filigreed brooch for Jane, a ring for her mother, and, the most important gift of all, a small gold pomegranate pendant for the Queen. It wasn't as grand as a queen deserved, but Catherine hoped the link with Spain would make Queen Mary smile.

It was a dizzying whirl of colour and light and scent, and Catherine was giddy with it all, and with the laughter of shopping with Diego. Unlike her father, he didn't grow bored with the task and he didn't pinch his coins. He helped her ponder ribbon colours, sniffed perfumes, smiled with her. He even played with several of the trinkets in the toy store until they settled on a doll with golden curls, like Isabella's own.

When they had finished with their task and dispatched the packages back to Whitehall, Diego bought her hot apple cider and roasted chestnuts from a cart. They strolled beside the river as they ate, watching the boats slip past.

Catherine glimpsed a father showing his small son how to tie the knots of the ropes next to their wherry. Their heads were bent together, so close, so trusting. She had a sudden, bright flash of memory of her own father, showing her her letters on a slate, patient and affectionate.

'What are you thinking of?' Diego asked. 'You seem so far away.'

She flashed him a quick smile, trying to hide her sadness. But he watched her so intently, as if he guessed. 'Just remembering something from when I was a little girl. How I felt as if things could never change, as if I could always be trusting of everyone around me.'

'Life does seem simpler when we are young, yes? When our family is all the world to us.'

'Yes. But you must have left home when you were quite young. To be a squire along with the Count of Feria?'

'So I did, when I was seven. My brother had been gone for many months by then and I was a little on the old side to be sent away to learn how to be a gentleman. Suarez and I got into far more trouble then than I'd care to admit! But we learned a great deal, as well. How to fight, how to dance, how to be gentlemen.'

'Your parents must have missed you.'

'It was what all boys in my family's position must do. I think my mother missed me. My father died when I was young and he was a busy man even before that, at the Court of Emperor Charles. But I remember his lessons with my first wooden sword.'

He looked so sad for a moment and Catherine gently touched his hand. 'You loved him.'

'I respected him and I know I must follow his example as a father.' He squeezed her hand and let her go, his smile turning distant. 'Come, the hour grows late.'

'But where are we going?'

'You will see. A surprise.'

They turned at a bend in the river and came within sight of the Tower. Her heart, so joyful only a moment ago, ached at what those walls contained. So close and yet so very far.

'Poor Father,' she whispered.

'Come with me, Catherine,' Diego said, taking her hand and leading her swiftly towards the drawbridge gates.

'Diego! What are you doing? We cannot go there without a letter of permission!' she cried, confused, afraid. Hopeful. Maybe they *could* get in, somehow. Diego seemed able to do anything.

'I'm a king's man, am I not? And you should see your father at Christmas, *querida.*'

She swallowed hard and followed him, feelings of fright and hope all tangled up inside her. He pounded on the porthole of the gate, which was quickly opened by a helmeted guard. Diego whispered something to him, the guard nodded and withdrew. A moment later, there was a metallic scraping noise and the gate was drawn back.

'This way, Don Diego, someone will show you to Sir Thomas Bridges.'

Catherine stared around wide-eyed at the same path she had walked only days before with her mother. It all looked much the same: soldiers and maidservants going about their business.

'Diego, what is this?' she whispered to him. 'How can you just walk in here?'

He glanced down at her, his face very austere and unreadable again. 'Just trust me in this moment, *dulce.* The King has tasked me to help many people in dire straits here. And remember what I said—much is hidden from us in this world, much we cannot know. But I will keep you safe. Do you believe me?'

Catherine nodded.

They were led to the parlour where Catherine and her mother had seen her father before. It was empty now, but a fire burned in the grate and a tray of wine sat on the table.

'I will leave you for the moment, to see your father,' Diego said. 'We don't have a great deal of time.'

She grabbed his hand as he turned to go, longing for

the solid anchor of him in those swiftly shifting moments. 'But, Diego…'

He kissed her hand, gave her a reassuring smile, and left, closing the door behind him. Alone in the silence, Catherine paced before the fire. A moment later, the door opened and she whirled around to see her father standing there, alone. He wore a fur-edged robe over his doublet, his cap crooked on his head as if he had dressed in a hurry.

'Papa!' she cried and ran to him. His arms closed tightly around her.

'Catherine,' he said, his tone full of surprise and joy. 'Whatever are you doing here? I could scarcely credit it when the guard said you were waiting. Not that I am anything but overjoyed to see you, but it's no simple thing to gain entry to the Tower.'

She remembered that it wasn't very difficult, not with Diego. 'Nay, I did not even know myself I was coming here when I left Whitehall. Diego de Vasquez brought me.' Walter led her to the chairs near the fire, holding on to her hand as they sat down. 'Father, what's happening?'

He shook his head sadly. 'Oh, my dearest. I know it hasn't been easy, these last months, and I have agonised about you and your mother. But I know your true strength, yours and Elena's. And I know this—Don Diego may be a Spaniard, yet you can trust him, as you can so few at Court. He took you the ring I sent.'

So it *was* Diego. 'But why?' Catherine demanded, her mind whirling.

'I cannot say more. Just that things will come right soon.'

Catherine didn't see how that could be, but she nodded.

'Tell me, Catherine—how is your mother, truly?' he said. 'I've missed her very much, though I fear she must not miss me.'

Catherine told him of the Christmas celebrations at Court, her mother's happiness in seeing her old friends, the Queen's kindness. She said nothing of her mother's sad-

ness late at night, when she knelt with her rosary and murmured prayers. She knew that if her father could tell her
no more, even her mother's confusion could not yet move
him to reveal secrets.

The guard who'd led them to the house appeared at the
door. 'It's near time for supper, Sir Walter,' he said.

Catherine's father nodded, and kissed her one more time.
'You must go now, my dear.'

'But, Father, I've only just arrived!' she protested, loath
to leave his side. 'I don't understand any of this.'

'Just trust me, my dear, for now. And trust Don Diego.
He will help you. He delivered my message, did he not?
And stay close to your mother.'

'But…' she implored.

He kissed her hand and, before she could burst into tears,
she hurried out of the room. Diego waited for her just outside the door and without a word led her back through the
gate and out into the real world again. The sun was sinking
in the sky, the wind growing colder.

'You know my father?' she said as they walked.

Diego nodded, his face unreadable. 'King Philip is very
interested in what happened in his wife's kingdom before
he arrived.'

'And you help him to do that?'

'His Majesty cannot be everywhere at once.'

'And my father—what's his part in this?'

Diego stopped at the edge of the steps that led up to the
palace. 'Your father is a good man, Catherine, you must always remember that.'

'I once thought so. I always imagined he cared so much
for my mother and me. They were a great love match, you
see. My mother gave up her homeland for him.'

'He speaks of her so fondly. It's rare to find such love
in marriage.'

Catherine glanced up at him, surprised by the sadness

in his words. He watched the street, pensive, distant. 'Was it like that with your wife?'

He took her arm and led her away, his face hidden by his cap. 'Truthfully, it wasn't. I had hoped for friendship and partnership, such as what my own parents had. My family and Juana's knew each other for a very long time. But we were very different people.'

'How so?' Catherine asked, wondering how any woman who found herself married to Diego could be less than ecstatic.

'I was gone a great deal for my duties and she was lonely.' He turned even further from her, his hand tight on her arm. 'I shall tell you, Catalina, a great secret, one I've never told anyone else.'

Catherine's breath caught in her throat. 'It shall never go further, Diego, I vow it.'

'I know that you're no gossip.' He smiled down at her, his eyes hard. 'She died in childbirth, but it was not my child she bore.'

Catherine gasped. 'Oh, Diego. I…' She took his hand in hers, but could think of no other way she could comfort him for such a shocking betrayal. 'I'm so sorry.'

'Sweet Catalina. Better to feel sorry for Juana. She was an unhappy soul all her life. But I vowed my own Isabella would never know a marriage like that. She will marry someone who will respect and care for her.'

Catherine nodded sadly. He'd told her the gravest of secrets. She felt so for him, longed to take away any hurt he had ever known. 'And I shall never marry at all. My family's situation—and my father told me never to trust anyone at Court.' Except for Diego. Her father had urged her to trust *him*. But soon he would be gone. The palace waited just ahead.

Diego smiled. 'What a strange pair we make, Catalina.'

'Indeed,' she whispered.

The bells of the chapel tolled the hour and she knew she

had to return to her chamber before she was missed. She went up on tiptoe and dared to press a kiss to his cheek, a promise to keep his secret. Then she dashed away before she could do as she longed to do and stay with him always. She feared she was more confused than ever before.

Chapter Ten

New Year's Eve

'Wassail, wassail, all over the town, our toast it is white and our ale it is brown! Our bowl it is made of the white maple tree, with a wassailing bowl, we'll drink unto thee!'

The tables of the Great Gallery were piled high with the gifts Queen Mary and King Philip had just given and received, and the night had begun to descend when the wassail bowl was brought out and song rang through the windowed space.

Despite its great length and gilded decorations, it felt like a more intimate gathering, such as the ones Catherine knew at home. Tables were set up for card games, where the Queen was laughing over the hand she had just been dealt with Mistress Clarencius and the musicians strolled through the crowd, playing.

Catherine sipped at her wassail and laughed with Jane and the other Maids as they exclaimed over the gifts of lengths of silk, brooches and rings, yet she found she looked all the time for Diego. She'd caught a glimpse of him when they first took their places in the gallery and he was talking intently with Feria. She didn't know if *he* saw *her* then. If he was sorry he had given her his secrets.

Queen Mary finished her card game and rose to stroll through the crowd, giving New Year's greetings. 'My dear ladies,' she said, stopping to smile at the Maids as they curtsied. 'How do you like your gifts?'

'Oh, they are wonderful, Your Majesty!' everyone declared and the Queen examined all of the pieces of jewellery before she turned to Catherine with a gentle touch on her hand.

'How is your dear mother, Mistress Catherine?' she asked. Elena had retired early with a headache, insisting that Catherine stay with her friends.

'I think the cold is affecting her,' Catherine said. 'She was sleeping when last I looked in on her, Your Majesty.'

The Queen clicked her tongue in concern. 'Poor Elena. I will send her a tisane, which I've found most effective. You mustn't worry about her.'

'The fireworks are starting!' one of the Maids cried and they all rushed to the windows. Boats decorated with lanterns bobbed in the water and in the distance the fireworks illuminated the river. Catherine knew the Tower was not far and wondered what her father did for that New Year's.

The darkened sky suddenly exploded above them, a crackling, glittering shower of red, white, gold and green. A flare of pure silver followed and a waterfall of blue stars. It was wondrously beautiful and Catherine stared upwards with everyone else, open-mouthed with delight, pulled away from her worries for a moment.

Why should she not have hope? It was indeed a new year, a royal baby was on the way, bringing new hope. It had never been her way to give in to despair and tears. She could not begin now.

She suddenly felt a gentle touch on her hand and looked up to find Diego smiling down at her. The fireworks cast his handsome face into shadows and light, making him seem unreal. Her perfect dream.

'Happy New Year, Mistress Catherine,' he said, his voice as soft and warm as velvet, deep with the touch of his Spanish accent.

'And to you, Don Diego,' she answered, feeling suddenly very shy. 'What is your wish for this new year?'

'To see dreams come true, of course. Is that not what everyone wants?' He took her hand and raised it to his lips for a gentle kiss.

Catherine longed to ask what his dreams could be. More power for his family? To see his daughter again? She barely knew what her own desires were, what she could have and what was beyond her for ever. 'Diego, I—I barely know what to think. I need quiet, I need time. Can you give me that? Can you leave me alone for a time?'

He frowned and for a moment she thought he would grow angry, would refuse to give her that time. But she should have known he would never be as other men. 'Of course. If you send me away, Catalina, I will go.'

'Diego,' she whispered. 'I'm not—'

'Catherine, we must change our gowns for the ball!' Jane called.

Catherine gave her a nod and glanced back at Diego. He still looked grim.

'May we speak later?' he asked quietly. 'There are things I must explain.' He pressed a small, wrapped package in her hand and she clutched it close.

'Yes, of course,' she said quickly and turned to leave.

In her chamber, her mother was asleep, the cup of the Queen's tisane on the bedside table. Catherine sat down by the fire to unwrap Diego's gift and found the beautiful volume of Spanish poetry bound in red leather and stamped in gold. 'To Catalina, to make her think of the sunny skies of Spain, from D.' was written on the first page, a bold, black slash of letters that looked just like Diego. She traced them with her fingertip, smiling at the thought that even when he was gone, she would have this tiny piece of him with her always.

'Hurry, Catherine!' Jane called and Catherine grabbed her friend's hand and followed her into the Great Hall.

She studied the men who gathered near the Yule log

fireplace, all of them clad in their finest cloth of gold and silver, dark velvets, pearls, but she didn't see the one she most longed for.

A trumpet fanfare announced the royal couple and the doors opened to admit Queen Mary on King Philip's arm. Mistress Clarencius carried her gold and scarlet train, while Ruy Gomez carried the King's of white and silver. The acrobats gambolled about them, tossing ribbons and sweets into the crowd.

'Round your foreheads garlands twine!' they sang, 'Drown sorrow in a cup of wine, and let us all be merry!'

The decorations Jane and Catherine and the other ladies had made were wreathed around the fireplaces now and over all the tables and chairs in loops of bright green and deep red. The acrobats danced between them, catching up wreaths to toss from one side of the room to the other.

Catherine suddenly felt as if she couldn't breathe as the crowd grew thicker, pressed closer. Her chest was tight in her closely laced stays and she felt as if the red and black hangings were moving closer and closer, shutting off any fresh air. What if they fell, enveloping everyone in their suffocating folds? Her stomach felt queasy with the wine and the heat. She turned to flee, to find some quiet corner, but her narrow path through the crowd was blocked by Susan Clarencius, who was scanning the crowd with a most worried look on her face. She held the Queen's white cloak over her arm.

'Oh, Mistress Greaves!' she exclaimed. 'Have you seen Mistress Dormer? The Queen left her silver pomander in her chamber and someone must fetch it at once.'

'I can fetch it, Mistress Clarencius,' Catherine eagerly offered.

Mistress Clarencius frowned doubtfully. 'Well—if you're quite sure. Of course you may go. I'll never find Jane in this crowd and I must return to Her Majesty.' She held out the beautiful cloak. 'And take this. The Queen fears the empty corridors will be chilled.'

'How kind of Her Majesty.' Catherine swirled the soft folds of the cloak over her shoulders and drew up the fur-edged hood. The corridors were indeed chilly, with only torches to light the way, set in their holders high up on the walls. The palace was quiet, too, echoing after the great uproar in the Hall.

Catherine shivered, rushing even faster through the royal apartments. Those spaces, usually so crowded with people, were empty. She'd wanted to escape from the crowd—now she found she wanted all the noise again. She wanted to look for Diego, to thank him for his gift. To tell him she hadn't meant to send him away.

She shook away his image and ran into the royal bedchamber. The candles there were already lit, the bedclothes folded back. She drew the Queen's fur-edged hood closer over her head and turned to the dressing table to search for the pomander.

'This must be it,' she whispered, snatching up the glittering sphere from the jewel case. It smelled of summer roses.

Beneath it, she glimpsed a pile of letters and the one on top caught her attention. *The matter of Walter Greaves...* it said and was signed at the bottom. *D. Vasquez.* A report on her father—by Diego?

She dashed out of the chamber, intent on finding him, questioning him. As she swung around the corner of the Presence Chamber, an arm suddenly arced out of the darkness, catching her around her waist and pulling her off her feet. A gloved hand clapped hard over her mouth.

Catherine twisted about, panic rising up inside her like an engulfing wave. She tasted the metallic tang of it in her mouth, thick and suffocating, like blood.

She twisted again, screaming silently, but it was as if she was bound up in iron chains.

'This is a lucky chance, aye?' her captor whispered,

hoarse and rough. A black cloud seemed to hover over her vision and she could see nothing. 'Most obliging of her to come to *us*, no guards or neglectful Spanish husband about.'

'It must be Providence, aiding our cause at last,' another man gloated.

Catherine managed to twist again, biting down hard on her captor's wrist. She landed on his thumb, tearing away a piece of leather glove. She tasted his blood.

'Z'wounds!' the man cursed. 'She's stronger than she looks.'

'Hold her down so we can tie her. No time to waste. She won't be alone for long.'

The two men shoved her to the floor, Catherine kicking at them. The Queen's cloak and her brocade gown weighed her down, wrapping around her legs, but she managed to land one velvet shoe squarely on one man's chest as he tried to grab her feet.

'Quite enough of *that*, you bastard vixen,' he shouted, and Catherine turned just in time to see a gloved fist flying towards her.

There was a sharp, terrible flare of pain—and then nothing but darkness.

Diego watched the swirl of the royal dance without much interest. The music, the laughter, none of it could hold any appeal to him now. Since Catherine had told him they had to part, everything seemed dark, when it had turned to vivid colour on meeting her.

He'd vowed before he left Spain that he would focus only on his duty. Perhaps his duty to *her* was to stay away from her, to let her live her own life once her father was released. But whenever he looked at her, only her, he felt alive again.

He studied each passing face, each lady in a green-brocade gown, but none of them was Catherine. She hadn't appeared after the fireworks. Had she nothing more to say to him?

Jane Dormer and another of the Queen's ladies strolled past, whispering together. Jane looked worried.

'The Queen sent her to fetch the pomander, so Mistress Clarencius says,' Jane said. 'But Catherine hasn't been here very long…could she have become lost?'

'Surely she'll return soon,' the other lady answered.

Diego frowned, a tiny, cold prickle of unease planted in his mind. Jane sounded worried about Catherine's whereabouts. She could be any number of places, of course, yet something told him all was not well.

'Mistress Dormer,' he called. 'Are you looking for Mistress Greaves? Can I be of help?'

'Oh, aye, thank you, Don Diego,' Jane said with a relieved smile. 'She was meant to fetch the Queen's pomander ages ago.'

Jane led him out of the hall, gaining Feria for their little search party near the gallery doors. They hurried along the shadowy corridors, which only grew emptier the further they went from the revels.

Diego and Feria exchanged a frown at the lack of guards, even near the royal apartments. Had they been given an extra ration of ale for the New Year? Were they slumbering nearby? Or had something more sinister sent them away?

'Sir Walter did warn the conspirators would make an attempt on the Queen soon,' Diego muttered to Feria.

'Would they do that here?' Feria whispered back. 'Snatch someone else by mistake?'

Diego shook his head, for the information from the Tower hadn't been so detailed yet.

'She should be here,' Jane said, gesturing towards the royal bedchamber.

But the room was empty, a few flickering candles illuminating the shadows. Nothing seemed disturbed.

'Perhaps she went back to the hall,' Jane said uncertainly. 'But how did we miss her?'

Diego was sure they hadn't missed Catherine. That

wary instinct was stronger now within him, a taut, ominous feeling.

Jane went to examine the dressing table while Feria checked the privy chamber and dining room next door.

Diego carefully studied the chamber, searching for any sign things were not as they should be. In the corridor just outside he found it—a glint of silver, the royal pomander, with an earring next to it. A pearl-drop set with a cabochon sapphire, one of the pair Catherine always wore.

'That's the Queen's pomander,' Jane said with a gasp. 'And Catherine's mother's pearl earring! She wore them tonight, I'm sure of it.'

Diego closed his fist around the earring, his gaze searching the floorboards for anything else. Crumpled in a corner was a torn scrap of leather glove, stiff and sticky with blood.

'Is this hers, as well?' he asked Jane.

She shook her head. 'She wore no gloves tonight.'

'We should get to the stables,' Feria said, taking Jane's trembling hand. 'They'll have to get away from the palace.'

'But why Catherine?' Jane whispered.

Diego wondered if it had something to do with her father. Were the rebels moving early? Had they discovered that Sir Walter was the royal spy and snatched his daughter as hostage? Or perhaps they'd mistaken her for the Queen herself, as she'd been alone in the royal chamber.

'I'll find them,' he said quietly, grim, determined.

'We'll help you,' Feria said. 'I'll summon my men right now. Jane, *querida*, inform the Queen what has happened. And search any hiding spots you know of in the palace, but do not go alone.'

Jane nodded, her face pale, before she dashed out of the room. Diego headed down the back stairs for the stables.

The grooms who were dicing there told him it had been quiet in the stalls all night; no one would miss the royal revels to go riding on such a night. But one servant had prepared a sleigh and horses much earlier.

It was for Andrew Loades.

'He said to be quiet about it, my lord,' the groom said. 'I thought maybe he had a secret meeting with a lady.'

'Was a lady with him when he departed?' Diego asked.

'Aye, he carried her. She was all wrapped up in a fine fur cloak.'

Diego crossed his arms. 'And which way did he depart?'

The groom scuffed his shoe along the floor. 'Along the river, towards Greenwich Palace? They were in a hurry. Eloping, mayhap.'

A lady in a fur cloak, carried off. That cold, icy fury inside of Diego hardened into burning steel. If the villain dared hurt her...

He had to find her and very soon. That was all that mattered in that moment, all that mattered at all. He loved her and he knew in that flash that he had to tell her that, tell her he was sorry he had not shown her how precious she was from the first moment he saw her. How precious their time together had been.

He strode back towards the palace. He would gather his men and fetch his sword. Master Andrew would rue his work this night.

Chapter Eleven

Catherine slowly came awake, feeling as if she was struggling up from some black underground cave towards a distant, tiny spot of light. Her whole body ached and she had to struggle to open her eyes. She knew she *had* to reach that light.

She forced her gritty eyes to open, her head aching as if it would split apart. At first she thought she *was* in a cave, she could see nothing. Something jolted painfully beneath her.

Then she realised her cloak was wrapped around her, the hood muffling her. And she remembered—she'd been dressed in the Queen's fine cloak. Knocked unconscious in the royal bedchamber. But where was she now? What did these men want from her?

Had they thought they were taking the Queen?

A cold panic threatened to swamp her.

Nay, she told herself, pressing that fear back down before she could scream and give away the fact that she was awake. She would *not* give in to these men, no matter who they were, what they did.

She had to get back to Diego, to tell him she hadn't meant it when she sent him away. That she loved him. Needed him. No matter what stood between them.

She took a deep breath, and heard the hum of voices, the clatter of horses' hooves. The jolt of wheels, carrying her away from Whitehall.

She slowly, carefully eased back her hood. Luckily they'd failed to tie her as they'd threatened.

'A bloody great fool!' a man shouted. 'I shouldn't have trusted your brother's word, not after he failed so badly last time. All he does in the Tower is drink and blabber.'

'How was I to know this was not the Queen?' someone else—the man who had grabbed her?—said. 'She is small and she wore the cloak. She was in the royal bedchamber!'

'How often do you see Queen Mary alone? She had terrible judgement in choosing husbands, but surely she is not a fool.'

Catherine frowned. She was not *that* small! But the man was quite right; it was foolish indeed to mistake her for the Queen.

'What do we do with *this* lady, then?' the first man said. 'She bit me! I'm still bleeding.'

'You deserve no less,' the other man, who sounded terribly familiar, said. It was Andrew Loades, she was sure. 'You were meant to catch the Queen! But maybe Walter Greaves's daughter will do as a hostage, if he has betrayed us.'

'I'll have naught to do with your foul plots!' Catherine cried, unable to stay silent any longer.

'Then I'll be rid of you just as your false Queen will soon be gone,' Andrew shouted. He grabbed for her, but Catherine was ready for him. She kicked out at him as hard as she could and, when he stumbled back, she leaped out of the cart, ignoring her cramped muscles. The snowy ground made her feet painfully cold in their velvet shoes, and she tossed off the Queen's cloak and ran as fast as she could over the slippery terrain.

Her path was lit only by the moonlight on the ice and she stumbled but forced herself to keep going. Her breath ached in her lungs, her stomach tight with fear, and she heard Andrew Loades shout after her. She didn't know which way to go, only that she had to get away.

Once, she tumbled over a fallen log and scraped her palms. The wind tore at her hair, battered her numb cheeks.

'Oh, Diego,' she whispered as she dragged herself to her feet. She had to find her way back to him.

She kept running and at last glimpsed bobbing lights in the distance, like lanterns, and heard voices shouting her name.

'Catalina!' one called and she knew that voice now as well as her own. It was him, truly him! Or was it just a terrible dream, a delusion of the cold?

'Diego!' she screamed. She ran towards those lights and saw that it *was* him, her beloved, his face frantic in the flickering light. She dashed the last few feet and threw herself into his arms. She felt safe, so very safe, at last. For the first time in months, she knew where she belonged. 'You found me, you came for me.'

'Of course, *querida*.' He kissed her, over and over, her cheeks, her brow, and held her close. 'I will always come for you, always be here for you.'

'It was Master Loades, he—' She broke off on a sob. She barely noticed the other men with them, racing into the woods to find her attackers. She shivered violently and felt her knees buckle beneath her.

'Come, *mi amor*, you will catch a terrible chill,' Diego said. 'We have to get you back to the palace.'

'I *am* cold,' she whispered. She had only just noticed the ice in her toes and fingers, the way she shivered. 'I could barely feel it before, but now I am too frozen to care. Isn't that odd?'

She swayed on her feet and Diego lifted her up in his arms, holding her close. She felt truly safe at last. Safe and warm, and exactly where she should be.

'We shall have you in your own chamber very soon, with a warm fire and plenty of blankets,' he said gently. 'Just hold on to me a little longer, my brave love, my Catalina.'

Chapter Twelve

Diego paced the corridor outside Catherine's chamber, listening for any hint of noise. All was silent, except for soft murmurs. All was blank except for glimpses of firelight when the door opened or shut a precious inch. Maidservants came and went, bearing trays of food and wine, fur blankets from Queen Mary herself, as well as the royal physicians in their black robes.

Jane Dormer appeared and stopped to give him a reassuring smile. 'She has a fever, but the Queen's doctors have bled her and given her a tisane for sleep, so she is resting now. I'm sure all will be well, Don Diego.'

'Will you tell her...?' he said, but then just shook his head. What *could* he tell her? That she had utterly transformed his lonely life?

That he couldn't bear the thought of being without her now. Of ever losing her smile.

Once he'd thought marriage to be a necessary duty, that partnership could be all to hope for, especially after Juana. Love was something only in poems. When he first beheld Catherine, first touched her hand, he realised he had been so wondrously wrong.

What if he lost her now, when he had only just found her? What if he could never walk with her in the sunshine of his home, never tell Yule tales with her, Isabella, and their own children? Never have a partner in his duty, a friend, a love.

No, he swore. That could never be. She had to live.

Chapter Thirteen

'Catalina. Catalina, *mija*, open your eyes.'

Catherine heard her mother's voice, but it seemed to come from a long distance. She had been dreaming of sunshine, a grove of sweet-scented orange trees, and now she was being pulled away from it, back to the cold. But she had to find her mother. She pried her eyes open and found herself staring up at the familiar bed curtains of her bed in Whitehall. A fire crackled in the grate and pale sunlight filtered through the window. It was daylight now—and she was safe.

Diego had come for her. But where was he now?

She turned her head to look at her mother and she found that even that small movement ached. She remembered it all now, being snatched from the Queen's bedchamber, Master Andrew. Elena and Jane sat by her bed, watching her with worried eyes.

'Madre?' she croaked. Even her throat was sore.

'You're awake!' her mother exclaimed. 'Thanks be to the saints.'

'Here, have a little sip of wine,' Jane said, offering a goblet. 'Queen Mary herself sent it. She's very worried, and most grateful, after the danger you faced in her name.'

Catherine took a drink and its rich warmth soothed her. She leaned back against the pillow, her eyes closing again.

'Shall I fetch something to eat?' Jane said. 'Some broth, or maybe a bit of roasted chicken? Or some comfits? I'll return soon!' She gave Catherine one more relieved smile and rushed out of the chamber.

Her mother took her hand. 'Oh, *mi dulce*, how worried we all were! When Don Diego carried you in...'

'Diego,' Catherine whispered. 'He was here?' She could imagine only him, of the way he'd held her so close there in the darkness as he carried her back to Whitehall, how he had kissed her as if she was precious to him. *Could* he love her, as she did him? She wished she could know what was truly in his mind, his heart, now.

'*Si*, but the Queen's doctor sent him away and said you had to rest.' Elena shook her head. 'How grateful we must be to him, for all he has done! All he does now, for all our family.'

'You—know?' Catherine said carefully. 'About Don Diego and Father?'

'Now that the Loades brothers have been found out, the plot has lost its danger. I should never have doubted Walter. They say he had warned that the conspirators were plotting to snatch the Queen. He learned it in the Tower.'

'Oh, *Madre*, how could we have known what was happening?' She hugged her mother, holding her tightly as all the fear and loneliness of months seeped away. 'We weren't meant to know. But now, surely, all will be well?'

'Of course, *dulce*, of course it will,' her mother murmured. She kissed Catherine's hair and urged her back down to the bolsters. 'Now, rest a while longer. I will be back very soon.'

Jane came hurrying back in, followed by pages bearing myriad covered platters, and Elena left with one more kiss.

'The doctors say you must be quiet for at least one more day,' Jane said, arranging sweetmeats on the table. 'Your blood must be allowed to warm sufficiently. Everyone feels quite safe again, now that you've caught the villains and foiled their wicked plots. How very clever you are!'

'It was my father who helped do that,' Catherine said.

Her father whose bravery had exposed a plot. Her father—
who would surely return to their family now?

'Oh, aye! Who would have guessed about Sir Walter?
And so very dashing of Don Diego to rescue you, like a
story in a poem.' She popped a sweetmeat in her mouth
and sighed happily. 'So romantic.'

'Romantic' Diego had not come to her that day. 'Not like
you and your Count, Jane.'

Jane blushed. 'Oh, well—I'm not sure how that will all
end. Our families are uncertain about the match.'

'But you love each other! I'm sure it must all come right.'
If only she had such certainties about herself.

'I hope so. Now, the Queen's doctors say you must rest,'
Jane said. 'I'll look in later.'

After she left, the chamber was quiet. Catherine closed
her eyes and was almost asleep when the door opened again,
softly. She smelled a familiar, delicious scent of warm citrus.

Her eyes flew open and she saw Diego standing there,
smiling at her, just as she had dreamed.

'Ah,' he said. 'The Enchanted Princess awakes.'

'Enchanted Princess?' she said.

'It's a tale my mother used to tell my daughter, about a
princess put under an enchantment by an evil sorceress.
She falls into a sleep for many years, until she's awakened
with a kiss.'

Catherine smiled. How she wished *he* would kiss her!
'Have I been shut up in this enchantment so long, then?'

He sat down beside her, so close she could feel his
warmth. 'Not so long, but to me it felt an eternity. The
Queen's doctors were being most strict about visitors.'

Catherine held out her hand and his fingers closed around
hers, holding her close. Giving her hope. 'Did you *want* to
see me, then?'

'More than I have ever longed for anything in my life.'
He bent his head to kiss her hand, lingeringly, softly. 'Ah,
querida, how you frightened me.'

'I should have known all along you were not trying to hurt my father,' she said. 'I should have known you better than that.'

He frowned. 'You once thought I was conspiring against your father?'

'The first time I saw you at the Tower. I thought someone had conspired to make the Queen believe my father was one of the rebels, as I knew he could not be a traitor. I thought you…'

'No, no, *querida*. My uncle had been your father's contact within the Court. When he died, I was summoned to take his place. I could tell no one the truth at first. It pained Walter deeply to hurt you and your mother, he loves you so much.'

Catherine nodded. 'We've always been the closest of families. I should've seen what he was doing—what *you* were doing. I should have trusted my feeling for you since that first day.'

He smiled, pressing her hand to his cheek. 'What feeling was that?'

'That you were honourable and kind and strong. That you had a sadness deep inside you, just as I have had for all these months. When you trusted me enough to tell me about your wife…' She gently stroked his cheek, wishing she could take away any pain he'd ever known. 'I never want you to be hurt again. I never wanted to be the one to add to your sadness in any way.'

'Oh, *querida*. It was only when I saw you that I came back to life.' He kissed her hand once more. 'You could never be like Juana at all. I have so longed for a return of light to my world, happiness, merriment. And I have found it, only with you. I cannot believe how fortunate I am to have found you here, of all places. You are the sweetest, finest lady I could ever have imagined. You make my life better just with your smile. You make *me* better. I want only to make you happy for the rest of our days.'

Catherine gulped down a sob, sure she was bursting

with happiness. 'Oh, Diego. My darling, wonderful, perfect knight. Can there truly be such happiness in the world?'

She sat up and caught him in her arms, his lips meeting hers in a perfect kiss. A kiss that meant home at last.

'We must marry,' he said roughly. 'At once. I shall go to your father, to the Queen.'

'And my mother.' Catherine remembered what Elena had said, that in a better world she would have fought for Catherine to be a Vasquez. Now that world had arrived. 'She will be ecstatic that I shall be Dona de Vasquez, shall see her homeland!' Then she remembered—her parents, their life in Kent. 'Oh. But we are only just together again. Where shall we live? What should we do?'

Diego kissed her brow, holding her close. 'Never worry about that, my Catalina. They are my family now, too, *si*? Just as my mother and Isabella shall love you. We must stay here until the royal baby is born, but then my family's estates will need me. Isabella will need me. We can take your parents with us then to Spain, if you like.'

Catherine remembered her mother's long-felt homesickness. Perhaps they would like Spain, as well. A new beginning. 'We shall all be together?'

'Together. Neither of us shall ever be alone again. I love you and I will make sure you will never be hurt again. Do you trust me?'

'With all my heart. I love you, too, Diego. More than I could ever have dreamed. It doesn't really matter what happens, because we will always have each other.'

Diego kissed her again and she knew that was the truth. They would never be alone again, come what may.

* * * * *

*If you enjoyed these stories, you won't want to
miss these other Historical collections*

Convenient Christmas Brides
by Carla Kelly, Louise Allen and Laurie Benson

Invitation to a Cornish Christmas
by Marguerite Kaye and Bronwyn Scott

Snowbound Surrender
by Christine Merrill, Louise Allen and Laura Martin

Author Note

I hope you have enjoyed spending time with Catherine and Diego this Christmas as much as I have! I love the holiday season and the Tudors certainly knew how to celebrate, with their music, dancing, feasting and wassailing.

I imagine that Christmas 1554 was one of Queen Mary Tudor's most happy and yet last happy times. She'd come through decades of neglect and persecution to fight for her throne, to combat the Wyatt Rebellion led by noblemen centred in Kent, which protested against the Spanish marriage and sought to dethrone Mary and replace her with Elizabeth—which Catherine's father finds himself embroiled in—and to marry her kinsman, King Philip of Spain. Sources say she fell deeply in love; his feelings were more doubtful—or should we say dutiful? Now England was reconciled with the Catholic Church and she was expecting an heir.

Things were not to be so merry for very long. By summer 1555 the pregnancy was known to be a phantom one—there was no baby at all. King Philip left to wage war in the Low Countries and Queen Mary plunged into depression. She died in 1558, leaving the throne to her despised half-sister, Elizabeth.

But I imagine Catherine and Diego's story ended on a happier note. They are loosely based on the true story of Jane Dormer and the Count of Feria, who also appear in our tale. Jane married her Count soon after Queen Mary's death and spent the rest of her very long life in Spain, as a patron of English Catholic refugees. She died in 1612; her husband, who had been made Duke in 1567, passed away in 1571. I envisage Catherine and Diego, along with her parents, living in Andalusia, raising beautiful children!

Catherine's mother, Elena, is also based on a real figure: Maria de Salinas, Lady Willoughby, one of Catherine of Aragon's ladies, who came with her from Spain and married an English nobleman herself.

She was one of the Queen's most loyal friends, defying orders to stay away when Queen Catherine was dying alone at Kimbolton and rushing to her friend's side at the end. Her daughter became the second wife of the Duke of Suffolk, after King Henry's own sister Mary.

For more information, and a list of resources for the time period, visit me at http://ammandamccabe.com.